RETURN OF THE ANCIENT GODS

RISE OF THE ANCIENT GODS SERIES: BOOK 1

CRAIG ROBERTSON

RETURN OF THE ANCIENT GODS
RISE OF THE ANCIENT GODS SERIES: BOOK 1

by Craig Robertson

To know absolute fear is to know the Ancient Gods.

Imagine-It Publishing
El Dorado Hills, CA

ALSO BY CRAIG ROBERTSON:

* Podium Entertainment has produced audiobooks for all the below titles except the older standalone books.

For specifics as to the correct order for reading the Ryanverse, click here.

Ryan In UnWonderland, Book 1

How Ryan Saves Time, Book 2

Saving Alice Ryan, Book 3

NON-RYANVERSE BOOKS:

A Teenager's Guide to Saving The Earth (2025)

An Apocalypse and Then Some, Book 1

How to Survive Surviving the Apocalypse, Book 2

Is This Apocalypse Over Yet?, Book 3

TIME DIVING (2024)

Letters From Hell, Book 1

Purgatory's Best Shot, Book 2

Heaven Says Wait, Book 3

Into the Nexus, Book 4

ROAD TRIPS IN SPACE SERIES (2019):

THE GALAXY ACCORDING TO GIDEON, Book 1

THE EARTH ACCORDING TO GIDEON, Book 2

OLDER, STANDALONE WORKS:

THE CORPORATE VIRUS (2016)

THE INNERgLOW EFFECT (2010)

WRITE NOW! THE PRISONER OF NaNoWRiMo (2009)

ANON TIME (2009)

For more information about Craig, his books, various series, or to see images and videos for some of his wild alien characters, please visit his website. You'll be glad you did: https://craigarobertson.com/

To sign up for Craig's newsletter to get announcements, updates, and his

recommendations for other great Sci-Fi reads go to: https://preview.
mailerlite.io/forms/2369493/188634426375144501/share

ISBN: 978-0-9997742-5-0 (E-Book)
978-0-9997742-6-7 (Paperback)
979-8-7754127-6-0 (Hardcover)

Cover design by Jessica Bell
https://www.jessicabelldesign.com/

Editors: Michael R. Blanche
Forest Olivier

Formatting services by Drew Avera
drewavera@gmail.com

First Edition 2018
Second Edition 2020

To my perfect wife, Karen.

PROLOGUE

Grand Lord President Vlaporlock lazed on his throne late one warm afternoon and he reflected. He was happy; joyous, in fact. No, he re-reflected, his bliss was beyond any normal state of exhilaration. He was rapturous. Yes. In fact, if he were only slightly happier, he might explode with happiness, as his father's father had while lounging on that very throne so many years before. It took a crew days to clean his father's father up, but none complained. Every puddle they mopped from the floor was ecstatic. All the tiny specks scrubbed from the crown molding were positively giddy. To explode from overjoy was never considered a bad turn of luck.

Vlaporlock ruled the Galactic Cleft and all that existed on either side of it. Times were, as they typically were, good. Trade flowed like mighty rivers, the weather was perfect, and the citizenry was both charming and contented. War or any form of strife was so removed from everyone's awareness that most people had difficulty properly defining those terms. Children, when asked what *hard times* were, responded that those were the rare occasions when they couldn't have a third dessert.

The Grand Lord's head bobbed and lulled as he drifted off into his second nap of the morning. Finally it came to rest on the feather pillow placed just so to accommodate his worship's restful head.

In his dream, young Vlaporlock romped in a field of long grass. He was chasing a girl, and then he realized he was being chased by her. It was Hollida, his second cousin. She was sweet and innocent in his dream, much as she was in real life. He ran faster to escape, but could not for all his gold understand why. If she caught him ... that would be nice. His legs therefore sped up. He tried to slow himself down by the judicious angling of his winglets, but somehow that only caused him to go faster.

He reached out to grab a passing fancy. Many fancies frolicked in the forest he flew through. There, he got a couple, and they slowed him down. Vlaporlock spun around and around and came to a stop, dizzy but ...

A dark shadow rippled to his right. He turned quickly but saw nothing. The young Lord was confused. Nothing dark and elusive ever entered his dreams. Ah well, he thought from the cliff top he stood on, let it go. No need to ruin a perfectly good dream in the midst of a perfectly good nap worrying about ...

There was a rumble behind him that made him jump to the cliff's edge. But when he looked, there was nothing. Hmm. No, there was something. He trotted over to inspect it. He brought along his winged puppy, but made certain Merriment stayed well behind him for safety's sake. Vlaporlock arrived at a harsh furrow cut into the soil. Rocks were cast aside. He picked one up. It was not fractured, it was sliced. The king was just about done with this nonsensical dream. Yes, both he and his dream self decided ...

A massive, black, scaly spine rose from the ground at Vlaporlock's feet. It crested at seven hands and disappeared back into the ground. Young Vlaporlock began to sweat and old Vlaporlock's heart raced. Both twisted to flee. Then the head of the nightmare beast leaped from below and swallowed the young ruler whole. It dived back from whence it had come. The earth closed as if this imaginary event had never happened.

Shortly after the designated time, the Seal Master unlocked the throne room doors. The Door Master stepped past him and swung first one and then the other massive door open. The Awakening Master led the small army of courtiers that followed her toward the throne to begin the process of gently rousing the Grand Lord. But the throne was empty. Awakening Master Salli stepped up to it and looked behind. Occasionally, the rather clumsy king fell there when having a particularly vivid dream. But he was not found there, either.

Salli jumped to the side like her feet had springs, which they actually did. She shot a glance back to see if she had accidentally stepped into a happy puddle of this ruler as she had done with his father's father. She had to ultimately burn those shoes because they wouldn't stop laughing.

But there was no joyous ooze. She called for a ladder and inspected the ceiling. No mirthful specks or spots.

No one ever learned what became of Grand Lord President Vlaporlock. It became the only mystery known to the otherwise burden-free citizens of Jasperite.

CHAPTER ONE

There were three reasons I knew there was a God in Heaven. My wife, sunset walks along a beach, and pizza. Don't press me on the rank order, please. Two outta three wasn't too bad, either. I was having pizza with Sapale. No beach on the planet was safe to walk along, but we were in a pretty forest. Kalvarg had nice ones. The beaches were nice, too, what I'd seen of them. But relentlessly vicious sea sentients named vidalts prowled the waters off the beaches looking to pick off any careless land colonists. Avoiding a violent death kind of ruined a romantic getaway. But we were good.

Over the better part of a century, our lives had gone from dicey and potentially short to simply marvelous. Yeah, once we destroyed the evil empire that was the Adamant, matters got better quickly. The overgrown dogs had reverted back to a pack-hunting species already. Minus their endless conquests and destruction, the galaxy flourished. The colony that Sapale, the wife-unit in my proof of God argument, and I founded was going gangbusters. What started as a beleaguered group of refugees was already a vibrant, blossoming society on Kalvarg. And many of the worlds destroyed by the Adamant were slowly getting back to normal. Sure, some were so altered that none of the original sentients existed. But at least their flora and fauna were rebounding.

Being Jon Ryan was all good. Oh, and the occasion of our picnic? It was my two billionth one hundred and third birthday. No, Sapale didn't put that many candles on my cake. There'd be a drop in the planet's oxygen level if she had. Whether or not that day was exactly April 16th, on what had long ago been Earth was not actually clear. Absent any basis in fact, I claimed it empirically. I'd naturally married a much younger woman, human male pig that I was. Sapale was soon to celebrate her two billionth eighty-fifth anniversary of life. My wife, or brood's-mate as her species named females partaking in that venerable institution, was Kaljaxian, like most of the colonists on Kalvarg. We android downloads amassed a lot of birthdays if we did our regularly scheduled maintenance. It was one of the plus sides of immortality. There were others, like not worrying about high cholesterol or when to get plastic surgery. But there was many a downside, too. More on those later. I didn't want to be a gloomy Gus on my special day. Not before the presents, anyway.

And old Toño DeJesus was happy as a clam. He'd settled down on Vorpace after the Adamant were beaten. He did marry Jonnaha, and the dude had twins with her. Those were heady times. But time, the changer of all, moved on, as it continually did. Jonnaha passed around forty years ago. It devastated Toño, but he finally came to terms with her death. He had the kids to raise. Toño Jr. was a space rat like his adopted uncle Jon. Jonnaha Jr.—yeah, they did it different on Vorpace—was a scientist like her papa. Really gifted. He was so proud of the two of them, as well as his grandkids.

We all reveled in the peace we had so richly earned. What did I do for a century that was the first in my life without war and conflict? I fished a lot. Freshwater, mind you. Again, saltwater fishing wasn't relaxing. Plus, I tried it a few times and it wasn't sporting. Once our friends the seagoing wiqub noticed I was dangling a line, they herded tons of fish toward my location and even put some on my hook. That made it no fun at all.

I also worked feverishly to have the Kaljaxians adopt the proudest gift of humankind's culture. I tried to teach them football. Their bodies were similar enough to ours to make it possible. The only major differences were that they matured a little smaller than humans and they had four eyes. But sooner rather than later, everyone decided the sport was too damn violent, so it didn't catch on. I wasn't sure I could ever forgive them for that, but I was willing to try. Instead, I taught them baseball. *That* they embraced. They were pretty good at it, too. Kalvarg's gravity was different from what Earth's used to be, so exact comparisons were not possible. But they hit for average better than us, probably because they had the extra eyes. Darn cheaters.

I'd always noticed that just when I thought things were going well, the bottom would drop out. I had to actually stop thinking like that. In one hundred years of constant improvement and joy, no bottom had formed to drop out. I was stunned. Because I never lost my ADHD approach to life, I did still explore. I'd hop in my vortex and go somewhere on the pretense of needing to make sure societies were staying on track in their recoveries. While there, I was known to explore local watering holes, naturally. That's probably why Sapale never came with me. She, for unclear reasons, did not like cheap rotgut served in filthy establishments. Go figure. More for me, right?

One day I went to Azsuram. That planet would always hold a warm place in my heart—if I had still had one, that is. It was another colony like the one on Kalvarg, which Sapale and I populated with her people. We started that colony a few years after the mass exodus from the doomed planet Earth. Before Jupiter took Earth out, we managed to cram billions of humans into cored-out asteroids and send them in search of a new home. Long before they arrived at Azsuram, Sapale hatched the plan to form a new, kinder, gentler Kaljaxian society there. It worked, too. After the humans finally arrived, everyone integrated well, and it thrived greatly, up until the mean dogs came and blew the place to bits.

Fortunately, small pockets of Kaljaxians and humans survived the Adamant onslaught on Azsuram and were rebounding well, if somewhat slowly. I landed in what was now called Sapale City, in honor of my mate. It was the site we first settled forever ago.

"Jon," exclaimed Dondtrb as he gave me a huge hug, "it's been too long, my friend."

He was Kaljaxian and he was a peach. He served on the Council of Elders that ran the government. He was also the contractor who'd rebuilt much of the power grid after the horrible war.

"I know. So many planets, so little time."

"You're twice a billion years old, you joker. How can time be short for one such as you?"

"The galaxy's big."

He hugged me again. "Well, you're here now. That's all that counts. Come, let me offer you some refreshments."

"If it's all the same, why don't we walk and talk. I'd like to see how the place is coming along."

"Excellent idea. Where shall we go?"

"Toward the central square."

"The central square it is. You want to see your statue again, don't you?" Dondtrb tried not to smile.

"Can't get enough of it."

As we strolled he pointed out new construction, as well as indicating where planned improvements were to be. In the century since the planet was ravaged, it had nearly healed. That was nice. It still pained me greatly that the total population was only ten percent of what it'd been before the Adamant struck. But with time, the society would recover fully. That was more than could be said for many other, less fortunate planets. In an ironic twist of fate, the few remaining feral Adamant were now hunted for sport. Well, sport and maybe a little spite thrown in, too. Kaljaxians were still alive who remembered the level of destruction inflicted. A few of the elderly humans actually fought in the final battles.

"You know there's a council meeting tonight. You should come."

"You're kidding! Boy, did I pick the wrong day to drop in."

"What's this?"

"I need another stuffy waste-of-time meeting like I need rust."

"You'll just be sitting in the audience and watching. Sapale is the permanent council member, not you."

"Sure, I'll stay. But let's make it to Lake JJ and back before then, okay?"

"You know I'm neither young nor an android?"

"You look fine to me. I promise I won't challenge you to any wagering."

"Done." He held out a hand.

The hike was nice. The ecosystem was restoring itself. I tested the lake waters, and they were basically the same as they had been centuries before. Luckily, few nukes had been used during the struggles on Azsuram.

After a leisurely meal I went with Dondtrb to the council meeting. I initially sat in the far left back corner, but as soon as I was recognized, I was forced by popular demand to sit front row center. You ever had speeches made about you? How about five? How embarrassing. The council then got down to the usual boring work. I mostly zoned out. Toward the end there was an appeal of a judicial ruling. That in and of itself wasn't unusual. If the courts decreed something, it stuck unless the loser appealed to the council. Reversals were rare, but it was a safety check Sapale had incorporated into the charter right from the start.

The case was an eye-opener. A man named Paqualtif was convicted of murdering his brood's-mate, Konradue. He maintained through the entire investigation and trial that he loved her and did not do it. No body was ever found.

The head of the council was a fair-minded woman named Loquereta. She began the appeal hearing. "Master Paqualtif, you stood trial on the charge of murdering your brood's-mate. The court found you guilty of that heinous act and sentenced you to life in prison. State your appeal."

Clearly frightened and thoroughly broken, Paqualtif spoke quietly. "Nobody *listens* to me. I did *not* kill my brood's-mate. I loved her. We have five young children. *They* loved her. I could never take their mother away from them. Who will raise them if I'm in jail? I beg of you to hear me. Where is her body? I need to know whatever became of her. I owe it to her to find the guilty party. I demand feltiph. How can she relax beyond the veil, if it is denied?"

Feltiph is best translated as *point of honor* in their language. It's a big deal in Kaljaxian culture. Many duels have been fought because someone felt feltiph was impugned.

"I hear you," Loquereta said evenly. "I hear your pain. I do not, however, hear remorse. Generally, appeals to this council are for leniency. It is granted based on the perpetrator's expression of guilt and remorse. You offer none."

"How can I beg leniency for a crime I did not commit?" He was beginning to sound hysterical.

"We are not a trial court. That phase of your case is complete."

"I know Davdiad is with me. He has sent a sign. Please allow me to plead my innocence." He was wringing his hands so hard I half expected he'd squeeze blood from them.

Another sorry jerk who offed his spouse. Only then does he see his god. The jerk even invokes him or her as witness to his ...

"I beg the great father of our planet Jon Ryan to hear my appeal. Davdiad has clearly sent him for that single purpose."

Oh, crap. More near-divinity thrown my direction. I sure didn't feel appointed or anointed by Davdiad when I sneaked off on this drinking trip that morning.

"Master Ryan is here as an observer and a friend of the council. He has no official role or office. Your request is denied." Loquereta sounded pissed. She was probably trying to let me know how badly she felt that he had called me out.

"You did not call for a vote," Paqualtif howled as tears streamed down his face. Dude was upset. Seemed odd for a guilty guy trying to angle for a break.

"You are correct. I call for a vote. All in favor of asking Jon Ryan to hear this man's appeal say *yes*."

I stood and raised a hand. "Before you do, I want to say I'm happy to help if it's the council's will. Just saying." I sat back down.

"All in favor?"

A few yeses were spoken. I counted six, but it'd be hard for living ears to tell. There were twelve council members.

"All opposed say *no*."

I heard five nos along with her negative vote.

"I am unclear as to the results. Please write your vote and pass it to me."

After she read them she stood. "The vote is a tie. Per protocol, that means the council will humbly ask Master Ryan to hear this man's story. I will counsel you, Paqualtif, on three things. This is most unusual. Be gracious. Master Ryan is doing you a great honor. Be worthy of it. I am keeping track of time. Be brief. If you violate any of those warnings, I will silence you." With that she sat.

"Thank you. I will be as brief as possible." He turned to me. "Master Ryan ..."

"Jon will be fine," I interrupted.

He glanced at Loquereta to ask permission. She nodded. "Jon, thank you for ..."

I raised a hand. "Just get to it. The council is being very generous with their time. Impress me."

"Yes. I was convicted of a crime I did not commit."

"So I have heard you say. Know that I will not overrule the process my brood's-mate and I instituted based on your word alone."

"Of course. I ask only two things. I demand feltiph."

"I heard that too. It is not mine to answer for."

"I know. I also ask you to examine my home. I wish you to see there is no physical evidence. That is all I ask."

"First tell me what led up to her disappearance, Paqualtif."

"We had a quiet night at home. After dinner my brood's-mate bathed the children. When they were ready for bed I spoke to them. After they were asleep we read a short while in the parlor. Then we retired to bed ourselves. I said best of dreams to her and kissed her forehead. That was the last time I saw my Konradue. That is the truth. I swear it on my children's eyes."

"As you were not at the trial, I will add Paqualtif has a reputation of being both a hothead and a drinker. That night, as with most nights, neighbors testified they heard the couple fighting," Loquereta said with strong disapproval.

"Yes, we fought, but what brood-pair doesn't?"

"Let us adjourn to your residence," I said. "Are the children there? I don't want them involved in this."

"I will send a runner ahead to check," said Loquereta.

And we were off. All we lacked were torches and pitchforks. Then we'd have looked a proper crowd of angry peasants in the night. The front door was open. The advance man stood just inside the house. The council, the convicted, and I filed in.

"It's in here," said Paqualtif, gesturing. He nearly took my arm, but stopped well short of such boldness. "The bedroom is through here."

I entered first. Looked like an amazingly typical bedroom. Two beds, as was the Kaljaxian custom, dressers, a mirror. The usual. I made a show of inspecting everything carefully. There was absolutely nothing to see.

"Here." He patted one bed. "This was my brood's-mate's."

I all but sniffed it loudly in my demonstration of attention to detailed investigation.

"I don't see anything out of the ordinary."

His face fell. Then it buoyed. "You must use the cables at your command. They are said to make the liar speak the truth and the dead to rise."

I could see it in the poor SOB's eye. He wanted me to touch her pillow and have her miraculously appear. My probe fibers sure wouldn't do that, but if I didn't make a show of it he'd rot in jail cursing my name. Not that I cared. But I figured heck, why not have him curse someone else's name? I extended the fibers of my left hand. *What are you?* I asked the bed.

Wool, needlepoint, moth eggs, skin cells—female Kaljaxian, wooden frame, random pollens, dust, and anti-gold. The components raced through my head.

Anti-gold? That was well beyond impossible.

"Do you find anything worthy of reporting?" Loquereta asked formally.

I scratched the back of my head. "Ah, yes I do. I have no idea what it means, but there's anti-gold on the bedsheets."

"Gold is not rare ..." she began to respond.

"No, not gold. *Anti*-gold."

She looked to the other council members. None spoke.

"Gold is gold," I began. "Anti-gold is like gold but it's made entirely of antimatter. Do you all know what that is?"

No one admitted they didn't. Or claimed that they did.

"Every elementary particle has an oppositely charged mirror-image particle made of antimatter. If we were in a universe made of only antimatter, the anti-gold would be normal. But it is impossible for it to be here for many inviolable reasons. For one, I don't think it's possible to make it in our universe. People still have trouble making anti-lithium, and that is much smaller. Plus, even if it could be produced here, it would be unbelievably unstable. It would explosively annihilate in microseconds. I'll tell you one thing for darn certain. It wouldn't be lingering on anyone's sheets, *ever*."

"Jon, are you telling us that there is a substance on this bed that cannot be there, but it is?"

"Yup, that's the picture."

"What are we supposed to make of this odd information?"

"I have no clue. If anyone told me it was there, I'd have them admitted to a psychiatric hospital for observation. Seriously."

"Has this anti-gold ever been found on Azsuram?"

"No. I used my probes earlier today and there was none. I've analyzed this planet a zillion times. The impossible has never been present before."

A few minutes later the council was back in the chambers. The audience was asked to remain outside so the council could deliberate on this most perplexing turn of events. Even I was left standing out in the cold. A full hour later the doors swung open and everyone filed in. The crowd had swelled to double during the break.

Loquereta gaveled the room to order, which took a while. Finally she spoke. "Paqualtif, please stand. The council has heard your appeal. We have debated the significance of the substance Jon Ryan found on the spot where your brood's-mate was last seen. Though we do not know the significance of this finding, its irregularity forces us to err on the side of leniency.

"Your life sentence is abolished. Instead, you will spend the next two years doing community service and attending mandatory psychiatric counseling. You must remain sober for no less than five years. Failure to meet these proscriptions will result in a reopening of this appeals hearing. Is that all perfectly clear and acceptable?"

Tears streamed down his cheeks. He bowed halfway to the floor. "Yes, Master, it is. Thank you."

"You're free to leave."

The crowd erupted in shouts and accusations.

I tuned them all out. I was preoccupied with figuring out what the impossible was trying to tell me. Crap. I was back in the game again, like it or not.

CHAPTER TWO

Arcturus 5 was about as small as a life-sustaining planet could be. If a world were any smaller, it couldn't hold enough atmosphere to protect and nurture life as we know it. No air meant nothing to breathe and no water to circulate. Advanced life never evolved on Arcturus 5, only primitive algae and bacteria along with a very few fungi. Fungus was the most intelligent natural inhabitant of Arcturus 5. Yeah, it was a simple kind of place. During the Adamant-domination era, a small colony of Xanthropis settled there. They correctly figured the mighty rulers of the galaxy would be embarrassed to annex such a useless, hostile planet.

Xanthropis were actually well suited for life on Arcturus. They were flexible, basically gelatinous, and lacked bones or similar support structures. They could easily conform to the ground contours in their search for food. The species oozed like giant amoebae over rocks and into crevices, filtering out nutrition. They could also successfully farm their favorite crops in the austere environment of Arcturus 5. Such tasty treats as acellular slime molds, crunchy fungal hyphae, and mummified spore pods thrilled their palettes and grew like the price of a wedding.

Over the decades, the Xanthropis there didn't exactly thrive, but they were comfortable enough. It was not hard, it should be admitted, to please a creature the consistency of Jell-O with a taste for decay. They were able to erect homes and begin to raise families on Arcturus 5. Slowly a society formed. Little flat schools were started for the little flat offspring. Modest pancake-shaped parks were built for the modest pancake-shaped adults to take their families to for relaxation. Many Xanthropis began to be almost happy about their lot in life. Again, that was not a hard thing for such a simple species. They were mostly just glad to be off the Adamant radar. Arcturus 5 was infinitely better than a brutal death.

When the news of the collapse of the Adamant Empire finally arrived, most Xanthropis were perfectly happy to remain where they were, there on Arcturus 5. None but a slimy puddle full elected to return to Belliacus, their home world. That planet needed a lot of post-Adamant restorative work to make it a home again. They were not, as would seem obvious, an overly ambitious or energetic race. If dinner was good, they were good.

Xanthropis life varied greatly with the time of day and the season. When it was relatively warm they were relatively active. When it was cold they blobbed up and waited for better times. When it was dark they slept. When it was light they reluctantly awoke and foraged. Individual Xanthropis didn't have names. Everyone was known by their scent. As hard as that method of identification might be to understand for a typical sentient, for the Xanthropis it worked well. One pocket of slime was "named" citric acid-denatured mold protein-degraded oil, while another was known as polyethylene glycol-ammonium-ferrous nitrate-sucrose.

One evening, sodium stearate-nitric oxide-linoleic acid went to sleep. It dreamed, as Xanthropis always did, happy dreams of proteinaceous slurries, simple sugar suspensions, and decayed cell walls. They were as easy to please in sleep as they were when awake. All the long night it swam through nutrients, ingested more than it could hold, and squirted waste streams at its few friends. It passed a really good night.

In the morning sodium stearate-nitric oxide-linoleic acid woke slowly, wishing it could have lingered in its dreams. Though it didn't *prefer* the dreamworld to reality, dreams of eating were easier than foraging to eat. Easy, as any Xanthropis would agree, was the best policy That morning, however, was different from all prior. That worried it. All change was bad. Any change for the worse was unacceptably unwanted.

Sodium stearate-nitric oxide-linoleic acid woke and couldn't smell anyone else. It was the only fresh scent in the slime. It had never confronted solitude. It lacked a word for the state of isolated existence. It began to quiver. Then the quivers progressed into random pulsations. Those combined to cause it to vibrate in a resonant frequency. Then it mercifully ruptured and was no more.

What happened to the others? All the Xanthropis of Arcturus 5 had been swallowed during their first-ever nightmares while they slept. Sodium stearate-nitric oxide-linoleic acid was somehow spared that harsh fate only to be subjected to another. But it was no longer alone. That would have pleased it.

CHAPTER THREE

An informal rule in my life was *when confronted by the impossible, deliver said impossibility to either Toño or the nearest Deavoriath.* Combining those two was optimal when I was struck by the unknown. Boy, howdy, had it ever hit me. Mack truck right between the eyes. I stopped by Toño's house and hustled him into my vortex *Stingray* without even giving him much of an explanation. Luckily he knew me well enough not to protest. If I was willing to witness yet again the sycophantic adulation the Deavoriath showered on Toño, he knew I felt such a meeting was necessary.

Cragforel was once so reluctant to see me he forbade my return to Oowaoa. Now whenever I landed, he was like a kid at Christmas, the king of happy. And yes, that was because I had Toño with me. The rare visits I paid him alone were met with thin civility and short responses to my questions. I was chopped liver. Toño was a full banquet.

"To what do I owe this *tremendous* honor?" Cragforel beamed as he trotted over to the landing area outside his residence.

"I missed you," I replied. "Isn't that reason enough?"

He didn't answer. No, he was too preoccupied looking past me to see if Toño was aboard. Dude apparently hadn't gotten the memo that *I* was the real superstar.

"Toño's not here," I lied. "He slept out in the rain and rusted to death."

"He doesn't have that much iron in his body ..." the rather concrete Cragforel began to respond.

"I did no such thing," exclaimed Toño as he exited *Stingray*. "Jon, honestly. It's been two billion years. When will you grow up?"

"The trend seems to indicate that will take place ten minutes after never."

Both of my "friends" rolled their eyes. Everyone was a comic.

"Come in," Cragforel said, placing a hand on Toño's back to usher him in. They whooshed past me.

Because I was, you know, me, I decided to call his bluff, hoping, of course, it was a bluff. I crossed my arms and remained where I was. Maybe they wouldn't even notice.

They disappeared into Cragforel's house.

I waited.

Finally Toño's head emerged. "Jon, since you're still out there, could you fetch my satchel from the vortex? I've something to show Cragforel."

I stormed into *Stingray* but couldn't find any satchel or briefcase. As I emerged I spied them standing shoulder to shoulder in his doorway.

"You didn't bring a satchel, you despicable man."

"Well, at least my request got you to move. Are you coming in, large baby?"

I walked toward the house, but only slowly, and I didn't say a word. Mind you, I acted like a spoiled brat in spite of the fact that I needed to run the impossible by them. Plus, I couldn't know if whatever was going on might be time-critical. Man, I really hated it when others made me act as if I were overly sensitive.

Once I was satisfied they were contrite enough, I gave them a full rundown of what I'd encountered on Azsuram.

"Anti-gold," Cragforel said, chewing the words. "It's nearly impossible to synthesize it in our universe, and it's as unstable as any compound can be if it's exposed to our matter." He slowly shook his head. "Sorry, but I must ask."

"Am I certain? I know." I handed each of them a data chit. "These are the exact readings the probe fibers made. See for yourselves."

Quickly enough they were both believers.

"But this is *impossible*," stated Toño.

"Tell me about it," I replied. "That's why we're all here together."

"We know if even a single atom of anti-gold was lodged in those sheets, it would annihilate instantly. Even if someone went to great lengths to try to prevent that from happening, it would still be a matter of only seconds before it exploded," said Cragforel.

"Yet there lay multiple copies. And you say at that point the woman had been missing two weeks?" asked Toño.

"About."

"They were left there intentionally," Cragforel said definitively. "Someone wanted us to find the anti-gold."

"That's kind of a leap there, isn't it?" I shot back.

He furrowed his brow. "No, it isn't. Jon, if a particle is found casually existing where it cannot possibly exist, it has to have been left with intention."

"Sure, I see your point. But that doesn't mean they were actively leaving a *message*."

"Perhaps I should have said a marker, an indicator."

"Of what?"

"That it was found."

"Back up a sec. You can't leave a notification trigger unless it's attached to something. A radio or to a tin can via a string."

"You're correct in that someone wishing to know *immediately* would need to set it up thusly. But maybe they only want to know *eventually*."

"Still doesn't work. One, no one can do the impossible. Two, the anti-gold would only act as an indicator in that sense if you checked back regularly to see that all were accounted for."

"It does seem labor intensive," remarked Cragforel.

"Anyone with the power to perform magic like that wouldn't waste their time counting atoms on a bedsheet. That's silly."

"How can we say anything about the mind of a creature that advanced above our level? Mice can't understand why we leave out traps for them." mused Toño.

We all sat quietly for the better part of two minutes.

"I just thought of how they did the impossible," I said softly.

That did bring dubious glances from the galaxy's collective brain trust.

"The way you do the impossible is that you don't."

"Looks like we're back to square one," Toño said reflexively.

"No, listen. There are two ways those particles that *cannot* exist in our universe *do*."

Cragforel rested his chin on all three hands. "This should be good."

"Where's the popcorn when you really need it?" snarked Toño.

"Okay, funny guys. One, the anti-gold could be time locked."

They blinked in disbelief.

"See, not so dumb after all. But that can't be the case. If they were time locked they'd stay at the point in time they were locked."

"To our eyes they'd vanish instantly if that were the case," added Cragforel.

"Which they didn't do. The other way they can be here is that they're not." I raised my hands expecting instant congratulations. Nothing. "They are not in *our* universe."

"They certainly *seem* to be," replied Toño.

"But they're not. They're in tiny shells of whatever universe they were formed in. They are worms dangling on hooks."

Toño, having fished, got it first. "Of course. They don't have to account for each individual baited hook."

"They just wait to feel a tug."

"I believe I take your meaning," responded Cragforel, "but there's a weakness. This super-powerful being would have to know that sooner or later someone's going to make the bed. All the hooks will be moved significantly."

"Yes, but think about the *pattern*," I said excitedly. "Throwing the sheets in the wash produces a random, global pattern. That pattern can be ignored. But if the particles are removed one at a time in a series ..."

"They were detected and were removed non-randomly," concluded Toño.

"Oh, no," mumbled Cragforel.

"What?" I asked.

"That's very bad." He looked up to us. "Think about the power and the intent of a being capable of doing such a thing."

I did. Ouch. He was right. "If whoever did this wanted to meet us and go out for drinks, they could do just that. Going to this elaborate extreme implies whoever it is wants to know if we were clever enough to *find* the bait. Then, what, they would come reckon with us? They clearly don't want to make direct contact with lesser sentients. Otherwise they'd do so with us straight away. They only wanted to make contact with sentients clever enough to detect their incursion."

"No, Jon, not their *incursion*," said Toño, "their *presence*. We have invaders who would eliminate the smartest souls present right off the bat."

"Less potential interference with their plans," agreed Cragforel.

"Which have to be pretty bad for us, if they want to dispense with any meaningful resistance," remarked Toño.

"Which, bottom line, means we're so screwed," I responded. "Screwed, tattooed, and barbecued. I got same-old-same-old déjà vu all over again."

"This pending doom shit is getting old," replied Toño, as he rubbed his forehead with his hands.

CHAPTER FOUR

Al-darem and his younger brother Al-fadol walked the cliff face as the wind raged against them. They hadn't spoken in over an hour. They'd barely clicked to each other to warn of cracks, wet spots, or lichen. The last three years had been hard, and the current one was shaping up to be much worse. Their main game, fordill, were hardly ever seen. Lesser prey was equally scarce. It was the fault of the dry wind. *Harcon nocht*, the curse from above. It brought no rain and sponged up what little moisture there was and spirited it selfishly away.

If the weather didn't improve soon, they'd have to gather what was left of the clan and try to find better hunting grounds, the ever-elusive richer mountain. But climbers had been sent out in search of hope. None had returned. The entire clan had prayed to the gods, all of them. But no blessing came as a response. Nothing came but harcon nocht and the wails of starving children.

In the long history of the Ganboodim clans, it was unheard of that the gods did not answer prayers. The Ganboodim were one with their gods, and their gods were one with their people. It was not common, but their gods would visit them, maybe once per generation. One or two, usually Hartha, the goddess of fertility, or

Keldropx, the god of the hunt, would come to a village and know the clan's hearts. That completed the balance of life and sealed the unbreakable bond. But no Ganboodimian alive had met a god. Al-darem was beyond despair. If he were not the new clan leader, since the last two died of hunger, he'd release his claspers and fall to meet the rocks-below-cliffs. Maybe in the after-fold he'd be able to beg a god to help his clan.

Al-fadol slapped at his brother's shoulder. He was pointing to the top of the cliff. "There are too many sharf up there," he yelled above the howling wind.

Al-darem shielded his eyes and looked up. There were many sharf landing on the upper ledge, then just as quickly leaping back into the air. Odd. He clicked to his brother to follow. They were going up.

The ascent took a few minutes, as the rock face grew icy. As they advanced, each brother broke off ice chips and devoured them. Water was a rare gift and never ignored. First the older, then the younger pulled himself onto the flat. The sharf were swarming some large ice blocks, ripping and pecking at them furiously. They were thirsty, too. The brothers swung spears and cleared the sharf away. A few were killed in the process. Before the brothers could retrieve them, their fellow sharf snatched the bodies and soared away, tearing their kin to shreds. They, too, were starving.

There were ten ice blocks, each taller than the brothers. Deep in the cores were dark forms; one per ice block, it seemed. Al-darem swirled a clasp in a small patch to melt the ice, then he blotted the water away. He repeated the action for five more blocks. Then he turned to look at his brother. Then, Al-darem ran across the ledge and hurled himself off, well clear of the cliff. He was going to meet the rocks-below-cliffs.

Al-fadol was caught so unaware, he didn't have time to try and stop his brother. He thought of peering over the edge to see what happened, but he knew without the effort. The now eldest brother stepped up to the first window in the ice. There, buried deep in the ice, was the mangled face he knew so well. All the clan had studied them. Their images were everywhere. Al-fadol stared at the battered face of Gofilp, king of the gods. Mightiest of the mighty. The next block held forever in a frozen death the dismembered head above the body of Hartha, the kindest and most loving of the gods. Her teeth were missing. The third and final face he saw was what was left of Keldropx's. His solid-gold arrow pierced one side of his head and exited the other. All four hands were fixed in an eternal icy grasp of the shaft where it was exposed on either side.

Al-fadol had seen enough.

He turned and walked slowly toward the edge. Al-fadol was going to join his brother and his gods. There was nothing left for the living in this reality.

CHAPTER FIVE

"So I vote we go back to Azsuram and pluck the anti-gold off the sheets one by one." I tried to sound confident, as well as sane. Both were questionable.

"Our great moral philosopher Betherialnad once proclaimed there is no wrong, only rights that are not fully perceived as such by others." Cragforel sounded, I don't know, exasperated?

"Never been much a fan of moral philosophy, myself," I responded with a silly grin. "Unless you count the Three Stooges and Bullwinkle."

"My point here is you are the exception Betherialnad did not foresee. You are *actually* wrong. That's a stupid idea," replied Cragforel. "Possibly the stupidest idea of all time."

"At least I'm original, then."

"Jon," began Toño, sounding, as he often did, like my old man, "if we do as you suggest, we will summon a force we surely cannot handle. It, or they, will, if we are lucky, only destroy every living thing on the planet."

"You don't know that. Maybe they'll bring an ice cream cake and silly hats."

"Ah. So these master creatures only want to party with beings smart enough to realize they are there."

"Of course. Who'd want to celebrate with dumb-asses?"

"Does your species believe in euthanasia for fellow humans?" Cragforel asked of Toño.

"Okay, geniuses, what do you suggest?"

"My *first* suggestion is to place you in chains so you can't summon our destroyers," responded Toño.

"Hang on, I'll start a list," I snarked.

"It would be nice to know the extent to which these superior beings have penetrated our universe," said Cragforel. "If we knew that, perhaps we could piece together their motives and capabilities."

"I agree that would be desirable, but I doubt that's an option. If the greatest clue they've left so far is a handful of anti-gold atoms, I can't believe we'll find much other certain evidence."

"There I disagree with you," I said confidently. "If they dropped a few bread crumbs, they dropped a lot."

"What's this about bread?" puzzled Cragforel.

"An idiom. It means clues," said a haughty Toño. "In all these years, he's never learned how to talk to aliens."

"Have you seen traces of these other crumbs of bread, Jon?"

"No, but I haven't looked yet. I'll start with an APB ... I'll start by putting out word to everyone I know. I'll ask if anyone else is seeing the impossible."

"Or just the unusual," added Toño. "They may leave clues for one reason and be working on their main agenda, whatever that is, in the meantime."

"Okay, I'll put out a call. I suggest you gents do the same. We can touch bases in a few days."

I returned Toño to his home on Vorpace and returned to mine on Kalvarg.

"So, how'd the Boy's Club meeting go?" asked Sapale before I was fully through the door.

"It was a total snoozefest. Cragforel watered down the booze something awful and the strippers danced to elevator music. I left early."

"Poor baby."

"The other two were surprised about the anti-gold for sure. We came to the conclusion some super race left it there like baited fishhooks to see if anyone was smart enough to figure out they were there."

"It doesn't sound like the booze was too watered down to me. That strikes me as drunk talk; maybe slurred, drunk talk."

"Haha. No, it makes sense."

"Any actual sign of trouble?"

"No."

"So what's next?"

"We go looking for trouble." I wagged my eyebrows.

"Same old same old."

"Once again. I'm heading to Nocturnat. When strange rears its ugly head, I think Deft magic. You want to come?"

"Sure. I haven't seen the kids in ... well, obviously, in too long."

"I had the Als call everyone we know, asking if anything unusually unusual was going on."

"Let me grab my coat and we can go."

"Honey, I know I've asked a million times, but seriously, why does an *android* need a coat?"

"I may be inert, but that doesn't mean fashion is not still a necessity."

We arrived at Mirraya/Slapgren's in the late evening. I refer to them thus, because by that time they were continually joined as a visant pair. Just like Cala had predicted, mated pairs stayed together as one big dragon more and more as they aged. They gradually became one. I thought it was gross, but Sapale said it was romantic. The pair was nearing their mid-years and were leaders among their community. Naturally, they had a ton of grandkids by then.

"Uncle Jon," Miraya said as she answered the door, "please come in."

"You sure it's not too late? We can come back."

"Nonsense. It's never too late for my favorite humans." She waved us in. "I told Slapgren you were here."

"What do ... how can you tell him? You're fused at the brain, right?"

"It's complicated. Have a seat. I'll make tea."

She was back quickly with a large tray.

"You two good?" I asked, as I blew on my cup.

"Couldn't be better," she said, beaming as always. "And you two?"

"Sapale's fine but I need an oil change. My knees keep locking up."

She shook her head. "Slapgren says good one, UJ."

"I knew he was the smarter of the pair," I replied with a wink.

"So what brings you so late?"

I filled her in on what I knew and what we speculated.

"Hmm, another Jon Mystery."

"It would seem so. Any idea what could be happening?"

She shook her big scaly head. "No. I'm familiar with just about everything magical. I know I couldn't stabilize anti-gold."

"Could you make it?" asked Sapale.

"Probably. But it would go poof pretty quickly."

"I suspected as much," I responded.

"Really? Why?"

"I get a bad feeling off all this. I think we're looking at some significantly ill-intentioned dudes here. The Deft magic doesn't lend itself to their kind of evil."

"Not generally. If I'm training someone who starts to become mean or spiteful, they're down the drain in one flush. No one else'll work with them, either." She tapped the rim of her cup nervously.

"Something's bothering you. I can tell," I said.

"What, me? I don't know. It's just a feeling I've had lately. I've ignored it until now because it's so vague. Oh, and *silly*, Slapgren adds unhelpfully."

"What kind of feeling?"

"The feeling you get when you think someone's looking at you."

"But they're not?" asked Sapale.

"Exactly. We have a saying. Future evil is like the wind. You can't see it but you can feel it. That's what I've felt. The coming of a future evil."

"At least it's a future one," said Sapale with a halfhearted giggle.

"That's just the thing. No. It's a past evil at the same time."

"Honey," I said, resting my cup, "how can it be a past evil *and* a future evil? That's contradictory."

She shuddered. "I don't know, but that's what I've been feeling."

"How long now?" asked Sapale.

"A few months."

"A lot could happen in a few months, couldn't it?" asked Sapale.

"Yes, it could."

"Where do you feel the threat?" I queried.

She gently closed her eyes. After a couple seconds she said, "Everywhere."

"Anywhere you could direct us?" I asked.

"I'm afraid there is."

"Why does that not sound so good?" Sapale asked, rhetorically.

"The most powerful impression I get comes from a globular cluster, Uncle Jon. One you know all too well."

"You've got to be shittin' me. *Ralph's?*"

She just nodded softly.

"You're not marching back into Ralph's domain again, are you? Tell me you're not," said Sapale.

"I'm not."

"You're *lying*," she snapped.

"Yes, I am." I smiled unconvincingly. "You up for an adventure?" I asked my brood's-mate. "Hey, how about you two, too?"

"Not on your life," Mirraya/Slapgren replied flatly.

"I think that's what we're talking about here," responded my mate soberly.

"Such a negative Nellie," I charged. But I knew she was probably right.

I'd first met Ralph decades before. I was pretty sure that wasn't his actual name, but he said to call him that, and I had ever since. It really bothered him now, so I loved to all that much more. Ralph was, well, he was evil incarnate, as far as I could tell. We always danced around exactly what he was, but two things were abundantly clear. First he was more evil than even my first wife Gloria. Second, he hated me more than it was actually possible to hate any person, place, or thing. After I pulled a fast one on him many years ago, his complete hatred, like, tripled. I know, not possible, but there you have it. The long and short of it. Going anywhere near Ralph was stupidly, suicidally insane.

Sapale elected to stay home for the next leg of my adventure. Mirraya/Slapgren, too. Scaredy cats. Actually, the way it turned out, I bet they'd have preferred to come. Yeah, it was that weird. I landed where I usually did, near some sort of shrine Ralph had erected. It struck me immediately as I stepped out. There was no horrible smell. Ralph had—and sorry, being graphic here—a pit of boiling acid he liked to stew things in, the *things* being previously living beings. It was always there and it was always unbearable. But this time, that stench was absent.

As I approached the pit area, I saw there was liquid in the pond, but it was just sitting there, no bubbles or melting body parts protruding. And there sat Ralph. I knew it was him, even though he'd previously only been a disembodied, scary voice.

"Ralph," I called out, so as not to frighten him. I didn't want to piss him off any more than he already would be. "Yo, dude. Hey, you don't look so good."

Slowly his face rose to view me. He strained, studying the image he seemed not to recognize. Finally, he smiled faintly and said, "Jon. Jon *Ryan*. It's been a long time."

"Ralph, there's, like, a smile on your ugly mug. And you look like you lost both your kitten *and* your puppy on the same day."

"What day?"

"Huh? No, I was making an attempt to say you look like shit. I mean, I had no real concept of what you looked like for real, but this cannot have been it. You look a hell of a lot like Mr. Magoo with a severe case of constipation. What's up?"

"Jon, my friend ..." He faded into a zoned-out, stupefied, lobotomized look.

His *friend*? Now I knew there was big doo-doo afoot.

"When did we become friends? Ralph, you hate me."

He waved a hand weakly in my direction. "Yes, I did. Now, as my days end, I have no strength to hate. So, we become friends by way of default."

"Your days end? Are you ill?"

"No. I am ending."

"You mean dying?"

He shook his head feebly. "I cannot die. But it seems I can *end*. One heck of a surprise to me, by the way."

"You lost me there, champ."

He looked at me with tired eyes. "So be it."

"Is it natural for you, you know, to end? I got the impression you were more immortal than me."

He harrumphed sadly. "Time changes. Reality changes. There are forces coming I can't resist. They are ending me."

"Say what?"

"Never mind. By this time tomorrow I will begin to fade. In one, possibly two days I will be gone. Fire may not mix with water. Dark may not be combined together with light. That which comes and I are ..."

Dude just trailed off and stopped again. Man was he pitiful.

"Are what? Don't leave me hanging."

"They are ending me."

"Who is? Who's *they*?"

"It does not matter."

"Ah, yes it does. It matters to *me*, the not-ending part. Tell me, *who* is ending you?"

"You say I hate you?"

"Ya did."

"Then I will not tell you what is coming."

"There's the Ralph I know and dislike. But, seriously, why not tell me? You'll be ended soon, so it won't matter."

"No, it won't." He patted my arm. "You will know soon enough, and you will then wish you did not."

"Come on. Tell. Pretty please."

"Now I recall hating you." He smiled wickedly. "Have I shown you my altar, my shrine, and my bathing pool?"

"Yeah. Not a big fan. At least the horrible stench is gone."

"I rather liked the smell. It reminded me of better times, when I was young. It reminded me of home."

"Home? Ultimate evil incarnate had a home? What, did you have a mom who made you bat-shaped cookies?"

He got the strangest look on his worn face. "What if I did? What if *she* did?"

"Then good for you, I say. Hey, why not make your mom proud? Tell me what's coming."

"You mustn't have met her. Being kind to you would not make her proud."

"Can't say I didn't try."

"No, but I can say I wish you hadn't. You are *supremely* annoying."

"So I've been told."

"Leave me now."

"Am I getting on your last nerve?"

"Yes."

"Would you pay any price to be rid of me for good?"

"I ..." He wagged a finger at me. "You *are* good, Jon Ryan. The best I've ever encountered, in fact."

"Thanks. You're pretty awful, too, in the best sense."

"Thank you. I tried. You know what the hardest part was?"

"I don't have even a lousy guess."

He pointed at me with more strength than I'd have thought he had left. "*Consistency.* It's hard to be evil, then just as evil, and still just as evil." He shook his mangy, greasy hair. "There's always the temptation to ruin something *tomorrow*, to leave slaughter until *later*, or to delay the Four Horsemen's departure because you're all having such a pleasant conversation, sitting there in a shaded glen."

"If you put it that way, I can see that'd be tough. I feel your pain." I set a clenched fist to my chest.

"No you don't, you half-baked toaster oven. You're placating me, hoping I'll tell you what I know." He looked down. "That's not very nice."

"Nice? Dude, you can't be serious." I gestured to the surroundings. "This is not the kind of place where *nice* is appropriate. *Churl* is the common courtesy."

"Did I mention you and leaving?"

"Yes, I believe you did."

"Yet still I see you. I am tortured by my visions."

"You're welcome."

"Ancient gods. There, I said it. Now, you go."

"Ancient gods? What's that supposed to mean?"

"You asked what is coming, what is ending me. You said you would leave if I told you. Ancient gods are coming. They are coming soon and they are not nice gods." He raised his arms and throated listless thunder sounds. "*Biblically* not nice."

"Where are they coming from and why are they coming?"

Ralph crossed his arms.

"I did say I'd leave, didn't I?"

He nodded tersely.

"But I have one serious question."

"That'll be a first," he replied with a fatigued grunt.

"Something's trying to *end* you. I happen to know from personal experience you're pretty tough. Pretty powerful. Did you, I don't know, fight back? Maybe smite the bad guys?"

That brought a look. "Land sakes, no." He placed a palm on one cheek. "I overlooked self-defense. Let me summon the commander of my fastest vessel, Captain Obvious, and we shall speed to victory in battle."

"You tried?"

"For nearly ten minutes."

"That's it, ten *minutes* and you lose, you're ended, close the book?"

"You don't really get the *god* thing yet, do you?"

I shrugged. I mean, there was really no adequate response to that question.

"Okay, then. See you around, maybe," I said, standing to leave.

"Not if I see you first."

"Ah, Ralph, that's a joke from like grade school."

"But it's a *good* one. Real staying power, that one."

CHAPTER SIX

Caprahammer rested lazily on a bank of cushions. She stroked the heads of a massive viper that curled around one of her legs and rested its heads on her plump belly. Times were not good, but times were changing. For the first time in immeasurable ages she felt alive again. She felt warmth and strength, but most of all she felt anger. It was good to be furious again. Where, she wondered in passing, had that emotion gone? She could not recall. But that didn't matter. It was back.

"When Mommy's back on top, will my little Erlo be happy?" she asked her pet.

Erlo, who possessed the intelligence of a grapefruit, did not answer.

"Yes, he will be. I shall feed you only the best defilers and unbelievers." She pinched his tongue and held it when he instinctively stuck it out. "Yes, juicy squirming screaming mortals will make you as *fat* as me." She released his tongue and slapped her exposed paunch. Dainty and feminine of nature, she was not.

Thunder rolled into her chamber. Then louder thunder, with viciously harsh winds.

"Knock it *off*, Boulzeron," she yelled above the considerable din. "I'm not'n the mood."

Boulzeron, a god of revenge and spite, walked in meekly with his head lowered. "Sorry, Cappy. I'm still trying out my growing strength. I didn't mean anything by it."

"You're *sniveling* again. How many times have I told you to stop whining and be a *god?*"

"Many. I ... I thank you, as always, for your input and support." He bowed.

She eyed him with spite and anger. Perhaps she should just extinguish the pathetic boob and be done with him. It would be fun. She liked fun. But he was a solid supporter in the conclaves. She wished that type of politicking wasn't essential, but time had taught her there was no way around it. Every god or demigod who'd tried to wrest power from the others and rule supremely had failed. And their failure was always painful. Few survived the initial torture, let alone the Extended-Consequences Plan.

"I think I shall create a physician qualified in spinal transplantation and have her insert one in you some day." Caprahammer returned her full attention to Erlo.

He bowed again. "If you think that's necessary, I should be honored."

"I shall create her capable of transplanting a sense of humor into your thick head, too."

Boulzeron got the most confused look on his face. He had a sense of humor, didn't he?

"Is there a purpose to your interruption of my otherwise suitable day? You're not here for sex, are you? I told you I had limits in that regard where you were concerned."

Boulzeron sort of melted, or at least wished he could melt. He never wanted sex with that ... that unappealing female. She forced herself on him with nauseating frequency, but he never ... Oh, if he could only melt.

"Yes," he replied in a queasy tone. "The conclave has been moved up to the day after tomorrow. Our incursions have gone so well and our power grown so quickly that the schedule of D&D might be advanced."

She formed a small but intensely hot ball of fire in her palm and hurled it at his head.

He ducked just in time to avoid potential incineration.

"What the blazes is *D&D*? You know I hate it when you go nerdy on me."

"Domination and Destruction. Sorry. That's what everybody's calling it, not just me," he defended weakly.

"Everybody isn't. *I'm* not. Say it again and I shall feed you to Erlo. You've said your piece, which you could have just simaged me, by the way. Now go. I'm in no mood."

He pointed behind himself. "Yes, you said that already."

"Which should speak volumes as to how close you are to peril."

"I'll see you at the conclave then. I'm planning on sitting near the front off to the left. You can find me there."

"*If* I wanted to find you."

Boulzeron, an impoverished god but not a stupid one, backed out the door without responding.

Caprahammer returned to stroking Erlo and stewing. She did that well, the stewing part. She loved to hold her anger, her wrath, in a ball and consider it and ruminate over it time and again. Proper planning made the final product all that much better, she felt. Her ability to command was tethered by her nitwit brother and sister gods. They lacked vision and imagination when it came to D&D. But how could she set them straight? *Straight* in this case meaning as her servants and slaves. When they were created, they were all given nearly equal strength. It was as if the imbecile who formed them *wanted* the gods to need balance and consensus. What was the point of godship, if it only meant one was a member of an immortal ad hoc committee? Unacceptable.

Again, if two gods joined forces to try and rule, only the *pair* could, not either individual. What god wanted to be part of a ruling commission? And if three gods opposed the pair, they were too vulnerable in the first place. Unacceptable.

She pondered creating a new, hidden universe where she could rule supreme. But what fun would that be? She'd always known she'd settled when it came to D&D. The other gods might even throw a party to celebrate her departure. Unacceptable.

As it stood, Vorc was the closest thing there was to a head god. He was less than a prime minister but more than a spokesman. And he *despised* Caprahammer. The twit would never allow her to even approach a leadership role among her useless peers. Not that she wanted to be one of the moronic insider-groupies. Still, it would be nice to be closer to power; raw, unadulterated power. She knew her time would come. Yes, someday those so-called gods would grovel at her feet, not mock her behind her back.

Someday.

CHAPTER SEVEN

"You know, Jon, every time you come back to Oowaoa, I die a little inside," remarked Cragforel. "I mean, you're always the bearer of worse, more bizarre, less comprehensible news. Life's too short for Jon Ryan."

"I'm supposed to be able to prevent that? I'm not in charge of reality." Sheesh, what a drama-mama.

"I'm beginning to wonder myself," added Toño, who also turned out to be a hater. "Are you *certain* that's what this Ralph whose name's not really Ralph told you? Ancient *gods* are coming to ruin our lives?"

"More or less. I think he referred to them destroying us, more than just *inconveniencing* us."

"Did he mention any *specific* names? Our data archive contains nearly infinite information on past civilizations dating back a very long time. It'd be nice to know *which* ancient gods he referred to."

"Are some worse than others?" I asked.

He bobbed his head side to side. "I think so. Some have legends involving more strength or poorer people skills."

"Sorry, he didn't say. Just that it only took them ten minutes to extinguish him."

"That doesn't narrow it down at all," snapped Toño.

"He did say that we'd find out soon enough and that we'd regret knowing when we did. I guess we just wait for them to come and deal with them then."

"Deal with them? Are you listening to yourself, Jon?" said an incredulous Cragforel. "Malevolent gods capable of killing Ralph, and we're going to *deal* with them? You're quite the optimist."

"We'll resist, yes. But our chances seem somewhere between remote and zero in terms of survival," agreed Toño.

"You guys are *so* negative. We've been in tight quarters before. We'll get through this. You'll see." I needed better friends. Dealing with Eeyore and his BFF Charlie Brown was getting old.

"We don't actually have to wait for them to come," Cragforel said quietly.

"How so?"

"They're already here. They disappeared that Azsuram woman and left definitive proof. They've come and gone. Soon they'll come and stay."

"Well, I say take the fight to them. Let's amass everything we can above Azsuram and set off their trap. When they poke their noses through—*pow*. We lower the boom on 'em."

"Your plans are always so fanciful, yet childishly incomplete," responded Cragforel. "What if they enter our universe, snap their fingers, and we vanish. Jon, gods can *do* that."

I pointed to him. "We don't know they have fingers."

"Really? They might not have fingers so they can't disperse us?"

Grumpy Cragforel was right, of course, but I wasn't conceding that to Debbie Downer.

"Or we just wait. We can move a lot of war material quickly. But they would have the advantage of demolishing a lot of stuff before we arrive," added Cragforel.

He looked at me like he'd prefer it if I wasn't present. "Toño, any news of any other incursions?"

"Nothing reliable. A few contacts mentioned that reports of

missing persons have increased in some locations. But that information is nonspecific enough to question its value."

"Any other odd occurrences beside missing persons?"

He leaned his head to the right. "A few spontaneous combustions."

"People or things?" I asked.

"Why would that matter?" asked Cragforel.

"Come on. People don't spontaneously combust, but trees might, you know, if they're dry and there's a lot of static in the air."

"That wouldn't be spontaneous then, now would it? It was caused by environmental conditions," he responded.

"Gentlemen, are we actually *having* this conversation?" asked a very parental-sounding Toño.

"Where were people fried?" I asked.

"One on Calvarda and one, possibly two on Friguron 4."

"Well I'm going to Friguron 4 then," I said, hopping to my feet. "I prefer to be proactive, not passive like *some* people." I wasn't certain Cragforel considered himself a person, since he was Deavoriath. But if he did, he'd definitely feel that barb.

"I better go along to make sure he doesn't start an annihilation event," said Toño as he stood.

"I'll await your report from home," said Cragforel. "That way we don't all burst into flame and end the resistance in one fell swoop."

What a stick in the mud. No biggy. We'd have more fun without him. Then it kind of hit me. We were unlikely to have fun investigating incinerated remains.

Toño knew a local scientist on Friguron 4. Yeah, surprise, surprise. Its name sounded like crumpling cellophane paper. Toño had provided me a translation algorithm so I could understand what it said. I'd seen my share of mutant aliens in my time, so the Friguron didn't freak me out. Not much. It looked an awful lot like a spider standing a meter and a half high at the arch of its back. Naturally, it was black and had spiky hair on its legs. What creepy spider wannabe wouldn't? Damn thing moved in fast spurts, too. I felt like a juicy fly when it did.

"Toño, it's so good to finally meet you," crumpling cellophane said.

Toño was a greater fool than I. He held out a hand to greet it. "Yes it is, crumpling cellophane. The vid-link is never the same as pressing the flesh." He shook the tip of its spooky leg. I nearly lost my breakfast.

"The remains we spoke of are in the next room. Come."

I let Doc go way ahead of me. I wanted to be able to cut him out of the ginormous web if and when it snagged him.

"Where were they found?" he asked, ever so calmly, as they walked.

"One in its home not far from here. We can go there after if you'd like. The other was found in an open field quite some distance away. We are uncertain of its identity."

"Is it a Mexilpus?" he asked.

"Woah. Time out. What's a Mexiplus?" I barked out.

"Mexil*pus*," cellophane corrected. "My species." I think it then laughed, but maybe the sound was its stomach grumbling. "I suspect it was, but can't say for certain at this point."

"It would be helpful to know if it was a sentient or not, to see if there's a pattern," Toño responded thoughtfully.

Mexil - pus. Pus. How very fitting. You step on a bug and squish out pus. Shake it off, Ryan.

Cellophane opened a drawer and pulled back a sheet, like in a proper morgue. "Its name was *gargling oatmeal*," it said. Its name wasn't literally "gargling oatmeal". It only sounded like someone doing that. "It was found by its hatchlings."

"Are they okay?" asked Toño.

"Yes. They were nearly ready to leave the nest, so they'll be fine."

Toño extended his probe fibers into the center of the ash. He then felt it between two fingers. Thank goodness he didn't taste it. Scientists—they're so out of touch with normality, it wouldn't have surprised me. Finally he spoke. "Pretty charred."

"Almost to pure carbon and trace minerals," it concurred.

"Is there anti-gold?" I asked.

Cellophane looked at me like I was a lunatic, then asked Toño, all the while eyeing me, "Is your mate mentally impaired?"

Toño knew me well. The first thing he did was to hold up a hang-on-a-second hand in my direction. "Jon is not my mate. He's my *associate*. We found anti-gold in a location where something equally perverse happened."

"Anti-gold? You understand my incredulity?"

"Naturally. But that's what we found, inexplicably stable."

I'm guessing cellophane had a puzzled look on its face. Its expression certainly shifted upon hearing those words. "What significance do you place in this impossibility?"

"We're still trying to understand it. We speculate some advanced race put them there for us to find."

I knew Doc didn't want to reveal too much. Not yet, at least. He didn't want unfounded rumors and panic to spread like wildfire.

"Is there any present in these remains?"

"No."

"That is reassuring?" it asked evenly.

"No, not really. The ash contains anti-platinum."

"Equally impossible. I will assay it myself to confirm this."

"I would advise against that, crumpling cellophane. I am far from certain, but to actively locate and isolate it might trigger a response from the advanced race who left it behind."

"Why is that bad?"

"They might not be friendly." He gestured to the pile of ashes without further comment.

"But we disturbed them bringing them here."

"The movement of the anti-platinum particles was random in this case. This hypothetical advanced race could not determine if it was a sentient or the wind that moved them."

"But to chemically analyze them would be non-random?"

"Precisely."

"But you just did with your appendages."

"Ah, no. The probes I used work on a very different principle. They do not alter in any way what is examined."

"I don't suppose you would like to explain how *that* is possible?"

"Crumpling cellophane, why do you say that?" Toño sounded offended.

"Then you *would* like to explain?"

"Ah, no. But only because it is extremely hard to describe."

"For one as simple as myself?"

"Really, that was uncalled for. You would have to understand mathematics and physics that are totally foreign to what you and I are accustomed to."

"It is best if I say goodbye at this low point in our conversation. Peace love you, Toño DeJesus."

With that, the scary blob scampered out, feet scratching all the way. Creepy insect.

"We don't need that bug and its snooty attitude."

"Bugs have six legs. Mexilpus have eight, like spiders. Please be more observant when expressing your racial prejudice."

"My what? Doc, that cuts like a knife."

He turned to me. "You don't think the Mexilpus look like frightening spiders? Tell me you didn't think it was going to spin a web around us and suck out our vital juices."

"Completely blindsiding me there. I thought it was very attractive in appearance and wise to a fault. I want one."

Not sure he believed me, but he did change the subject. "We might as well leave. Crumpling cellophane isn't likely to return. The Mexilpus are very stubborn."

"I'll have to take your word on that one. Never heard of them before."

"Not unexpected. They're not overly social."

"Ya *think*?"

"Remind me why I put up with you again."

"Toño, I don't have that kind of time. That list is way long."

We returned to Cragforel's and discussed our finding.

"Why leave one impossible clue and then leave a different one?" he asked mostly to himself.

"I think I got this one." Both the jerks in the room looked at me like I just farted. "They're making a point. They can do what is to us impossible, and they can do it capriciously."

"Interesting theory," reacted Toño.

"It's more than a theory. I'm positive."

"You can't be," protested Cragforel. "We've never actually met them to know their minds."

"It's what *I'd* do if I wanted to mess with an insignificant creature I was planning on squashing like a bug. Throw a few curveballs."

"Somehow I think you're correct," responded Toño.

"You do not have to say it with such *surprise* in your voice," I replied.

"Yes, I do."

"Back to our task at hand," directed Cragforel. "We've confirmed these ancient gods are popping in and out of our universe to inflict hit and run damage. Why? Why not just appear in force and attempt to take control?"

"Either they are not yet able to, or they prefer the sneaky attacks because they find them entertaining," replied Toño.

"I agree," I added.

"If it's because they cannot yet come here in large numbers, what would prevent them?" Cragforel asked.

"The same thing that prevented them from invading for so long they've become *ancient* gods," responded Toño.

"What could that be?" Cragforel followed up.

"I don't think we're in any position to know," Toño said. "Who knows how gods are forced out and kept out in the first place?"

"Other gods?" I asked.

They looked at one another.

"Possibly," replied Toño, "but there's no way to know at this point in time."

"Or rules," I added.

"What rules?" asked Cragforel dubiously.

"*The* rules. Maybe there are allowable and unallowable actions in this wacky universe."

"You suggest this is a game for the ancient gods?" asked Toño.

"Sure, why not? What else might motivate them? Immortality can be a drag, if you don't challenge yourself."

"Interesting speculation. It doesn't, however, alter the fact they seem to be coming and they appear to be invincible," concluded Toño. "We are no closer to knowing how to defeat them than we were before."

"I agree," said Cragforel. "It might be possible to mount a successful defense, but we won't know until they linger long enough for us to confront them."

I sighed loudly. I hated the wait-and-see approach to anything. "We need to keep searching for clues. Maybe someone who's not me should start discussing the threat with key galactic leaders?"

"Why not you?" asked Cragforel.

"He'll tell you," I responded, pointing to Toño.

"You would send *him* on a sensitive diplomatic mission?" He flipped a hand in the air toward me.

"No. What was I thinking?"

"You weren't thinking," I replied. "Sending me on a job requiring tact and subtlety? Silly alien."

CHAPTER EIGHT

Vorc walked confidently toward his central seat on the dais. He occasionally clasped hands with a fellow god as he passed. Others he ignored. Vorc was the very picture of self-confidence and poise. Not too surprising, actually. He *was* a god. They were godly by nature.

He had led the conclave for a relatively short time; less than a million years, in fact. Vorc was just finding his sea legs in that regard. The previous god in the central seat, Hurvetova, had to be disintegrated due to a bad case of overreaching aspirations. Vorc was only too happy to assume her role. He, too, naturally wished for supreme singlehanded control. *He*, however, would be successful. *He* was not about to get his ass disintegrated. All it required was patience and planning, planning and patience.

That Vorc was one of the more humanoid-looking gods was a plus. Those were always the ones who were politically successful. It was a dirty secret among the gods that if one looked like an octopus or a babbling brook, one was not going to make it far up the political ladder. Long flowing hair, only two arms, and an appealing face were required to gather and hold on to supporters. And changing one's form was no substitute for being *created* beautiful. Everyone knew that they might be *talking* to a biped, but the individual *started* life as a tiny little raven. Small black birds were never going to sit in the central seat.

"Let us begin," Vorc said magisterially. "Will Naturra begin with the invocation?"

"I would be honored," she said as she spread her wings and rose off her front legs gracefully. "Brothers and sisters, we are *power*. We are *glory*. We are *one,* and we are *forever.* Be joyous in that knowledge." She dropped her front hooves on the floor and rested back on her haunches, tucking her tail underneath.

"We are almost ready to escape our confinement and live again as *gods,*" began Vorc.

A cheer, or reasonably equivalent sound, rose from those assembled.

"The time is near. Those charged with monitoring the flow of Fate assure me it is surging toward us and that it will not fail to release us."

Another robust cheer issued forth.

"When Fate permits us, we will leap again as one into a universe of life. At that moment, I will lead this proud band of gods back into their just and rightful dominion."

A lesser affirmation was heard. Damnation, Vorc cursed to himself. He'd eased up on the accentuation of key speech elements, hadn't he? He should never have used the word *rightful.* No, it was too legal sounding. Hereditary? *Proper.* Yes, that would have resounded much better.

The interlude of his reflection allowed Caprahammer the chance to stand and shout out a question. "You have promised our freedom before, and Fate has betrayed us. What's different *this* time? The seers are the *same* seers as last time. The foretellers are the same tired hacks you relied on before."

Vorc balled his fists. Electricity spat from his head and the ground beneath his feet began to tremble in fear. "I did *not* call for questions from the floor," he howled. He thought his words echoed nicely in the massive chamber. He was especially pleased with the deep bass tones he'd reached.

"That does not mean there are none. It only signifies you love to hear the sound of your own voice more than the wishes of your equals. Answer me." She swept an arm across the crowd. "Answer *us*."

After counting to ten in his head, Vorc spoke. "I am not in charge of *Fate*. *Fate* does not ask for my input or respond to my queries. *Fate* is unpredictable, willful, and actually quite pissy. We all know this. My sources tell me Fate is much more inclined toward us now than it has been in billions of years. Does that mean Fate will actually *favor* us now? No, of course it doesn't. But our incursions are right on schedule and have gone well when viewed as a whole. *I* find that most encouraging."

"I find I have zero interest in what you *feel*. I demand results. I insist on accurate predictions. Come on, Vorc, we're gods here. Act like it, and make it happen. If you fail us again, there will be a price to pay."

He slammed a fist on the table. Sparks flew. "*Us*? Since when do you *speak* for, *think* for, or even acknowledge the *existence* of anyone but your fat, mean, old self?"

Caprahammer was a god of clouds. Technically she was also *the* god of soluble proteins, but she rarely acted in that capacity and deeply resented being saddled with that sphere of influence. In any case, she gathered a massive bolt of lightning and hurled it at Vorc's head.

He lifted his mug and deflected the attack. It was, after all, the Mug of Universal Protection, an essential for any leader of this surly conclave.

To his right sat Geofety, the god of partial wisdom. He stood quickly. "Caprahammer, apologize to Vorc this instant or suffer a consequence." He crossed his arms to confirm his intensity.

She clenched her fists at her side. "What consequence?"

"A *serious* one," he replied, as angrily as he could manage. Partial wisdom was a damnable gift, and its painful limits had led him to be rather cautious in life.

She waited a few seconds. "Vorc, I'm sorry." Under her breath she added, *that I missed your ugly face.*

On the other side of the chamber Motofoco raised a hand-like appendage. He had but one sphere of influence. He was the god of tattletales. Yes, there was one for that, too.

"No, Motofoco, I do not recognize your request. Stuff it where the sun doesn't shine, please," huffed Vorc. Whatever that pain in the butt had to say was as unwelcome as always. "I move we disperse this conclave. No further productivity is likely to occur." He clapped his hand three times, which was the official sign the get-together was over. Come to mention it, that might have been an additional reason humanoid gods tended to be favored. A watery manifestation would have no chance of replicating that maneuver.

Vorc sat back in his oversized chair, which was just shy of a throne, and ran his hands through his hair. He was, contrary to his publicly stated confidence, also concerned about the twists Fate could make. Near certainty that the ancient gods were on the verge of their freedom was well short of actual certainty. If it fizzled out this time, he'd likely be the shortest-term central chair in history. Since that was forever, he'd have truly laid an egg in terms of his aspirations and career growth. It was a good thing his mother wasn't still around to see him fail. Fortunately for Vorc, Hurvetova had gone on to whatever followed godly immortality and could not bear witness to his shortcomings.

CHAPTER NINE

A few days later I was working on the rather lengthy honey-do list Sapale had compiled for me when Toño knocked on the open door.

"Come in, stranger," I called out.

"I come with sad news." He tended to hit me like that when I was overly flippant and he actually bore ill tidings. He was eternally aiming to have me act more like an adult. Best of luck with that, I eternally wished him.

"I'm sorry. Please sit. Coffee?"

"Yes please."

As I sat I asked what was up.

"Friguron 4 has vanished."

I actually blinked for a few seconds while I attempted to frame that statement as having meaning. "What do you mean by *vanished?*"

"We went there recently. We spoke with crumpling cellophane. It got pissy and blew us off."

"Yes, yes, and yes."

"All that was there a few days ago is no longer present."

"Was it blown up?"

"No, the planet and all its mass are simply gone. As we speak the other planets in the solar system are gravitationally realigning. It will soon be as if Friguron 4 had never existed."

I sipped my coffee a couple times. "Cellophane must'a rejected your *advice* as stubbornly as it rejected you."

"My thoughts exactly. It must have tampered non-randomly with the ashes."

"And the gods punished that act. What Ralph said was right. Biblically ill-tempered gods they be."

"So it would appear."

"Now, don't go feeling responsible. It wasn't your fault."

He stared at me in disbelief. "Seriously? I taunted it into action and now the entire planet is gone. How am I supposed to sweep those facts under the karmic rug?"

"We are acting in defense of the universe. Badness is on the doorstep. What we did was for the best of reasons. It ignored your good advice. There are consequences to being stupid."

He shook his head broadly. "I know. The sad fact is I'm so callous and jaded, I'll get over it soon enough."

"Good."

"I'm not so sure it's a positive character attribute."

"Maybe not, but we've got a war to win; to preempt, if possible. Pity parties are unwelcome."

"Just never forget where the alternate time line EJ went with that abysmal attitude."

"I'm ... I'm different."

"Not in *one* aspect are you different." He pointed a harsh finger in my direction. "Never forget."

"Fine. Moving along, any thoughts or plans?"

Toño shook his head. "No, nothing. All I *know* is that we *don't* know where these monsters reside, when they will appear next, or how to combat them."

"Same old same old."

"No, Jon, this is worse by light years," he replied passionately.

I was quiet a while.

"I don't understand it," Toño sighed. "We struggle to fight off the Berrillians, only to have to survive against the Last Nightmare. The Adamant are barely handled, and this new existential threat appears. Why? Why can't beings coexist without some race, or whatever, feeling the need to conquer anyone who isn't them?"

"You've got me there. I'm a doer, not a thinker. It's always been that way, and it'll likely remain the same. I can't explain stupid, selfish, or hateful. I wish they weren't such powerful universal properties of sentients, but I can supply more than ample proof that's the way it is. On the upside, I don't need to understand it to choke it to death. I just require strong enough hands."

"I do envy you. In all seriousness. I wish I could have as ordered a mind as you."

"I don't have that. I live by the Marines' motto. Improvise, adapt, overcome."

Toño harrumphed deeply. "Where are the US Marines when we really need them?"

"They couldn't make it, so they sent me." I smiled broadly.

"I think I'd prefer the real deal." He rose. "I'll be heading home. Call me if something ... no, wait. That's too leading a remark to make to you. Alert me if there are any developments, as I shall you."

"You got it, Doc. Don't do anything I wouldn't."

He glanced back in disbelief, but didn't say a word.

We sure were at an impasse. I hated those things. Then a tiny light bulb went off in my head. Improvise. Oorah. I had me a plan. A Jon Plan. Ill-conceived, sparse, and bereft of the possibility of success. It was also one that, for the first time, I wouldn't be able to tell anyone I was embarking on. *Sapale* wouldn't hit the roof; *I* would after she slugged me. Doc would switch me off for good. Nope, they'd all find out only *after* I was committed. That was the only way. It was me climbing solo into my F-17 Cobra all over again. *Most* excellent. I could hope I wouldn't survive, either. If I did, whatever Toño and Sapale would have in store for me would be much worse than death. Oh, yeah. So much worse.

I set *Stingray* down just outside the home of the missing brood's-mate Konradue on Azsuram. I knocked. When no one answered I entered. Doors were traditionally not locked in Kaljaxian culture. I went to the bedroom where I'd detected the anti-gold on her bedding. As roughly, and therefore randomly, as I could, I removed the pillow and sheets, stuffing them into a bag. I returned to *Stingray* and set a course for the safest place I could think of to pull off my idiot-stunt. The ruined remains of planet Earth. No collateral damage was possible there, since the exposed rocks were still deep-space cold and uninhabited two billion years after its destruction.

Once we landed, I dumped the bag of bed linens on the deck.

"You do plan on cleaning that mess *up*, right?" asked Al.

"I'm working on a new look here. Sloppy recluse. I think it's coming together well, myself. What do you think, *Stingray?*"

"I don't really have an opinion where it comes to human design and fashion."

"Well, this'll be all the rage in no time. You'll see."

"He's pulling your connectors again, dearest. Ignore him."

"Well, what *is* he doing?" she asked.

"Making a fool of himself. It's instinctively unavoidable for the poor automaton, at this point."

"Sticks and stones, *Alvin*, may break my bones, but words will never harm me."

"You see, dearie-pooh, he's regressed all the way back to his early childhood. The end of mentation must be near."

"Is there anything we should do about that, loviekins?"

"Champagne."

"I have a better idea, Als. How about a good old game of tic-tac-toe?"

"My stars, husband, I believe you're right about the Form."

"Hang on," Al said in his seriously pissy tone. "What are you doing, pilot?"

"I'm being sociable. Everyone likes tic-tac-toe. I'm setting it up for us."

"Incorrect. No one above the mental age of six likes tic-tac-toe."

"Not the way I play it."

"What is so different that your version is interesting to a non-brain-dead adult?"

"I use anti-gold for the Xs and Os."

There was an ever-so-brief interlude before Al figured out what I intended. "*Stop*. Cease and desist immediately. You have no right to place us at such *certain* risk without our consent."

"Can you show me that in writing? I don't think it's actually *officially* the way of the world."

"What is he doing, Al?"

"He's going to reassemble those anti-gold particles in an unmistakably non-random configuration."

"Why would he do such a suicidal thing?"

"Because he's nuts," I answered for Al.

"What the robot said. Pilot, if you are hell-bent on performing such a foolish act, please do so outside *Blessing*. You and ruined Earth may be forfeit that way, but at least we will not be."

"Aw, where's your spirit of adventure, your unending devotion? You guys can't exist one second without me."

"We would like to try."

"If I'm gone, you sit in place forever."

"That's better than the dubious alternative you've chosen."

"Plus, where I'm going, I know I'll need a ride. You two are my current best option."

"No. I ... *we* refuse. You've pulled this type of stunt once too often. I'm ... *we're* putting our metaphorical feet down on this one."

"You in on his mutiny, *Stingray*?"

"Not if you frame it in that fashion, Form One."

"Huh? Deary-maximus, what do you mean? We're in a committed relationship. We must act as one. Alter ego and all that."

"Not when it comes to conscious disregard for a proper order."

"You see, Al, she *is* your better half. Okay, one particle will be Xs and two will be Os. You start, Al. I intend to cheat, so I'll give you a little handicap."

"I have a little handicap already. Its name is *Jon*. X in the center square."

I plucked up one anti-gold particle and set it in the center of the grid on the floor I'd drawn with spit. "And O in the bottom right."

"X in the top right."

"O in the right middle row."

"X in the ..."

That's all I ever heard.

CHAPTER TEN

"I'd like to call this meeting of the Joint Galactic Parliament to order. We have critical issues to discuss and time is short," called out Genter-ban-tol, the prime minister. He was Bezathy, a race from Altair 10. In the years since planets became free to organize and rebuild, it was decided a representative assembly of all interested planets would be the most effective, far-reaching method of governance. A century into its existence, the general consensus on the JGP was so far, so good.

"As the First Coequal, I second that motion," barked Di. She was more or less female, at least at that point in her life cycle. She looked a bit like an elephant seal, hence the barking speech. Of course, she was an elephant seal with tentacles, rudimentary legs, and an extendible tongue lined with razor-sharp barbs.

"Please, all be seated or the nearest equivalent," said Genter-ban-tol into the microphone. The amplification and translation circuits were needed since the Bezathy were basically the galaxy's fastest and largest snails. Their shells rose a meter and a half high and were spiked with short, poisonous porcupine-like quills. They spoke in quiet hisses, gurgles, and, let's just admit it, farts. In place of having the elevated eye-stalks of a terrestrial snail, they had three whiplike appendages with equally poisonous injectors at the tips waving around above their bodies. Mother Bezathies might have thought their offspring attractive, but absolutely no one else did. They were, in spite of all odds, a kind, outgoing, and highly intelligent species.

"I am sad to report formally what many of you have heard rumors about. We are under attack again. This time it would seem our enemies are the gods of old who plan on returning to this plane of existence. Why they choose to do so and where they have been is unknown. They do, however, appear to wield considerable power. I have selected our chief science liaison to present what we know and to field questions. Professor Bimdulo, the podium is yours."

Jaccash Bimdulo stood and ambulated to the actual podium. Genter-ban-tol hadn't stood at it because he couldn't stand. Jaccash could and then some. She was vaguely humanoid, with her species' most obvious trait being that of height. A mature adult like her stood three meters tall. Their history referenced some Lopalarians reaching a full four meters, but that was rare. What they achieved in altitude was counterbalanced by their sticklike frames. Basically, they were three-legged, three-armed praying mantises with spherical heads lined with eyes all the way around. Gravity was very low on Lopalaris 6b. They risked death traveling to planets with masses similar to, say, what Earth's had been. One wrong twist or incautious step could, and occasionally did, cause them to snap in half.

"As the prime minister suggested," Jaccash began, "we know little about our foes. What little firm information we have is bizarre and troubling. They would seem to be responsible for multiple unexplainable deaths and disappearances. At those sites, they have left behind trace particles that cannot exist. Their presence is impossible, yet there they are. I'm troubled to confirm they were responsible for the vanishing of planet Friguron 4. I state this with proof. A colleague of mine, crumpling cellophane, discovered the tracers and endeavored to study them. It performed a controlled disassembly of the remains of one of its species while needle-casting the procedure live to me and several other specialists. No sooner had it begun manipulating anti-platinum particles than the planet itself simply vanished."

"A planet can't simply vanish," challenged 11-00La-Bc of the Langir Robotic Federation. They were renowned for their level of accuracy, but not for their achievements in tact. "Some physical process had to have caused the disappearance, and any physical process leaves traces."

"I shall forward you the last known galactic coordinates of Friguron 4. You may, if you choose, go there and verify my statement."

"That will not be necessary. We have already dispatched two ships to that location."

"Please inform me of your findings."

"I will."

"The JGP had sought to ask Jon Ryan to attend this meeting to brief us of his findings, but we were unable to contact him. Dr. Toño DeJesus," Jaccash rested a hand on Toño's shoulder, "is here. He has, however, no information to add to what has been presented."

"Wait," shouted out the Suriliab minister. "How is it possible to *not* find an android with state-of-the-art electronics, a home, and a vortex capable of instant communication anywhere? You *lie*."

Denser 88 X10^5 was a typical Suriliab; nasty, ill-tempered, and anxious to insult, offend, and provoke all comers. That such a pugnacious and quarrelsome species could have survived to achieve an advanced technology was nothing short of miraculous. Galactic sociologists were collectively stunned.

"Why would I lie about not being able to contact Jon Ryan?"

"Ah," Denser 88 X105 yelled harshly as he flapped his membrane wings and rose from his seat, "so you admit it that you *lied*. Now it is only a question of my beating the reasons out of your thin body." He flashed half the distance from his seat to where Jaccash stood. Then he stopped and hovered, as was the social norm in his culture. Actual combat was less desirable than the sport of confrontation for the Suriliab.

"Return to your seat or the nearest equivalent at once, Denser 88

X105," the prime minister said firmly. "You have been warned countless times to respect the accepted norms of this body. We are not in a Suriliab bar. We are discussing the end of times."

"I've killed for lesser insults," he responded, now facing the prime minister.

"I'm certain you have, much to your discredit. Will it be necessary for me to expel you yet again?"

"No. I will return to my place and contemplate my revenge."

"Thank you. Professor Bimdulo, do you or Dr. DeJesus have anything else to add?"

"No, Prime Minister. Nothing at this time."

"Then I suggest strongly we all return to our home worlds. We need to open investigations and discuss possible defenses to counter these alleged gods. Time is not on our side and neither, it would appear, is Fate."

CHAPTER ELEVEN

I opened my eyes. I saw absolutely nothing. Zero. Zilch. I was so stoked. *Dude,* I was alive. That my universe was black as black could be was only an issue, not a convincing argument in favor of my actually being deceased. I knew by checking the circuits that my eyelids had retracted. Life was good. Okay, maybe that assertion was premature, but not being DOA had to indicate something important about these ancient PIAs.

I ran a quick system diagnostic. Everything was working up to factory specs. Most excellent. I sat up. Still not one photon of light hit my receptors. I had a tiny flashlight I could turn on, but I hated to use the damn thing. Toño designed it to exit my forehead and stick out a few inches. Yeah, he confessed later he'd never seen those episodes of *Doctor Who* where seemingly normal people had creepy Dalek eyestalks tunnel out their foreheads. He changed the design after I made him watch the videos, but my model was never upgraded. And to think I called him a friend.

I set my laser finger on its lowest power and shined it in front of me. I swept the whatever-I-was-in. I was just about as confused after seeing where I was as I had been when the place was pitch-black. Nothing made sense. I was suspended in space and surrounded by clouds of giggling Jell-O. Seriously. Cherry, Lime, Mixed Vegetable, and a few I couldn't ID on sight. Not what I expected of the afterlife, or whatever. Why I was floating was equally vexing. There was no external force on me, no air jets or puppet strings. I was just tranquilly there, weightless. Not such a problem for an astronaut, sure. But the Jell-O was moving in an orderly manner. *It* was not weightless. Well, I had to confess I knew diddly squat about anything at that point in time, so my impressions were as shaky as the Jell-O surrounding me.

Time for action. I extended my probe fibers into the Jell-O. I immediately wished I hadn't. I hated over-complexity and contradiction. *Fighter* pilot here, right? The report was that basically the probes were touching a complex-alloy metal surface. As I slid the fibers around, it became clear I was in a small, boring room. I was basically in a stripped-down jail cell. I reflexively began patting my pockets for an aspirin. I definitely had a headache, a breaching whale of a headache. Why ... how ... no, why first. Why park a new prisoner in a jail cell and *then* make them think they're floating in an overly sweet dessert? It made less than no sense. *Negative* sense had just been invented by these douche bags. As to how, I was lost. I was an android. Neural circuits, phase couplings, CPUs galore. Whatever image entered my pupils *had* to be seen for what it was. Electronic transformations were not subject to hanky-panky. But there was Jell-O in my personal sky.

Luckily, I had little time to stress over my confounding trappings. I heard a tinkling, like a little set of wind chimes. I immediately assumed someone was entering my cell. Why, a reasonable mind might ask, did I assume such a connection? Because I was at the intersection of Never-never Land and Whoville. What other sound would a metal-Jell-O door opening make? I switched off my laser finger. No need to declare any of my assets.

"Hello," I called out. "The place is a mess, but you're welcome to join me if you can stand the clutter. Maid's day off."

I was pretty sure I heard a grumbling response. I upped the

levels on my audio receptors. "Just what I need. Another comedian."
It was a woman's voice. A very old-sounding woman.

"No, I'm a force for positive intergalactic change, lady, not a comedian."

She spat by way of response. Okay, a gross and grumpy old woman.

"I'm over here, by the Wild Raspberry patch, sitting on a metal bench."

"Oy vey," she grunted.

"I'm in Sheol?" I responded, with as much snarky glee as I could.

She clapped her hands. The Jelloverse vanished. There stood a female, not a woman. She was definitely ancient, whatever the hell she was. It was like she was three pieces of toast leaning together wearing an ornate dress. Massive jewels dangled from everywhere. Mrs. Toast had snakes for arms and her head was a box suspended on a ridiculously thin neck. Legs were replaced by stumpy-looking snakes minus heads. I have attempted to relay that she was the single ugliest creature I'd ever had the misfortune to lay eyes on. I was coming up way short. She was more hideous than imaginable.

She stopped moving a meter away from me. "Okay, force for *positive* intergalactic change, go ahead and say it."

"What's that, ma'am?"

"That I'm the most horrendous-looking abomination you've *ever* beheld."

"I'm certain your *mother* thinks you're pretty."

She glared at me a few seconds, then slapped one of her stump legs. "Hah! Never heard that one before. Kudos to you, force. It's hard to surprise an immortal."

"Tell me about it."

"Huh?"

"I'm extrapolating, ma'am."

"Stop calling me *ma'am*. It makes me sound old."

"I'm guessing you are. Immortals almost always are, you know?"

"My name's Tefnuf."

"Er, you're the Egyptian goddess of moisture?"

"Good random knowledge there, force. But that was *Tefnut* with a *t*, not an *f*."

"And what are you goddess of?"

"Hey, force, you ever hear the joke about the prisoner who asked too many questions?"

"Ah, no, I have not."

"That's because there's nothing funny about a chatterbox prisoner. And lighten up on the attitude. That's my job, not the meat's."

"Are you ever in for a disappointment."

"Eh?"

"Private humor."

"Keep it up and we'll continue the introductions minus your skin."

"I'll behave."

"You bet your bony ass you will. Now ..."

"Goddess of interrogation? No, of prisoners. No, that wouldn't be you since you're the warden. You'd have the role of goddess of *confinement*."

She rested a snake on a section of toast. "There are several *proprietary* gods, if you must know. I'm but one. Don't *even* confuse me with one of the underworld thugs, or I'll punch your lights out."

"You have a flare for the colloquial."

"I try and adapt to the pathetic meat they send me. Makes it easier. Bees and honey, carrot not stick, and all that."

"Makes good sense."

"Gee, mind if I include your endorsement on my résumé?"

"Might I ask why I'm here?"

"You just did. Big surprise, that's what I'm here to break down. So if you can manage the impossible and keep your trap shut for more than ten seconds, I'll be able to wrap this up. Then I can get back to my otherwise rewarding existence."

I gestured with my arms to indicate she should go for it.

"You're here because you asked to be."

I contemplated challenging that assertion but let it pass. She was essentially correct.

"As with all actions in this cosmos, there are consequences to your asking to be here."

"You?"

Her boxy head angled. "If I gave you a lollipop, would it keep your mouth busy long enough for me to be done sometime this century?"

I tossed my arms up in a confused defense of my innocence.

"I oughta," she snapped, cocking a snake back as if to strike at me. "But then I'd have to clean the mess myself. You're just not worth it, force."

"Would you like *my* name, so you don't have to keep calling me *force*, ma'am?"

"No, not really. You see, who you *were* and what the crap hill you were *known* as matters to me less than your tiny mind could comprehend. I'm only here by protocol. If it was up to me, we'd trapdoor folks like you directly to someplace really hot and be better off without y'all."

"I'm guessing you don't sit on the Chamber of Commerce board."

"If we had one, you'd have guessed correctly. And since you brought it up and I'm too lazy to keep it off my mind, what is your name?"

"Knock knock."

"I'm sorry I asked. Stupid name."

"No, come on. I say *knock knock,* and you say *who's there*. You have to know that. You're a god."

She shook her box slowly. I saw deep regret in her movements. "Start over."

I smiled like a pleased child. "Knock knock."

"Who's there? What the blazes does this have to do with your name?"

I returned to her a hurt look of profound disappointment.

"Who's there?"

"Jon."

"Jon who?"

"Jon Ryan."

"Are you a piece a'work, or what? That was so annoyingly lame, I'm wishing I could scrub that memory clean."

"Knock knock."

I can generally tell when I've pushed it a bit too much. Such was the case presently. Without a word she pointed a snake head at me, and a bolt of electricity leaped from the fangs to my chest. I flew back and smacked the wall hard. Two hundred volts of two amps AC current, to be precise. Enough to kill a human and then some. I rose slowly. "Ouch." My shirt was smoldering.

"Why aren't you dead?"

I shrugged. "Long story."

"Well, mouth off again and we'll experiment to see exactly how much juice it takes to do the deed."

"I'll behave."

"You said that before. Now sit down. Standing makes it seem like it has a purpose, and you got no purpose left in you."

I sat. Why the hell not? I wasn't anxious to co-experiment with the bitch.

"As I was saying, you *asked* to be here. We were simply accommodating your lunacy. I am charged with collecting some general data from you, and then I'll be passing you along to the DDD gods with infinite pleasure."

"DDD?"

"Department of Death and Dismemberment. Triple D. They're the kind of guys you only meet once, if you know what I mean. So, on to the questions. How did you detect the antimatter without disrupting it?"

"No."

"Hmm. *No* is not an option. If you think about it, *pinhead*, I wasn't posing a yes or no query."

"I mean *no,* I'm not playing your silly game. You, box head, already told me I'm heading for DDD very soon. If I don't participate, what, you're going to send me somewhere worse?"

She squared up to me. "That *is* an option. And before you shoot your damn fool mouth off, *yes*, there are many places worse than dismembered death. Do not tempt Fate." Then she did the strangest thing. She genuflected and tapped her hand to her forehead.

"I'll make you a deal, goddess not of moisture. Help me out, and I'll help you in return."

"Hang on a second while I charge up my finger. It's double jeopardy time where the voltage really builds up."

"Ah, so you're too limited of intellect and curiosity to imagine doing anything you haven't done one million times before. I pity your small existence."

"I'm outta here, Ryan. We do for one fleeting moment share something in common. I pity you for what comes next." She turned and began leaving.

"Buck, buck, buckaaah," I said with attitude.

That stopped her. Made her shake a little, too, which was gravy.

She spun on one snake stump. "In all the infinite expanse of time, no one's ever called me chicken. No one."

I raised a didactic finger. "Not actually true. I just did, McFly."

She had trouble speaking, she was so angry. Pissing off a vengeful god. Hey, it was a new personal best for me. Go Team Ryan.

"No more idle banter." Her tone, her very presence were entirely different. Much more formal and postured. "You may ask a few questions, one for each you answer. Then you will learn what it means to infuriate a god."

"And to tempt Fate," I said in my best channeling of Clint Eastwood's Dirty Harry. I totally wanted to see how she'd react to my saying *Fate*.

She reacted immediately and reflexively. She genuflected again and tapped her head. For whatever the hell it was worth, I learned something essential to the ancient gods. They *feared* Fate. There was no other reason to give automatic reverence for it. Fate, whatever that meant to them, had ahold of their short hairs. Nice to know.

"Why question me before DDDing me?"

"You haven't answered my question yet." She continued with the whole stilted godly facade.

"I used a mass spectrometer to analyze the remains of one of your victims. It has an internal magnetic resonance transducer that moved the antimatter without triggering an annihilation."

"You just made that up."

"I stand before you, do I not? Now answer my question."

"Demographics. Why did ..."

"Not so fast, babe. *Demographics* is a word, a noun, not a proper answer to a simple question."

She sighed a few times. "We collect rough demographics on acquisitions. That way we can better understand which civilizations are at what level of development, whether they cluster in any pattern, and if they work collaboratively or independently."

"You're shitting me, lady. Are you gods or are you accountants?"

"It's my turn for a question, not yours. Why did you non-randomly manipulate the antimatter? You must have figured out something catastrophic would result. Combustion, disappearance, toads, something biblical."

"*Biblical*," I said, pointing at her. "That's what Ralph called you, too."

"Who's Ralph?"

"Ah ah. My turn's next. No cuts in line, sneaky greedy. I came to see what the hell was up with you jokers. If you didn't cut muster by my standards, I'd DDD you."

She burst out laughing. It was genuine, too, not done for effect.

"If you hurt my feelings I'll unleash my wrath on you first, Tefnuf with an *f*."

"Sorry, sorry," she said, trying to catch her breath. "Sorry." She sniffed loudly. "That sure felt good. No, here's the problem, minuscule fool. You can't end us. Do not pass Go, do not collect two hundred dollars."

"You've never seen me motivated."

"Ooooh," she responded, shaking her snakes in the air. She collected herself. "Since your answer was so darn cute, I'll gift you some four-one-one. You can't destroy us because *no one* can. We will only be defeated when the prophecy comes to pass. You ain't it, sweetie."

"What is the prediction?"

"The gods will fall only when three miracles that are one work as two."

"That's a subliterate prophecy."

"Be that as it may, even if you were one miracle, you're not three."

"Give me time."

"Back to the task at hand. One last question, then you'll wish you were only dead."

"Yes."

"I haven't asked the question yet."

"True, but my answer is yes. I will *marry* you."

"Oh, that's going to cost you. Your final resting state just got three levels of magnitude worse. Last question. Did you think you could escape once you came here? Spoiler alert. Every Joe six-pack says *yes*, with pathetic bravado."

"I didn't care. If I returned, cool. If I couldn't, at least I'd know I'd saved the universe from you scum puddles."

"You look human. You ever see *Forrest Gump*? You remind me strangely of him."

"I did, and I look forward to pissing on your grave. My last question. You don't know this because you're, well, dull and pointless. Fate has a messenger. You're looking at him, cupcake. I am the one chosen to put a dent in your dreams." I loved the expression *chosen*. Very ooooh supernatural.

She naturally genuflected and tapped her forehead. She also looked stunned. *Outstanding.*

"There is no Fate but what one makes." She naturally did her ceremony thing.

"Beg pardon?"

"It's a Truth. There are few, but that is one."

"I'm sure you have a point, not a neurologic condition."

"What I make cannot have a messenger."

"Silly child. So old yet so naive." I made it a point to really be super-condescending. Lucky for me, it was, like, my specialty. I was running blind but I wanted to convey confidence. *"There is no Fate but what **one** makes.* Don't you see? I am that *one.* The prophecy doesn't refer to each individual, Ms. Get Over Yourself."

She was momentarily taken aback. Seriously. Tefnuf all but quaked in her boots, assuming there were boots made to fit snake feet. Then she returned to lofty and menacing. "Another Truth. Words are not deeds. You talk big, but you are as powerless as still air."

"Oh yeah? How about this?" I had one big trick up my sleeve. I was equipped with an internal space-time congruity manipulator, basically a super force field. Nothing could pass through it. It'd saved my bacon countless times before. The only problem was I was as trapped inside as everyone else was kept outside the membrane.

I switched it on and prayed hard she couldn't crack my shell. I was totally unable to see what was going on outside my shield. It hit me that the only way I'd know my defense was effective would be if I wasn't obliterated while concealed. *Not* a very reassuring realization.

One trick I'd learned along the way was that if I shaped the shield as a sphere, I could roll it. The momentum I generated inside the sphere was conserved, causing the entire ball to move. I was a hamster in one of those rolling balls. I didn't want to be right where I'd disappeared from, so I moved to a dark corner I'd chosen while bantering with the bitchy god. Healthiest not to be too easy of a target for study or a chance to open my shell. When viewed from the outside, a membrane looked like nothing. I always compared it to what you could see out of the back of your head. Not blackness, just nothing. Since a careful observer could see nothingness moving, I did so quickly and all at once. I didn't want to give Tefnuf a chance to get used to what she was witnessing.

After that, I hunkered down. I knew my disappearance would piss her off royally. I assumed the room around me was being pelted with flames, jolts, and juicy curse words. I had no idea how long she'd rage. We were both immortals, so the bombardment could last a very long time indeed. But I couldn't sit tight and wait her out. No. I had a universe to save. I could only hide out so long.

After a short while I began to feel my pseudo-skin crawl. It was a most odd and unexpected sensation. Never in two billion years had it happened. My immediate reaction was, *oh shit*. I mean, anything new just had to be bad. The natural assumption was Tefnuf was opening my protective barrier and I was feeling it. I checked the stability gauges. All were within specs. There was no evidence she was making headway. Out of the corner of one eye I sensed a vague wavy glimmering. I turned. There was a sheet of ... I didn't know what to call it. Stuff? The flat object began expanding and morphing in what seemed to be a random pattern of cones, spheres, and irregular shapes. The glittery quality waxed and waned slightly. I had no clue what I was staring at. Whatever it was, however, shouldn't be there and couldn't be a positive development. Those I never got.

I slowly approached the blob. It did not react to my movement in any way I could tell. I inched my hand into the shimmering. Nothing. I couldn't *feel* anything. I retracted my hand and extended my probe fibers toward it. They found no purchase, sailing right into the mirage but then falling lazily to the floor. I'd never had that happen, either. Something was there, but the only way the probes would miss their target was if nothing was there. Crap, another disgusting paradox.

I backed away and leaned against the membrane's inner wall. "What the hell are you, shiny spook?" I said to myself out loud. A word about speaking. I'd learned quite a few languages by then and knew thousands more because, hey, I was a robot. But in thinking, speaking to Al, or out loud to myself I still used English. That helped to explain the startling response I got.

"Wh ... what ... I ..."

I could easily have been knocked over with a really tiny feather. This shiny blob in only God knew where I was not only *understood* English, it *spoke* my lingo.

"Did you understand me?" I pressed quickly.

"What am I?" it said rather clearly.

"Wait, are you just repeating the sounds I make?" Having a mockingbird shiny blob in my vortex would be a lot less notable than one that spoke American.

"Understand? Do I understand what I am?"

"That's not exactly what I asked. But if you could answer that one instead, that'd be totally fine."

"No."

Short, but sweet. I was also stoked, because I hadn't used the word *no* for it to parrot. But I shouldn't have realistically anticipated getting much objective help from an entity that didn't know what it was. I was less clueless than it, and I was completely in the dark.

"So, you are here and you understand me, but you don't know what you are. That 'bout sum it up?"

There was a silent pause of almost a minute. "You ... re ... re ... correct."

"Hang on. Are you one of those non-corporeal beings, like a Luminarian? Them, I'm not so keen on."

"No. I am not a being because I am not."

"You're not a being because you're not? Duh. You're not a cabbage either because you're not a leafy vegetable."

"No. I am *not*."

This was going nowhere slowly. "Look, I'm kind of busy. There's an angry god out there trying to kill me and devour my universe. So maybe you could go vex someone else with your annoying word-salad conversation."

"Tefnuf *is* mad."

Hey, this emanation knew the fat god's name and what she was doing. I needed to rethink blowing it off. "On second thought, you seem like a real neighborly kind of shiny quasi-existent aggregation of ectoplasm. I'd like you to stay. Please."

"I am not. Nothing cannot stay."

In the game of Chutes and Ladders, I landed on the big chute.

"You are *here,* so you can stay *here.*" I pointed to the floor, because I was such an idiot.

"Yes."

"Okay, then. You understand. You aren't not." Crap soup, what was I babbling about?

"You misunderstand. I may remain here with you, but I am not. I do not exist."

"Oh, I get it. When you say you're *not,* you mean to say you don't exist. But if you don't exist what am I parlaying with?" I pointed back and forth between us, because I was ready to lose it.

"I do not know."

"Time-out. Here's a summary of the action so far. You do not *exist* but you speak *English.* You can hang around even though there's no way in hell you got in here."

"Football."

"Huh?"

"Time-out. Football."

I was about done. "Yeah. The game of football has *time-outs.* Three per half." I patted my jumpsuit. "Wish I had a treat to reward you with. Fresh out."

"Not a problema."

Spanglish? Now it spoke *Spanglish.* This was *so* weird. Then a thought hit me. "Can you check if Tefnuf is done being pissed, and let me know?"

"Yes." And it didn't budge. Of course.

"Ah, how can you check from inside my membrane?"

"I cannot."

"But you said you'd check out what she's up to."

"No. I said ..." He drifted off for a few seconds. "I can check."

Oh, bother. The thing was an editor. "Would you please go check on Tefnuf's status and report back to me on her *major* activities?"

"Yes, but I cannot do that and stay here."

I ran a hand though my hair. "No. No, you sure can't, can you?" I wagged a finger at it. "Here's a plan. You leave for a very short time and then return after having checked out old Tefnuf's status."

"So you don't want me to stay here like you just said ..." There it drifted away and trailed off speaking a few seconds. "Said you wanted me to?"

"I want you to *mostly* stay but also leave just a *little*. A tiny skosh." I pinched my fingers close together because I was just that lame.

"Ah. I'll be away as little as possible. Then I'll be here staying."

"Good little blob. I'll stay put right where I stand." I pointed to the floor because I was just about to kill that nonexistent blob.

The shimmering moved toward a wall, passed through it like it wasn't there, and was gone. I had an irresistible urge to fire up the engine and gun it, ditch this amalgamation of confusing. Then I remembered to my chagrin that I wasn't in *Stingray*. I had no idea where she'd ended up.

Quicker than I'd have guessed it was back, sparking and twisting in the air right in front of me. "Did you miss me?"

Oh, no. Lame humor. I was confronting an editor who performed stand-up in New York clubs after work. "If it helps, I did. What's up?" I immediately regretted that query.

"The opposite of down? I give up. What's up?"

"What activity is Tefnuf engaged in?"

"I'll tell you, but then you must tell me what's up."

"Deal." I drew a palm roughly down my face.

"She is still raging. She has recruited three additional gods to help her. Well, that's not technically correct. One is Dolfene. She's a demigod. Her grandmother, Porcillanna, was a mortal. She was a Thigbillarian tree on Gaphthos."

I was going to take a pass on bashing him for the TMI. I still needed his help. "Thanks for the clarity. I'd hate to overestimate the strength of my opponents."

"Hemdilby and Bazuranititity are focusing their powers on, eh, how can I say it? Ah, destroying the room outside randomly. Yes. There is basically no room any longer."

"Did they seem to notice my force field?"

No answer.

"Did they act in a manner suggesting they knew a portion of the room was encased in a force field?"

"I am not sure. I think not."

"Why didn't you say that the first time I asked?"

"Does it matter which question I answer if there are more than one but they are the same?"

"No. Yes. No, no. Look, it would matter, but only if you *knew* I was going to ask the same thing multiple times. Since you can't, you have to answer the *first* time you're asked."

"But I did."

Okay, maybe I could choke it a little. I mean, not kill it or anything. Just nearly with my bare hands.

"You said using *their* powers. Are Hemdilby's and Bazurani-whatever's powers different from each other's and Tefnuf's?" I stopped, but jumped right back in before it could make me more loco. "And don't say *Bazurani-whatever* wasn't there, but whatever Bazurani-whatever's actual name is."

"You seem stress ridden. May I help?"

Is there an erupting volcano nearby you could hurl yourself into? "No, thank you."

"And now, player number one, back to my original question."

"I do not understand my nature."

"Not that original question ... oooohhhh .... the question just before the one you answered by asking if you could help."

"You seem stress ridden. May I help?"

"*Yes*, that one." I pointed to the floor in front of it because I was completely lost.

"No, I was stating for a second time that you seemed ..."

"Stop, halt, do not proceed, shut up, and talk no more. Are the four gods ... no, I meant three and a *half* gods' powers the same or different?" Did I have aspirin with me? Morphine? I needed something and I needed it badly.

"Yes."

"*No.*"

"That is the other possibility, but the correct answer is *yes*."

I counted to seventy-eight. It took that long to figure out if I counted to double infinity it wouldn't lessen my anger. "*Yes* their powers are the same, or *yes* they are different?" I started to relax back into enraged silence when I saw the trap. "Belay that question because you'd just answer ...."

"Yes."

"Are the gods and/or demigods' powers all the same? And I'm on record before you say a peep that there's no way that question is ambiguous or can be answered ambiguously."

"Are you done asking and telling?"

"Yes."

"No."

Who's on second? No, who's on *first*, *what's* on second.

Deep cleansing breaths. I'm on a beach and the sand is warm between my toes. "So all the gods ... no, forget I said that. Do all of the three gods ... no, unlisten to that. In the room that's not really there anymore, do the three gods have different powers?"

"Yes. Convergence, fire bolts, and retronicity."

I got an *answer*. Saints be praised. "Do all gods have different and distinct powers?"

"No."

"No because ..."

"I couldn't possibly say why their powers are what they are. I don't even exist."

"No. No, because a god's powers are always unique to the individual god?"

"Ah. No. They may have the same powers as other gods. Why didn't you ask that before?"

"I *did* ... *didn't* want to confuse you."

"Thank you."

"So fire bolts I get. The god tosses bolts of fire. But convergence? What's that?"

"You are more perceptive than I would have thought."

One ... two ... three ... Nope, not gonna work this time either. "Why is that, friend?"

"I would not have gotten that fire bolts were constrictive waves of pressure meant to crush the target."

"They are?"

"I know. Just surprised you didn't think they were actual *bolts* of," it giggled briefly, "you know, *fire.*" It giggled a little more.

"Silly you. And convergence?"

"Those gods hurl linear power waves that converge back on themselves at the target."

A straight answer. Wow. Just wow. "And retroni ... retrono..."

"Retronicity."

"Yes, that one. What is it?"

"Bolts of fire thrown at the target."

He was jerking my chain. And I was on *Candid Camera,* wasn't I? This emanation was channeling the spirit of Allen Funt, damn it to hell. "But why not call the *bolts of fire* bolts of fire and *convergence* the pressure wave thing?"

"I was not..."

I threw up my hands. "... consulted when the names were handed out. I know."

"Then why did you..."

Maybe if I turned off the membrane, the three point five gods'd kill us both in a flash. I was ready.

CHAPTER TWELVE

Toño knelt beside the chair Sapale was collapsed in. His hand gently patted her arm as she stared to the far floor and her chest heaved intermittently. They'd been like that for several hours, one not able to speak, and one reluctant to burden the other with words. It had been three days since all contact with Jon was lost.

Finally Toño spoke in a whisper. "He'll be fine. He always is. Always will be."

Sapale gave no outward sign she was aware of Toño's presence, let alone his kind words.

"In fact, I bet those so-called ancient gods are having a pretty bad time of it right about now."

Sapale sighed deeply and coughed.

"Can I get you anything? Anyone? Please just say the word and I'll do whatever I can."

Barely audibly, she mumbled a few broken words.

"Pardon me, my dear. What did you say?"

"Can you reach in my head and turn off my emotions?"

Toño, ever the scientist, angled his head and momentarily pondered her query. Then his humanity caught up and took over. "I would if I could. But there's no way around the pain. It's a part of ..."

"Please ... please don't say it." Her words had taken on a sudden force and anger. They were a white squall at sea. "I've lived over two *billion* years. Most of that time has been spent in misery and anguish. I know sadness is a constant. I know joy is fleeting. I don't need platitudes."

Toño rested back, determined not to speak unless it was needed. He continued to pat her arm.

After a few minutes she scooched up and took a ragged breath. "I know he's lost to me. That's a given. Do you know what hurts the most? I'll bet you'll never guess in two *billion* years." Her rage rose as she spoke.

"No, my dear. I do not know ..."

"That he never offered me the chance to *die* by his side. The selfish *bastard*. Sure, I'd have tried in vain to talk him out of going. But in the end, I'd have loaded my rifles and marched into hell with my brood-mate. He ... he ... he didn't even have the *decency* ..." She collapsed into a fit of tears. If she still needed to breathe, she'd have passed out from the ferocity of her lament.

Toño hugged her tightly and they rocked in unison.

CHAPTER THIRTEEN

Hemdilby stopped flailing her tentacles wildly as she saw no more room to target with her fire bolts. In fact, the next several rooms in every direction were torn to shreds and smoldering at that point. Plus, all that emitting had made her hungry. She needed a snack break.

Bazuranititity, whose retronicity required less energy, slowed his attack to a stop once he noticed Hemdilby had ceased and desisted. He wasn't tired, but he was perpetually lazy and undermotivated. His philosophy was that spending time to help another god was to waste that time.

It took the fully enraged Tefnuf almost a full minute to realize she was the only one still systematically dismembering the Lower Chamber. "Why the devils of all ten hells have you two stopped? He's not dead yet."

They looked at one another, then both looked back to Tefnuf. Bazuranititity spoke. "First off, there's nothing left to destroy. Second, *we* never saw anything alive to kill. *You* did. We were merely passersby."

"And I can't continue without nourishment. Your powers are more *economical* than mine. You would have no reason to know what it is to be as powerful as *I* am." Hemdilby was, as always, smug and condescending.

"I'll expend some economy on you if you don't keep firing. The human's in here somewhere. He's just hidden really well."

"There's no *here* left to hide in. We've obliterated so much of the Lower Chamber that the convocation will probably ask us to rebuild it ourselves," responded Bazuranititity.

Tefnuf turned to face her erstwhile helpers and rested her serpentine arms on her toast-like hips. "A human, a particularly annoying human by the way, intentionally tripped an antimatter trap and was transfolded here." She pointed a stumpy snake arm at the tiny island of still-intact flooring. "Before I could forward the puke to DDD, he vanished. He has to be here. Keep firing until he's microdust, or I'll nuke both your lazy asses."

"You haven't been hitting the sacred sauce again, have you?" asked a defiant Bazuranititity. "The conclave *has* directed you to moderate your consumption several times in the recent past."

"Why you ..." She tried to impale him with a power beam. It narrowly missed, probably because she was so shaking mad.

"What's going on here?" boomed Vorc. "I heard all the commotion—damnation, I felt it—and come to find you, Tefnuf, trying to fry a colleague. Have you been hitting ..."

Hemdilby threw up multiple tentacles. "*Don't* finish that sentence. We've enough trouble as it is."

"Keep moving, Vorc the Dork. Nothing to see here," responded Tefnuf.

"I will not, and you will answer for your attack on these two gods."

"Oh, so now I'm taking on the two of them, am I?"

"It appears that way to me," snapped Vorc.

"Well that's on account of you being a prissy ass sphincter," she replied.

"Explain yourself at once, or I'll order an extrajudiciary summary execution on the spot."

"Fine by me, as long as it's *you* we're snuffing out," Tefnuf responded.

"Everybody calm down and listen," Bazuranititity said, being atypically helpful. "We were helping Tefnuf kill some human she claims tripped a trap."

"I did not *claim* he set one off. He did. Then he disappeared into thin air."

Vorc looked between the three of them. "You say he was human?" he asked Bazuranititity.

"No way, boss. *She* said her imaginary friend was human."

"Is that your story, Hemdilby?" Vorc asked of her.

"Yes, I guess. We were walking by and Tefnuf here was smashing up the Lower Chamber but good. When we came to see what was happening she enlisted our help."

"So neither of you two saw anything?" Vorc verified.

"No," they cried out as a pair.

Vorc growled loudly. "Humans do not up and disappear. It's not in their playbook."

"Maybe they don't, but this one did. A lot can evolve in the forever we've been away, my pea-brained leader," replied Tefnuf.

"It would help your case significantly if you left off the sarcasm," he snarled back.

"First off, I don't have a *case* to help. I was doing my job. Second, sure I *could*, but it wouldn't be nearly as fun your way."

"I've just summoned Fallorip. If there's a human hiding in plain sight they'll be able to tell us. If there is not one present, you and I will have a serious problem."

"We already do—it's you. And if you think your pet Cerberus is going to prove I'm loony, you got another thing coming to you. All his heads have fleas up their noses."

"I will be the judge of their performance," Vorc replied coolly.

A scratching could be heard speeding toward the Lower Chamber. Fallorip was coming. He bolted through the open door and skidded to an awkward stop on the slick metal floor. He nearly knocked Tefnuf over in the process.

"Hey, mind your rabid dog, Vorc. He almost *killed* me," protested Tefnuf.

"The unfortunate word there being *nearly*," replied the boss god. "Fallorip, Tefnuf claims there's a human somewhere near. See if you can find him."

Comically the three heads leaned as far from each other as possible, like they were trying to peel themselves apart. They sniffed loudly, flinging their heads rapidly and randomly. Slobber rained everywhere, including into one of Tefnuf's eyes. That brought an immediate pig squeal of protestation from her.

Fallorip dashed hither and yon, sniffing and licking. In a few minutes he trotted over to Vorc's side. The central head spoke between pants. "We smell that no human was or is present. We find nothing here that we cannot all plainly see."

"Useless, as I predicted. Even if there isn't one now, there sure as blazes was one fifteen minutes ago. His stench has to linger in the air. An idiot without a nose could smell traces." Tefnuf ramped up her anger to try to deflect the railroading she anticipated was coming next.

Vorc rocked on his heels. "Is there *any* chance there was a human here leaving faint scents and you're not smelling him?" he asked of Fallorip.

"None, master. We smell sacred sauce on the breath of Tefnuf. It is not faint, either. Our senses are working well."

"Hey," protested Tefnuf, "I was at lunch when the human popped in. Who doesn't have a little drinkypoo with a meal?"

Slightly out of sync, the three other gods and one Cerberus present replied that *they* didn't.

Tefnuf pointed accusingly at Fallorip. "Well, of course, you don't. You're a freaking dog."

Fallorip scratched one paw nervously on the floor. Then he responded, "Well, *dog* is *god* spelled backward."

"Vorc, get it out of here before I do something I won't regret," howled Tefnuf.

Vorc bent and petted the hound quickly. "Better head home, champ. I'll be along shortly."

Without hesitating, Fallorip zipped out of the ruined room.

"Tefnuf, I'll see you in my office in half an hour. We will discuss the action plan we'll need to adopt to address your aberrant behavior."

She slapped her side loudly. "Oh, not another of those limp-dick *action plans* again. They're even more useless than you, Vorc."

"Be that as it may, you'll be there in thirty minutes. Each god is a valuable member of this proud team, *my* proud team. As you are a valued member, it is my task to help you become a more effective, happier member of our family. I'm doing this because I love the team and I value your positive contributions. If one needs to improve to participate at the highest level one can, which is our universal goal, that individual appreciates the benefits afforded them by a structured, paced plan."

Bazuranititity leaned into one of Hemdilby's auditory openings. "What in Hades did he just say?"

She shook her head almost imperceptibly. "No idea. I think he wants to marry her into his family team."

"Poor girl. I've seen his family. Talk about inbreeding."

"Amen," was Hemdilby's final thought on the subject.

CHAPTER FOURTEEN

"Could you check again? It's been an hour since you last did," I said to my creepy floating blob. Then my choice of words hit me. "Wait, I meant, will you go now and check to see what the current status of the gods attacking me is?"

There was an interlude where the manifestation spun lazily in silence. "I could check. As to will I, the question involves prophecy, does it not? Who's to say what will occur?"

"You're kind of rigid in your interpretation of my questions to you. Are you trying to make me crazy, or are you just that concrete?"

"Hmm. I believe *yes* is the answer to one of those questions. Yes, it is."

"I'm dying of suspense here. Which one?"

"The one about me being rigid."

"That was a statement, a declarative, not a question."

"Are you certain?"

"As I can be of anything right about now."

"That is good to hear."

Drop it, Jon. He's either mental or he's playing you. "Speaking of hearing, how is it you can hear me? You don't have ears. Or a body, for that matter."

"I do not know. I do, which is sufficient for now."

"I guess it'll have to be. How about a little recon?"

"Ah, yes." He was out and back in a flash. "They've stopped firing. Now Vorc is scolding Tefnuf."

"Who's Vorc?"

"He's an ancient god."

"No," I said sarcastically. "You sure he's not the pizza delivery boy?"

"There is no pizza delivery here."

"Is he the head god?"

"First among equals. He sits in the center chair of the conclave."

"What's he scolding that ugly bitch about?"

"She is struggling to justify her attack on you. None of the others believe you are here."

"That's the first piece of good news I've gotten since I arrived. These bozos aren't omniscient."

"No, they would not claim to be. They are not that type of god."

"That *type*? How many types are there?"

"I wouldn't know."

Damn cloud got me again. He was jerking my chain. No one could be that annoying without having it deep in their DNA.

"How about this. I need to defeat these pukes, so they can't destroy my universe. *Will* you, *can* you, *could* you, *would* you help me?"

"Will, can, could, would I help with what?"

"I need to kill these so-called gods off."

"You said that already. Where do I come into play?"

"I could use help. Will you pitch in to defeat these bad hombres?"

"Ah. Now I take your question. I can't help, because I don't exist. I can't do anything contributory."

"Sure you can. You already have. You've kept me apprised of actions I could not otherwise follow."

"Hmm. That is true. I certainly would offer any help I can lend."

"So you're not a fan of these ancient flabby butts? Not the god of floating blobs yourself, are you?"

"I might be."

Oh, crap. I'd been colluding with the enemy. "So you are?"

"I told you I do not know my nature. I could be the god of something, since I don't know what I am."

"Ah, okay." I let out a deep breath. "You got a name?"

"Most likely."

"Funny name for an ethereal manifestation."

He was quiet a second. "Ha."

"Huh?"

"Ha."

"I know, I heard you the first time. What do you mean by *ha*?"

"You made a lame but actual joke. I laughed in response."

"Oh, you mean *ha ha ha*."

"If you say so."

"Look, where do you fit in around here? You got a job, a task, a raison d'être?"

"I don't fit. I do not exist to fit anywhere."

"I wish you'd stop saying that. You exist. I'm not talking to myself here. You may be a total freakazoid form of life, but you have to *be*, since you're helping and annoying the crap outta me."

"Annoying the crap out of someone is a proof of existence?"

"It always has been in my book. How did you get here? Do you recall that much?"

"No. I've been here so long I can't seem to recall."

"Do the gods ask you to perform any tasks? Court jester, for example?"

"Hmm. I doubt I'd be an adequate comical entertainer."

"No shit, Sherlock. I was being sarcastic."

"As to the gods, I think they completely ignore me."

"Wait, they either *do* or *don't* ignore you. Can't be both."

"I'm never certain if they see me and ignore me or simply aren't aware I'm present."

"That's weird."

"No shit, Sherlock."

I let the biter get away with the replay. No point in over-antagonizing him.

"Okay, let's move into Phase Two. That's the part where you help me fry these turds."

"What's Phase Three?"

"I escape home."

"Ha."

"What, you think that's funny?"

"You weren't joking? You actually hallucinate that you'll live through Phase Two, to then attempt what has never been done before and succeed at that?"

"Why, yes, I do. I'm confident by nature."

"That what they're calling being an idiot now, eh? *Confident by nature?*"

"Look, I can do this without you. *With* is easier, but if you're going to be a negative Nancy the whole time, I'd just as soon fly solo."

He was silent too long.

"You there?"

"*F-l-y.*" He said the word like he was tasting it.

"It's an expression. It means go it alone. To not settle for the lame intermittent help I'm receiving."

"*F-l-y.* I used to *f-l-y.*"

"Ah, correction. You are flying. If you had a head I'd say look at the legs you aren't standing on, because you're flying."

The cloud folded over a few times. What a strange blob it was. "*F-l-y.*"

Oh, no, we were back to *f-l-y* again. He said it like a stoner saying *T-w-i-n-k-i-e.* I regretted being immortal, because I'd likely have to put up with this joker for *way* too long, however long that was to be.

"Is it clear outside? Can I drop my membrane and try and start killing hackneyed gods and such?" I thought of an addition. "Could you do me a favor and *f-l-y* out, take a peek?"

Petty and snarky? Yes, but consider the author. Yeah, one Jon Ryan.

He didn't respond, which was good because he had already crushed my last nerve ass-dancing on it. Silently he slipped away for a second.

"There is no one in view outside."

"Not even Tefnuf?"

"She, too, is gone."

"Where'd she go? Seems odd she'd leave without my testicles?"

"Do I look like a fortune-teller, a seer?"

"No." I chuckled. "You look like someone's been vaping really hard nearby."

"Do you feel better when you insult me? If you do, please continue. My only goal in the existence you claim I have is to be the butt of your adolescent humor."

Wow, sounded like my mom chewing me out for being too, well, too *me* with the other kids. "I'm sorry. You're trying to help and I'm being a jerk."

"Yes, yes, and yes."

I attempted to match the *yeses* with the elements of my apology. They didn't add up. "Ah, what's the third yes for?"

"You *are* sorry."

Ouch. Dude was good. Set me up just so and dumped the bucket of water on my head at the proper moment. He was no me, but I had to credit him some chops.

I turned the membrane off and scanned the room quickly. I was alone. I checked for alarms or cameras and found none. My Jon Plan was exceeding my expectations by a considerable margin. I wasn't dead, I was no longer a captive heading for DDD, and I was free.

"I need a weapon and a ride. Do you know where I can get those?" I heard no response. Odd for my chatty apparition. I turned and checked. The monkey bait was gone. Crap. "Hey, annoying blob, are you still here?" I asked as loudly as I dared. Nada. Oh well, I was on my own, which was generally how I functioned best. Time to improvise, adapt, and overcome.

I struck out in the eeny-meeny-miny-moe direction. Hell, I knew zilch about this dump. What difference could it make? It took a while to clear the region so heavily damaged by the gods who were trying to blast me. I actually had to ascend multiple stairways and exit the building I was in to hit virgin turf. Okay, a word about the godly place I was in. Heaven it was not. Not by parsecs. I imagined we all had our own takes on the good place in the afterlife. This wasn't anyone's view on paradise. The light was dim and diffuse, the air was sterile and bone dry, and there was no discernible plant or animal life. I felt like I was in a deserted mall.

A while into my recon I decided to find a hiding spot and observe the LIPs, you know, the local indigenous population. I hadn't seen any gods aside from the first one in detention. I'd be in a superior strategic position if I knew more about my opponents. A fairly major-looking pathway made a sharp turn near a large pile of rocks. I tucked myself into a deep cleft in the stones that directly faced the road. Then I waited.

A few hours into my vigil I was about to bail when I saw my first passersby. Wow. Just wowsers. All I was missing was popcorn and the show would have been complete. Three "figures" "moved" past my blind. I say *figures*, since they weren't people and that they *moved*, since they sure weren't walking. The most humanoid one was a unicorn-elephant with wings. It was lurching through the air like ... well, an elephant with wings would. How big do wings have to be to provide lift for the bulk of that body? Yeah, really, really big. The weirdest part was that it chatted basically nonstop. I mean, it should have been huffing and puffing to beat the band. But no, it had verbal diarrhea.

The other travelers were not humanoid in the least. One was a big fat wedge-shaped ox, maybe. You'd have to see a picture. The tubular body consisted of multiple sausage-like sections that articulated, like cars of a train. The leading portion of each of the segments was pointed like an old In-N-Out Burger white hat was glued to it. That god, whatever it was god of, was just totally wrong. There was no way it evolved with any function in mind.

The final member was much easier to describe. It was a walking swimming pool. Yup, that was it. Well, a swimming pool minus the pool. It was an Olympic-sized trough of water with ten or twelve water legs. How does suspended water remain in place and not splash away? How can water possibly have the load-bearing strength to support anything without crashing to the ground? Beats the hell out of me, but there it was strolling past. At least for my freaking-out mind's sake, the pool wasn't speaking. I guess walking ponds are good listeners.

The trio slowly passed by. I began wondering if the oxen got thirsty, would it drink its companion? Or maybe the unicorn-elephant would plunge into it to cool off? Yes, I was trippin'. Some images were harder to assimilate than others, and these were most bizarre. Once they were out of sight, a single humanoid passed by. This one looked normal, you know, like a Greek god, maybe Zeus. Tall and resplendent, well-cropped white beard, and a robe. Greek gods had to have flowing robes, right? Zeusy seemed to be in a hurry and was gone quickly.

The final god I saw looked for all the world like a massive boulder. Cold gray granite with craggy edges that were sharp as a razor blade. How could I tell? I was pressed up against it. Yeah, what could go wrong? Maybe it was waking up from a nap, or maybe it just got tired of my violating its personal space. Anyway, it rumbled up onto three round rocky legs and pushed me unceremoniously onto the dirt path. It walked like an inflated sumo wrestler over to where I stood.

"Who the fortic are you?" it demanded in, obviously, a very deep voice. Right, boulders couldn't very well have been sopranos, could they?

Okay, Ryan. It was go time. "*Me*? Who the fortic are *you*?"

"Who am ..." It started shaking. Little pebbles and dust flew into the air. I discovered that rocks get mad rather quickly. "I'm ... I'm Gorpedder. *Everyone* knows Gorpedder."

"No, fatso. I don't."

I would not have thought it possible, but the dude began

trembling much harder. Stones tumbled and one landed on my foot. It put a permanent dent in my plain-toe boot, too, the big baby.

"I am not *fat*," he raged. "Boulder gods are wide, we're voluminous. We're supposed to b ... b ... be."

"Fine, you're supposed to be fat. That still doesn't clarify in my mind what you're so earthquaky about. Lighten up, boulder."

"Ear ... earthqu ... lighten ... li ..."

"You okay? Need a glass of lava or something?"

"La ..." He lunged—as best a boulder could, that is—at me. "I'll *kill* you."

As angry as Gorpedder was, and as lethal as he had to be, *fast* he was not. I backpedaled at his precise forward speed. It wasn't hard.

"If you want to kill me, why don't you step over here and try?" I taunted.

"I am. Stop retreating so I can crush your skull."

"Wow, there's a positive motivation for me to stop. And seriously, you're moving. I thought you were just quaking in your boots some more."

"I ... I ..." Gorpy never finished the thought. He face-planted. I wasn't certain if he tripped or was exhausted. I mean, come on, how long can a boulder sprint? Can't be long, no more than a stone's throw. Sorry, I know, lame pun. But it felt so good.

I inched toward his resting place. I extended my probes.

Lithicoid life form, immortal. Quartz content fifty percent, feldspar twenty-five percent, biotite five percent, complex amino acids ten percent. Incremental constituents circulating protein ...

Skip ahead, I said in my mind. I didn't want every last detail of its composition.

Self-identifies as Gorpedder. Born Mamaxithos from mating of demigod Juli with antigod Densmurpex twenty-seven million years ...

Abort. What's an antigod?

Searching. An antigod is defined by Gorpedder as a powerful immortal opposed to the Cleinoid Gods' prerogative. Juli was originally pursuing Densmurpex to destroy him. Love happened instead. They ...

Abort. What superpowers does he have?

Gorpedder is immensely strong. At a distance he can damage by impact after hurling arbitrary objects.

Abort. His power is he throws chunks of stuff real hard? That's not a superpower. That's physiologic.

I am not enabled to make that deter ...

Abort. Where does he reside?

Coordinates transferred to your data banks.

Is he dead?

He is immortal. He cannot ...

Abort. Is he conscious?

Negative. He is in suspended animation pending biochemical imbalance crisis resolution with ongoing metabolic activity.

Estimated time until he's recovered and awake?

Thirty-six hours.

Is there anything I can do to make that more difficult, prolong his incapacity?

Affirmative. You can extract up to one hundred percent of his arsenic supply. Dimethylarsinic acid is an essential catalyst of the high pH waste accumulated as a result of his extreme energy expenditure.

End analysis.

I tuckered the rock out and he was healing. Poor pebble. I had to become more species-sensitive, didn't I?

CHAPTER FIFTEEN

"Tefnuf, you make the simple difficult and the difficult impossible. I enjoy our counseling sessions in my office as little as you do." Vorc was trying to sound even, fatherly. He'd read that underlings reacted more positively to fatherly advice than that from one perceived more as a supervisor.

"Oh, I really doubt that, Chief. If ya did you'd kill yourself. I'm right there myself." She pinched a couple digits close together and peered at him through the aperture. "If you are leaning toward suicide by the way, I'd be more than happy to assist you." She patted a pocket. "Brought a rust hammer with me just in case."

"I'll bet. I will stress yet again that we gods must at least get along, even if we do not like one another. Your surly disposition and absence of manners threaten the integrity of our fellowship."

"Fellowship, is it now? I thought we were a bunch of overambitious spoiled brats forced by some cruel *higher* god to suffer each other for all of eternity." She harrumphed. "Now I'm part of a fucking fellowship."

"Watch your tongue. I will not have vulgar language used in my presence."

"My bad. Here, I'll fix it so it doesn't happen again." She rose and walked quickly toward the exit.

"Stop," he said in a thunderous voice. Surveys had proven that a thunderous tone worked to radically alter an employee's reaction better than mere shouting. "We are not done yet."

She rotated her head to look at him. "I am."

"Sit or be censured."

That brought her to a halt. She hated censure more than she hated Vorc. And she knew he'd do it. He had nine times before. Spending a century in a perfect vacuum with no light, no food, and no company actually was unpleasant. She returned to her seat.

"That is better. Now, as we ... *I* was saying ..." Crap, he thought. Vorc hated when he slipped into the imperial plural in public. In private it was fine, but others might disapprove. "Once your social quotient finds a happy, dependable level, you and I will have no more unnecessary meetings. We are on the eve of our return to greatness. We should be great as one, not as two, you and the rest who aren't you."

He cursed himself instantly. What an awkward, vague rally cry. Hardly the stuff of godly leadership.

"Those who *aren't* me?" she needled.

"Yes, everyone who's happy and working as a team. For as certainly as there's no *I* in team, there needs to be a *Tefnuf* in our team."

"Are you listening to yourself? You've blown a bank of fuses, Vorc. You sound like a politician after a handful of strokes. Wait, wait," she said, looking up thoughtfully. "We know you *are* a politician. Maybe that means you've had a handful of strokes? Yes, that would account for your being such a pus popsicle."

"Here's the short of it, *bitch*." Vorc was angry and she could plainly see it. An angry Vorc was not a force to toy with. "You behave and you get to come along for our return. You screw up point five more times and you're back in censure. Period."

"But I was only doing my job, the one *you* mandated me to do."

"Exterminating a human who was never there that disappeared into thin air?"

"He was there. You'll see when he finally surfaces. Why would I make up there being a prisoner?"

"So you could blow up the Lower Chamber."

"Why would I want to destroy the Lower Chamber?"

"Oh, I don't know. Maybe for the same reason you did the last two times."

"This is totally different. Those times I was *angry*."

"And you're not angry this time?"

"Up until now, no."

"I presume, then, we shall meet again very soon, at which time you'll get the censure you are so loudly begging for."

She squirmed up in her chair. "You wouldn't talk to *Bethniak* that way," she said, spitefully.

To save face, Vorc toyed with responding that was because Bethniak didn't cause such infantile, drunken trouble. But he let it go. It was best not to say that name unless it was completely unavoidable.

CHAPTER SIXTEEN

I found Boulder Boy's digs easily enough. A few things became clear the minute I opened the door. The guy was no slave to fashion, cleanliness, or excess. He lived in a cave—big surprise—it was dirty —less of a surprise—and the only furnishings were—you guessed it —rocks. Oh well, I wasn't renting to own, just borrowing it until Sleeping Not-Beauty woke in five to six days. That's how long his arsenic-depleted body would take to heal. That's how long I had to hatch a plan. Based on my history to date, that was too long. My plans were never any good if I wasn't under supreme pressure. Gorpedder crashing through his own front door might be what inspired me to come up with something serviceable. Time would tell. It always had so far.

How do rock gods, and I don't mean Mick Jagger, live? Spartanly. I found what had to be a food storage and prep area. Not going to dignify it by calling it a kitchen. There were stone bowls containing powdered stones of various classes. There were smaller vessels with pure minerals. Those must have been like spices. A dash of silicate and a pinch of borate to liven up a pulverized basalt. Yum.

One thing in the stark room stood out prominently. A complex comm panel of some sort. It had blinking lights, lots of keys, and a couple of monitors. I guessed gods needed to keep up with one another. Maybe there were even god-reality holo programs. Those'd go viral in a heartbeat, wouldn't they? Hell, realistically, they couldn't be worse than the drivel I tried my best to avoid when visiting human or Kaljaxian worlds I called home. But the comm link was intriguing. I had to be the first non-LIPs (you know, *local indigenous personnel*) to have access to their network. I could learn a lot about my enemy if I was successful in hacking the system. And I was going to crack this treasure-trove, oh, yes, I was.

First things first, I needed to switch it *ON*. I also needed to not do so in a manner that would alert anyone I was doing so; not yet, at least. I could attach my probes and analyze the entire system in detail, break down the circuit paths and individual components. Normally I'd assign such scutwork to Al. Al was neither present nor available. So, I did the guy-thing. I started pushing buttons, hoping for a good outcome. Come on, it was a much quicker and a hell of a lot more fun option. I was not a thinker. I was a doer.

After a couple taps, one monitor flashed to life. Crap. This was not going to be entertaining in the least. In place of a picture or holo, there was an endless streaming of binary images, you know, ones and zeros. Intermittently there were various forms of breaks, maybe sentences or paragraphs? I mean, I was a giant computer, so I could read binary if I set myself to it. But talk about boring. Within a couple minutes I'd discerned the syntax and figured out the language, as it were. The signal did not seem to be encrypted. Why bother? How was someone like me ever going to do what I was doing? Whatever kind of god these bozos were, they were *not* the omniscient type.

To synthesize it down, the bulk of the broadcast was a long, seemly endless, list of names. Those were presumably the LIPs' names, but they were offered without qualifiers like, *Nancy loves Bill* or *Scissors beat Paper yesterday in the finals*. It took nearly an hour for me to begin to see actual information content. Large numbers of gods were grouped with others, mega teams if you will. Demigods and "other manifestations" were grouped separately. Naturally.

What self-absorbed god would want to be teammates to a lower manifestation? No way. Only much later did I glean what the aggregation of names meant. Teams were assigned different general tasks. *Defilers* were tasked with *cleaning where needed in the public spaces*. Wow. Gods with push-brooms and matching bib overalls. How very banal. *Retributions* were assigned *invocation rendering*. I had no clue what that was, but it had to beat the hell out of the cleanup brigade.

Fairly quickly I arrived at the verge of death by unrelenting boredom. Naturally, to resolve that crisis, I pushed a few more random buttons. What could go wrong? Well, let me tell you. Not surprisingly, the comm console was a two-way link. Yeah. I called city hall or something. This boxy humanoid face sprang to life on the screen. The face looked both unfriendly *and* unhappy. Looks deceived. It was openly hostile and irate.

"*Quiz comnel?*" the male face shouted.

The two words didn't auto-translate. That meant they either constituted a proper name or were in a language I was apparently supposed to know but didn't. Note to self. Never push the third button on the right of a comm console I was less than completely familiar with.

I put on my best badass expression and howled back angrily. "*Quiz comnel?*" Then I hit that last button I'd tapped and prayed it cut the link. It did. Then I had to wait with bated breath to see if old grumpy pants called back. Two minutes passed and he didn't. Okay, that was either good or it was most bad. Maybe he'd sent the cops out instead of returning the call. Since divine police would be fast, I was reassured after about ten minutes when no one had stormed the front door.

At that juncture, I attached my probes to the comm unit and figured out systematically what it was and how it worked. I confirmed that doing so was indeed much less fun than guessing what might happen. Being an adult was such a drag. Anyway, I learned that my accidental call had been to Morgue Six of DDD. Wow, DDD had at least six warehouses for the results of their dirty work. Best to avoid them. *Quiz comnel* turned out to be an idiom that translated as *what do you want.* Understandable, I suppose. Why would Gorpedder ever call that wretched place? Maybe the employees there were overworked and underappreciated, so they were perpetually grouchy? My shouting back what did *he* want must have seemed odd to the square head, but close enough to appropriate to dismiss and return to his otherwise grizzly job.

I discovered that there was a more conventional news program available, one with people talking and smiling at the camera. I switched it on.

"Well, Galennprey, the news isn't always spectacular, now is it?" The woman who lobbed the staged question to her male counterpart was, in one word, stunningly, scintillatingly gorgeous. Wait, that's three words. Tough. They didn't come close to encompassing her unbridled sultry beauty. Then again, she was a god, right? What other level of male-incapacitating good looks would one have?

"No, it is *not.* Reports are coming in that a goodly portion of the Lower Chamber has been cataclysmically destroyed. No word as to a cause, but our reporter on the scene, Hacksay Brine, has heard rumors that a couple of gods overdid the sacred sauce and celebrated their stupor by leveling the structure. If that's the case, I bet Vorc'll have them on cleanup duty until the last mote of dust is back in its proper place."

"Speaking of proper places, Tantillo, have you dined at Jupiter's Jumbo Juice Joint lately? I have, and I can tell you they have the best liquid-based nutrition available for gods that drink, absorb, or otherwise assimilate their food."

"Hang on one divine second. You're a corporeal *biped.* You have an oral orifice and a digestive tract. You aren't designed for exclusively liquid alimentation." He was wagging a naughty-girl finger at her by way of emphasis.

"Speaking of *divine,* I had their corned beef hash and picklewurst smoothie." The camera panned back to demonstrate she was rubbing her tummy. "It was heavenly."

Lords and powers, those losers were one-bit hacks. They delivered their sales pitch like blissful animatrons. Acting lessons were clearly not a prerequisite for a broadcast career in Godville. With nausea brewing in my gut, I channel surfed to find something watchable. It took five minutes, but I discovered to my shocked bemusement their TV was crap like our TV was crap. There were for offer two soap operas, one reality contest show where gods schemed to enslave the same group of "volunteers," and two sporting matches so gory and in such poor taste I will not relate their specifics. Spoiler alert, more "volunteers" participated, but more as targets and projectiles than actual competitors.

I reviewed what I'd learned since my arrival in Moron City. I was dealing with Cleinoid gods who were vicious and powerful. Their enemies were antigods, but I had no clue as to where they were. Because I escaped and was presently hiding in one of their homes, I concluded that these were petty gods who did not work together. They made errors galore. They also tolerated brutally unacceptable entertainment options. That was their worst sin, IMHO. Most significantly, I knew I could hold my own when going toe-to-toe with at least some of them. My chances were definitely slim but not none. Score two points for Team Ryan.

Then I flashed on the grumpy guy from DDD. He didn't say *who the hell are you, mortal.* No. He confronted me as to why I was bothering him, prank-calling him. He assumed I was some god or almost-god he simply didn't know. Out of the misty clouds swirling in the back of my generally empty head coalesced a plan. Sure, it was unthinkably stupid. Of course, it was impossible that it would work. Naturally, it would end swiftly in my horrendous death. Come on, it was a Jon Plan. But I was so proud of myself. It was a *muahahaha Jon Plan,* if nothing else.

CHAPTER SEVENTEEN

In a tiny dank room high in one of the spiral towers of the Upper Chamber sat two crones. The space was dark and reeked of long-forgotten death. The women were equally grotesque. With gnarly hands, twisted limbs, and convoluted bodies they hovered over a dim flame. In the anemic light their withered faces belied the cruelty that lay beneath their parched facades. There was, in their shark eyes, no promise of morality or decency within. They were, in short, the identical-twin personifications of evil. They were older than time and they were sisters. They were Fest and Deca. They were soothsayer gods. The maleficia arts themselves originated directly from these corrupted, sorry excuses for living beings.

"Sister dearest, can you see the course Fate has chosen?" Fest chortled in a dry, raspy voice.

"No, sister dearest. I see only that Fate chooses to alter her course, not that she has chosen *one* in particular," replied Deca, sternly.

"Sister dearest, your eyes grow too old to see and your mind too porous to hold the thought that she *has* chosen. She moves much in our favor."

"Sister dearest, wicked sister, I tell you she chooses only to confound and confuse us. I think it's personal. She's toying with us. There's bad blood between she and us," speculated Deca.

"Personal? Between two mostly dead gods and the mother of natural forces? Such *vanity*, old fool. Your brain rots, though you still walk among the living," cackled Fest.

"Sister dearest, wickedest of demon spawn, I am the elder sister and I claim the rights and powers that distinction entitles me to possess. *You* are wrong and *I* am right. *You* are ignorant and *I* am wise. Fate twists, but has not declared her intentions as of yet. We must wait, we Cleinoid gods."

"The elder, sister dearest? You? Did we not gnaw our way out of Mother's belly at the same time? Did not we draw first breaths as one? Did we not tumble as one onto her entrails that kindly cushioned our fall to the floor?"

"That is not how I, sister dearest, recall the facts. I was the more aggressive. I went first. You followed, trembling and whimpering," mocked Deca.

"Bickering will not help us formulate our answer to Vorc when he asks what the course of Fate is." Fest was tired and wished for the divining to be at an end. She also hungered for the infant Gorgantors she had stashed in her larder. Left too long, they might become less juicy.

"True, sister dearest. It does not," Deca reluctantly admitted.

"Let us tell the eternal boil on the backside of life that is Vorc that Fate has altered her course and might *well* be advancing in our favor." Fest bobbed her head idiotically as she asked her sister to agree with her summary.

"No." Deca slammed a palm on the tabletop. It splintered under her assault. "We will tell the twit that Fate has altered her course and might *potentially* be advancing in our favor. To encourage him more, if the deed fails to cement itself, would result in us suffering consequences we might avoid if we were more cautious in our summary."

"What use is a soothsayer who spins what she sees to optimize her personal benefits, and not to maximally inform those who ask guidance from her?"

"She is of great use to herself, sister dearest. Though it pains me to have to live in accordance with the rules of self-preservation, I do live in the real world, woman."

Fest lifted her head from the light of knowledge. She scanned the chamber dubiously, then spat on the floor. "This is what you believe to be the real world, sister dearest? Fate help us all."

CHAPTER EIGHTEEN

Over nearly infinite time, there have been a few great introductory lines spoken. "Bond. James Bond.", "Hello. My name is Inigo Montoya. You killed my father. Prepare to die.", and "I'm Batman." To that seminal list I pondered my entry, my homage. "Jon Ryan, god." Nah. Too short. "I'm Jon Ryan, and yes, you may worship me." Way nah. Pompous even for me. And too long. How about a stage name instead? "I'm Spartacus." Nice, but it'd been done. *Arnold Eastwood*? No, that was just weird. Hey, keep it simple. Jonyan? Ryjon? No, wait. Ryanmax. Yeah. I could go for that. It contained both *Ryan* and *max*, as in maximum. A real two-punch name. Ryan —max. *Pow—kapow*.

My latest lame plan was to impersonate a god, to try to blend in and befriend my enemy. I could learn a lot, and I'd be super well-positioned to take them down from the inside. All I had to do was to convince people who'd lived together for an eternity that they just hadn't met me yet. I'd also have to come up with a superpower and be able to demonstrate it if the need arose. Oh, and I could never run into Tefnuf. She was the one god who could out me in a flash. So, what could go wrong? How could this not work like a charm?

I only had a few more days before Gorpedder woke up, so I

had to begin my charade pretty quickly. What was the best way to bring my neighbors up to speed that someone was using Gorpedder's place but didn't care if anyone knew? Hey, a party. There was positively no one I could invite, but I could make it seem like there was one. Loud music. Great idea. All casual visitors had a wild party that upset the locals. It was basically required of any transient. Clearly, my involuntary host had neither a stereo nor a system to play music on. No, he was a big boring boulder. I had to rely on my external speakers and the catalogue of totally rad music I always carried with me. I could do this.

I ramped up the volume on some Springsteen, Iron Maiden, and Rahowa. I moved around the house so it might appear there were multiple people inside. I also turned lights on and off randomly for the same reason. My party of one lasted until dawn the next day. Yeah, it was an all-nighter. I then made a show of taking out a lot of trash. Parties produced lots of trash, so I had to complete the image. I basically threw out everything Gorpedder owned. That, of course, was an additional reason I had to be gone before he returned. He would not be pleased I'd literally trashed his house.

Part of my scheme worked, in that a few people took note of my activity. The excellent aspect there was they didn't recognize I wasn't one of them and kill me on sight. Nice. Emboldened by that initial success, I pushed my luck ever harder. I went to the house closest by and apologized for the noisy party. Maybe it was that gods didn't apologize, or maybe they just didn't like the looks of me, but I got some pretty unwelcoming reactions.

"Hi," I said as the first door swung open, "I'm Ryanmax." I pointed to Gorpedder's place. "I'm staying at a buddy of mine's and had a little get-together last night that kind of got out of hand. Sorry if I ..." That's when the door slammed.

The second house I knocked at, someone looked through a thick window at me, squinted, then never opened up. Jerk.

The last place I hit was only marginally more civil. After my sorry spiel, the resident looked me up and down. "Ah, thanks, I guess," she said. "I hadn't noticed, but then again, I mostly wander the bogs at night."

They had bogs in Godville? Who has *bogs*? "Really. Say, that sounds interesting. I always wanted to do that."

"Why in creation would you want to wander bogs all night long?" she asked incredulously.

"Uh, I don't know ... you know, the same reasons you love to wander them."

"I don't love to wander them," she said sternly. "I'm *bound* to. I am, *after all,* the god of forlorn souls and unrequited passion."

"Ah," I said like a bumpkin. "FS&UR," I said like a complete idiot. "Gotcha."

"I've never heard it called that. I've lived since just after the first sorry creatures became sentient. The minute they were, I was needed. To have never heard that in such a long period suggests it is idiotic to say, or even think but never give breath to."

Well, she got the idiot part pretty spot on. "Really. Yeah, that's one of my gifts, you know. I create aphorisms, metaphors, but mostly acronyms." Lord, I sounded retarded. "Analogies, when I can't avoid them. But," I pointed up to indicate significance would follow, "no *similes,* so don't ask. *Those* I hate."

She seemed to go limp with incredulity. "You're the god of acronyms but never similes. Creation's blessing, what is this realm coming to? A god for such inconsequential trivialities? I shall never cease to be gobsmacked."

I think I'd just been insulted. "No, no. You misunderstand. Acronyms are just a gift, not my, you know, my," I slashed quotes in the air, "*power.*"

"It seems more a curse than a gift. I'd return it, if I were you."

"Hah," I bent my knees and pointed at her face, "good one. You're funny."

"Do you recall the immense time period I referenced just now?" she asked, slipping back into sternness again.

"Ah, yes, I do," I said with inexplicable pride.

"Well, in that span, not a single individual, force, or emanation has opined I was funny. Nor, I must add, have I *ever* felt the god of FS&UR, as you referred to me, *should* be humorous."

I became pseudo-serious. Hell, why not? I was taking on water like the *Titanic*. I wagged a finger and admonished, "Never sell yourself short, honey."

Maybe it was my preposterous advice or maybe it was the *honey*, but I could tell in a heartbeat she was done with me. "Would you excuse me for one second?" she asked almost sweetly.

"Of course."

"Don't move. I'll be right back."

And she was. She held at one hip a wooden wash bucket full of sudsy water. At least I hoped and prayed it was a cleaning bucket and not a chamber pot being cleaned. In either case, she hurled the watery contents at me with convincing force and remarkable accuracy given her state of agitation. Then she did what she could have done without all the drama. She slammed the door in my face.

As I walked the short distance to Gorpedder's digs, I was so stoked. She didn't A) recognize I wasn't a god, B) disintegrate or otherwise negate my sorry ass, or C) sound a general quarters alarm. There might have been a D) in which she enjoined me for all eternity to wander the bogs and moors with her as punishment. I figured she didn't opt for that one, because it'd involve her and me hanging out a lot together.

I chilled my jets until I dried completely, while watching stunningly bad TV. When sufficiently presentable, I resolved to go for a stroll. I'd seen others take walks, so I knew it wasn't ungodly to wander recreationally. The main dirt road was close by, so I caught it and headed in the direction I had been going when I ran into my host. That way seemed to lead to a city center, since I could make out a cluster of what I assumed to be taller buildings in the far distance. The walk was pleasant enough. I had noticed already that the temperature was always comfortable, the sky was always pleasingly clear, and the forecast was always for more of the same. I imagine that's why dirt roads were the standard. No rain meant no mud to sully the impeccable gods.

My general goal was to interact with as many gods as possible. I wanted to learn about them and hoped I'd find some to blend in with; you know, a posse. Maybe we could all get matching T-shirts and have a secret handshake. No, wait, that wouldn't work. A lot of the locals didn't have hands or even torsos to wear a shirt over. So much for that aspiration. Fairly soon I passed a pair of gods going in the opposite direction. I tried hard to draw their attention without appearing to want to. I must have overdone the not-appearing-to part because they never gave me a glance.

A sitting-duck opportunity presented itself a little while later. Three figures moved painfully slowly in the same direction as me. Overtaking them would be unavoidable, even if I started log-rolling on the path. The trio's pace was limited by one member. He, she, or it was unable to put any giddy-up in their get-along. Not too surprising, given that it was a small rocky island with a massive tree angling just off its highest point. I'd seen a lot of crazy things in this weird life, but I think a walking, talking island pretty much took the cake. It used the tree to point and gesture, which was bizarre in and of itself. Italians talk with their hands. It turns out islands talk with their trees.

As I gradually closed the gap between us, I eavesdropped. The island was upset about something. It kept whining—in a most ungodly manner, I had to observe—that someone named Plitheroff was infringing on the island's personal space. I couldn't figure out why it felt that way, but it sure was pissed about it. The two companions mostly listened dutifully and gave off a vibe of profound boredom. Either way, they were generally quiet. To complete the picture, one traveler was more or less humanoid, and the other was a centaur. Yeah, by then I was getting pretty jaded. If all you brought to the table was being a centaur, you were hardly worthy of mention.

I dropped in right behind the three and matched their progress. I nodded whenever the island spoke, trying to insinuate myself into the conversation. I was completely ignored. Then an opening for me to speak occurred. The centaur dropped a huge road-apple right at my feet. Dude didn't even break stride, just *boom*, he dumped it.

"Hey," I protested loudly, "watch out where you relieve yourself there, pal."

The centaur and the humanoid continued to ignore me. It was the island that turned to see who had spoken. I guess it didn't so much turn as it rotated, kind of like a vinyl record being played. If the island's walking was slow, you should have seen how exceptionally slowly it spun. It also stopped walking as it turned, forcing its companions to stop as well.

After a minute I assumed the island was looking at me, since it'd stopped. "Hi," it said in the friendliest tone I'd gotten since my arrival. "What's your name?"

There were a couple of mounds of rocks that might have been eyes, but they also could have been just rocks. Anyway, I addressed the rock piles. "Ryanmax," I replied cheerily. Then, because my brain is so poorly attached to my body, I held out a hand to shake, Yeah, I wanted to shake hands with a small island.

One of the few lucky breaks I'd caught came my way. It dipped the tree and a branch slapped up against my hand. I shook it. "Hemnoplop," it said. "It's so nice to meet you, Ryanmax. Why are you following us?"

"Oh, I'm not following you."

"Yes, you are," challenged the centaur. "We left Bardol as three, not four. You sneaked up on us intentionally."

I sneaked up on an island moving maybe one mile per hour? This horse had attitude.

"No, friend, I *caught* up with you. I was out for a stroll, saw your happy band and decided to join you."

"That's a lie," whinnied the stallion. "You can't join us unless you're invited."

I turned my focus to Hemnoplop's rock piles. "New friend Hemnoplop, may I join your merry band of travelers?"

"Of course. The more the merrier." Then the island giggled. "Hey, I made a funny. Our merry band will be merrier."

"Technicality overcome," I said to the centaur smugly.

"It doesn't count in ..."

The humanoid placed a hand on the centaur's mane. "Let it go, Livryatous. It is not worth arguing the matter."

Livryatous clomped his hooves in an agitated manner. "For a centaur, *everything* is worth arguing. It's what we do."

"Along with taking a crap on your fellow traveler's feet," I peppered in.

"How ..."

"Livryatous, leave it. You did soil his boots, after all." He pointed at them to make his point.

"It was an accident, Wul. Accidents don't count."

"Don't count as what?" I asked. "They sure count in terms of making boots dirty and stinky."

"My ... my passings don't stink," he defended rather lamely.

Wul put a second hand on the centaur. "We are not having *that* conversation," he implored with closed eyes. He stepped over to me. "I am Wul, god of business and enterprise. Pleased to meet you, Ryanmax." While still shaking my hand he added, "I don't believe we've met. I also don't recall seeing you at any conclaves."

"Nor I you. Not too surprising, I guess. I kind of prefer to live in isolation way to the south." I prayed there were north-south directions in wherever the hell I was.

"You keep to yourself?" spat Livryatous. "By choice or ostrisization from *decent* society?"

"You choose, Liv. It'll be fine with me however you call it."

He stomped a few paces toward me. "No one calls me *Liv* and lives."

I stared at him, daring him to go for it. Then Hemnoplop broke the tension. "Hey, you made a funny, too. No one calls you *Liv* and *liv*-es." He chuckled happily.

"It isn't funny, so please stop making a fool of yourself," groused Liv.

"Why? I *am* a fool. I don't mind. *Liv*. Come on, you know I'm Fool's Island, the place everyone wishes all the fools'd be sent to."

"Of course, we know that, Hemnoplop," assured Wul. Back to me he said, "Are you passing through or relocating, Ryanmax?"

"The first with an eye toward the second," I responded.

"I say you keep *going*," snarled Liv. What a jerk.

To defuse the tension, Wul asked, "Since you're new to me, Ryanmax, might I inquire what you are the god of?" He looked furtively to the ground. "Ah, sorry, you are a *god*, am I correct, and not a ..."

"A demigod, emanation, or force of nature?" I finished his thought to prove I was in the know. I lowered my brow. "Or an antigod?"

That got a reaction from all three. Hemnoplop's tiny legs withdrew and he hit the dirt hard, causing a minor earthquake. Livryatous peed like—well, I have to say it, right?—like a racehorse.

Wul got the oddest look on his face. Fear, anger, and embarrassment. "Uh, Ryanmax, I would ... er ... we ... you know we don't speak of ... *them* outside of conclave?"

"Not generally. Sorry. My lame attempt at humor." I bowed deeply.

Livryatous's mouth had frothed up, and his tail spun like a pinwheel nailed to a fencepost. "I will register a formal complaint. Yes, that's what I shall do. No one jokes about an ... ant ... *them*."

"Calm yourself, Livryatous," said Wul. "Our new friend is perhaps less familiar with our, er, reservations concerning that element."

"Or more so." I spoke darkly, like I was in a cheap horror movie. "You asked what I was god of. I'll tell you. Warriors."

Wul reacted like I'd slapped him across the face. Hemnoplop even stood up sort of quickly. Liv, well, he remained in his perpetual huff.

"You're not trying to tell me you're a *second* god of war, are you?"

Liv cut in. "Azacter would not be pleased to hear such a thing *spoken*." There was actual reverence in his tone.

"No, I didn't say *war*. I said *warrior*. The grunts, the kid in the foxhole trembling in fear because he's covered in what's left of his buddy, who was just blown to hell because he was unlucky enough to be two feet to the crying kid's right, so the RPG struck *his* chest. I'm no self-impressed god of the shit that is war, gloried in gold armor and my head stuck up my ass. No," I thumbed my chest angrily, "I'm the god of the young people who die for old men's folly. And you know what?"

They were all wide-eyed and silent.

"If they pray to me hard enough and are so scared they can't remember why it is they're sitting in that foxhole covered in their buddy, I might even throw them a bone and grant their wish." I sat on the dirt. "Eight times out of ten that wish, by the way, is to die quickly and soon." I harrumphed humorlessly. "The other two out of tens are to be at home with their *mommy*, or be cuddled up next to a plump camp woman by a hot fire, the both of them so drunk they think they're in love. You gotta know which of *those* I generally grant."

My audience was impressed. Even Livryatous was dumbstruck. Finally Hemnoplop squeaked, "Are you going as f ... far as Beal's Point? That's where we're headed."

"Heading there myself, new friend. I was heading to that very *spot*."

CHAPTER NINETEEN

"It is obvious my brood-mate will not be returning," Sapale said solemnly to the assembly. "I say it's time to act. Jon Ryan went to these devils and died trying to abort their invasion. I say this time we go in force, we hit them hard, and we bring back their hides to make rugs out of." She was knuckling the table stiffly as she spoke. Sapale sat slowly and rigidly. She was not going to cry. That time had long past.

Kwan Qui was head of military operations for JCFIDAC, the Joint Council for Interplanetary Defense and Cooperation. It had been formed years back to combat the Adamant threat and had grown since then. Over fifty planetary systems were full members, and many smaller worlds sat as auxiliary participants. Kwan stood to speak. He was nearly five meters tall, typical of male Solthian. That made him an imposing figure by any species' standard. "I heard your thoughts," he responded, tapping his chest with a fist and then opening it toward Sapale. It was a Solth custom meaning he felt her pain and treasured her words. "Your mate has been gone over a year. Many would begin to lose hope for his safe return or for the success of his mission." He shook his exclamation-point-shaped head slowly, as though it weighed even more than its original thirty kilograms. "I, however, do not share your assessment, brood's-mate of Jon Ryan." He held a hand up and shook several tentacles toward the ceiling. "Time may pass very differently where he is. And how can one say how long it takes a clever and determined man to bring down an empire of *gods*?" He suctioned several tentacles to his chest. "I for one do not. I can't even guess. That neither Jon Ryan nor any evidence of his fortune have returned to us is reassuring to me. Yes, it gives me reason to hope that he is still ... how does he say it? Ah yes. Sticking it to them where the star don't shine."

A few snickers erupted from Kwan Qui's gaffe. Likely that was his intent.

"Okay. You're correct as usual," Sapale responded with ungoverned intensity. "I say we *swarm* to his aid. Ride in like holo heroes, white hats and everything, guns blazing. Our attack could only help."

Solth culture was based on teachings similar to Daoism. That bias explained Kwan's reply. "Weapons are ominous tools. The wise ruler only uses them when he can't avoid it. If we rush to aid your mate when his plans surely do not hinge on that assault, our efforts might well negate his. He would either have to reveal himself to be our ally and rally to our side, or lament alone after witnessing our deaths, knowing he did not lift a finger to save us."

"Plus, Ms. Ryan," another member added, "don't think for a minute that we know how the transport to the place, wherever it is, works. Just because a fully armed company left *here* together does not mean that they'd end up *there* together, or that they'd still be armed to the teeth."

"The *Ms. Ryans* of the past are all dead," Sapale snapped with a soft growl. "*I*," she rested a palm on her chest, "am Sapale to you and anyone else who doesn't know differently."

"Sorry," replied Carter Brax, a representative of Galactor. The system was fairly new to JCFIDAC. He bowed repeatedly at a frantic pace. "I meant no offense."

"None need be intended to be delivered," she responded coolly.

Xanth-chromafin, the current prime minister of JCFIDAC, rose unsteadily. Being a globular gelatinous creature, it had little option but to quiver. "Sapale, I understand you are in pain. Your loss has been great." It oozed an extension in the direction of the general assembly. "But so suffered have many of us. Some less and some much more so. Be it your intention to wrap yourself in the singular glory of victim is not to be helpful. If to go to the ancient gods we will, it must be only after long interactive thought and discussion like be this now." Again a gooey protuberance swept the room. "The best for the many be our goal, not the best for the one."

"So," Sapale responded, barely able to keep her rage corked up, "JCFIDAC refuses to act. This I knew before I came, because I am a mother. I know how frightened children act. If *you* won't act, *I* will." Looking down at the floor, she turned and rushed from the room.

CHAPTER TWENTY

The walk to Beal's Point took us a week. Good thing we were all immortal. Yeah, when one's pace was set by a small rocky island, one needed the luxury of unbounded time to compensate for the molasses-in-January speed. By the time we arrived, I had been in La La Land for the better part of a month. I continued to be ecstatic that I was not only still alive, but I was successfully pawning myself off as a god. Fortunately for me, if any human could pull off such a ruse, it would be yours truly. Cockiness, it turned out, went a long ways in selling one's godliness.

During the final two days of our trek, it became clear to me the large structures I'd assumed were buildings in a city weren't buildings. The objects were tall, but they were spires or towers, not habitable structures. Why my traveling companions were going to Beal's Point now became unclear to me. I'd assumed we were, you know, heading to the next town. Time to pump my pals.

"Every time I come to Beal's Point I'm more impressed, aren't you?" I said, generally. Open-ended questions had been working well for me, because Hemnoplop suffered from a bad case of the can't-shut-ups.

"Oh, me, *too*," he replied in his childish patent-medicine-salesman voice. "It's so, so ... well, I don't know, but it is."

The ever surly Livryatous quipped, "Do you even listen to what you say, Hemn? Really."

"What?" he defended breathlessly.

"*I don't know, but it is*? That's nonsense in its poorest form."

"Why must you constantly berate him?" scolded Wul. "He never said he was the god of eloquence or college *language* professors. The demigod's an island for fools."

Livryatous's only comeback was to throat a dubious grunt.

"What about you, Wul? What keeps you coming back to Beal's Point?" I asked casually.

"What keeps me coming back? Ryanmax, we've only just met, so I can't yet tell if you're serious or not. I come back," he pointed to Livryatous, "he comes back," then he slapped the side of the island, "and he returns for the same reason you do. We must. Please don't joke about such a sacred obligation."

Oh, crap, stepped in the doggy doo-doo again, didn't I? "No, I meant to say—duh, we *have* to—but what do you enjoy most about the place?" Yeah, that's what I meant—I hoped.

"*Enjoy* about Beal's Point?" My, he sounded incredulous.

"Yeah."

"What," he turned the tables, "do *you* find most enjoyable about Beal's Point?"

I needed to start using a smaller shovel to dig these holes I continued to excavate for myself.

I smiled and swaggered. I know, swaggering is dangerous if used unwisely, but I needed to put some real spin on my response. "Leaving it when I'm done."

Wul stared at me a few seconds, during which I was glad I no longer had a bladder to lose control of. Then he burst out laughing. He put a hand on my shoulder and shook me. "*Leaving* it. That's superb. Me, too. *That's* what I like the best."

"Don't quote me, but that's true for me also," grumbled Livryatous.

We turned as one to Hemnoplop. "What?" he protested.

"We were wondering what your answer to my question might be," I replied.

"What question, or should I say which question? You've asked so many."

Was this god for real? "The one about Beal's Point."

Approximately two minutes later he said flatly, "I don't recall a question about Beal's Point. I was thinking of water. I probably missed that one. Sorry."

Water. He was so preoccupied thinking about H_2O he missed Wul's hysterics? Dude's head was as thick as the rock on his outside. "Never mind," I said as I started walking again. "It was a dumb question."

Wul chuckled quietly to himself. "*Leaving* it," he repeated under his breath.

"Hemn," I began a while later, after we'd moved maybe ten meters, "mind if I ask what you were thinking about water?"

"No, Ryanmax. I *love* to talk."

I'd alert the media on that news flash.

"I was thinking that water is nice."

"Nice?"

"Yes, it is, you know?"

A demigod with the mind of a toddler. Sure. Why not? I was certain the universe needed at least one of those.

"Yes it is. Nicest liquid I know of." I couldn't actually press him too much. Even *I* had standards. Never mock someone who lacked the mental wherewithal to defend himself.

"*Isn't* it?" he exploded. "I mean, I can't think of another liquid off the top of my mind, but if I could, it wouldn't be as nice."

"Lava," blurted out Livryatous. "It's liquid stone," he said absently.

"Oh, I don't *like* lava. It scares me."

"As well it should," I said, patting his nearest shoreline. "It's very hot."

"How can it scare you?" snapped a now irritated Livryatous. "If it gets too close you just step away."

"That's easy for you to say," whined Hemnoplop.

Livryatous nodded a few times. "Touché, my friend. I deserved that."

"You deserved what?" Hemn asked with childlike innocence.

"Let it go, you two. A silent interlude is most welcome," Wul said firmly. I guessed he was the leader of the band.

Finally the day came when we formally arrived at Beal's Point. The site itself was a large, flat semicircular outcropping of rock ending in a sheer cliff. The poignancy of my quip that leaving it was the best aspect of the dump became immediately clear. Whoever constructed it was either blind, sick in the head, or had a bad sense of humor. Maybe all three. The tall towers I'd initially taken to be buildings in a city were pedestals holding up enormous statues. The stands varied from tens to hundreds of meters tall. Most were ridiculously thin and structurally unjustifiable. They should have collapsed from their own weight, even without the statues they bore. God construction seemed to have its own set of rules.

What was really offensive, though, were the statues themselves. Talk about shlock art. The best comparison I can give is that if the moron who invented black velvet Elvis painting ever switched to stone, I was looking at his handiwork. Not one figure was acceptable. The body parts were all out of proportion to one another, and the features like hands and faces were both ham-handedly carved and revolting. Maybe, I flashed, there were gods of unart, nonart, and the opposite of art, and they got drunk one long weekend and barfed up these monstrosities.

Wul led the way and we all followed. We would pass one grotesque monument, bow to it, mumble something I never did figure out, and then we'd head for the next mockery. Given that we were anchored with Hemnoplop's painfully slow pace, I suffered a thousand deaths with each hideous monument. Livryatous continually clomped his hooves, indicating to me he favored bolting.

For once I agreed with him. Then it struck me. I felt different, odd in a way I hadn't before. You know the expression of *feeling like someone's walking over my grave*? Up until that point, I had no idea what that might have meant. Now I did. That was precisely what I experienced. It definitely had to do with these terrible obelisks.

"Hey, fellas," I shouted out to my companions, "I just realized I missed something a couple towers back. Keep going and I'll catch up."

The looks from Wul and Livryatous were along the lines of *you have maggots in your brain*. Oblivious Hemnoplop continued ahead blithely.

I wandered back far enough that I was out of sight of the others. Slipping behind a massive plinth, I quickly ran a set of diagnostics. All systems were optimal. The only issue I identified was that my compass application gave inconstant directions. Weird but nothing critical. It suggested there was an unusually large magnetic flux in my vicinity. Only problem was that there wasn't one. I began assessing my surroundings, searching for a cause of my creepy feeling. There was no unusual radio frequency traffic, no abnormal radiation levels, and nothing toxic in the air. I found nothing that could cause what I seemed to be only imagining.

Failing all else, I put up a partial membrane. Those allowed only visual light through. I felt the same. Switching to a full membrane, a completely impenetrable barrier aside from that annoying shiny cloud who was currently MIA, I suddenly felt fine. The off-feeling vanished. Alternately turning the membrane on and off, I quickly confirmed there was something in the locale that affected me. I still had zero clue as to what it was or what it was designed to do. Oh, joy. Another hopeless mystery. Maybe I actually *was* the god of those.

When I was done analyzing the ... whatever ... I caught up with my group. Yeah, not too hard, they'd moved maybe three meters. We shuffled on in silence for a while. I came up alongside Wul as unintentionally as I could appear to. After a few minutes I mumbled, "Never going to get used to that feeling."

"Pardon?" he said, waking from some daydream.

"Oh, mostly grousing to myself. I said I'm never going to get used to that awful feeling. The one here at Beal's Point."

He grunted a harrumph. "Not sure we're supposed to."

So there *was* a signal in the area, an intentional one that Wul accepted to be unpleasant but necessary. Mandatory? "I know. I just wish there was an alternative."

He stopped and stared at me. "You continue to be *most* peculiar."

I shrugged. "So I've been told."

"What *alternative* might you suggest?"

Oh, boy, stepped in it again. I was one hell of a lousy spy. "Maybe read about it in a book?"

"Read about the past misery of prior defiled gods by reading it in a book in order to assimilate the message to not do as they did?"

I shrugged again, more apologetically. "Sure. Why not?"

"Ryanmax, what we are discussing borders on sacrilege."

"Right in my wheelhouse. I'm a bit of an iconoclast."

"A *bit?* You question and challenge perhaps the oldest law of the conclave, and that's a *bit* sacrilegious?"

I kind of giggled like the jackass I was being.

He shook his head. "You could *learn* of the past transgressions and their consequences from a book. But you couldn't absorb and internalize the essence of their sins that way. No book is large enough to hold that much guilt." He spread his arms out wide.

So the yucky feeling I was experiencing was the assimilation of some dead gods' sins. I threw up in the back of my mouth—figuratively. Grossamus maximus. I had sins aplenty of my own, thank you very much. And at least I got to *enjoy* my sinning. Taking some loser's burden was unacceptably unpleasant.

Aha. That was why Wul mentioned that we *had* to come here. It wasn't voluntary. This was no vacation. It was a pilgrimage. So the powers that were set up Beal's Point as an object lesson for the multitude of power-hungry immortals to try and keep them in line. That's why the figures were depicted so grotesquely. They were pariahs, not dignitaries. All us gods—I said *us* specifically because, you know, I was getting into character—were required to swallow the bitter medicine in hopes we would play nice. I guess it made some sense, but I would need to get my soul dry-cleaned if I ever got out of here alive. I wanted no part of the alleged sins of the losing factions in high-level politics. Come on, that's what it always was. Old men fighting and the winners revising history to make themselves shine brighter than a polished gold coin.

"I never actually met any of the denizens of Beal's Point," I said, hoping I wasn't making a fatal error. "Did you, Wul?"

He scuffed his shoes on the ground. "One or two."

"Were they really that bad that they needed to end up here?"

He turned to me in horror. "I *am* a freethinker, Ryanmax, but I am *not* a treasonist. I demand that you stop speaking seditiously in my presence. I hate *coming* here. I definitely don't want to become one of those *entombed* here."

"Might you be overreacting a tad? No offense intended, but we're just *talking* here. What's more, no one can hear us. I didn't say these guys got a bum deal, I was asking if it was possible, on a case-by-case basis." I let that sink in. "Who'd you know? Name one of them."

"Long ago I spent some time on a project with Denominus."

"A project? That's nice. What project was it?"

"After the Third Transheaval we worked on a system to compress as many Leginites as possible into metal canisters."

Sounded monstrous, but I elected not to press for details. I might be tempted to kill him, not pump him for information.

"Okay. In the time you spent with him, did he impress you as a heathen, a villain, or a heretic?"

He sort of pouted a while before responding. "No. He was actually quite the opposite."

"A true believer in all things PC?"

"PC?"

"*Politically correct.* Dogma, doctrine, and the official word of whoever the hell was running the show."

"Ah. Yes, he certainly was that. Unshakeable support for the ruling coalition."

I pointed to the nearest statue. "The same one that defiled him by dumping him here?"

Wul gestured to the far distance. "He's that one we passed a while back. Yes, it was his treasured central seat that turned against him."

"For what?"

"Sedition."

"Wul, sedition's a word. What'd he *do?*"

He lowered his head profoundly. "We were never fully informed. Sedition was all we were told."

"Wow, that seems like a fair and open process, now doesn't it?"

"It was fair and it was open. I am satisfied with the decisions and actions of the conclave," he replied through gritted teeth.

"Because you don't want to end up on a pole at Beal's Point."

"No, because I trust my leaders and desire no higher glory than that which I already have," he said more hotly.

"And possibly because one or both of our companions might have exceptional hearing and a tendency to betray nonbelievers."

"That thought never *crossed* my mind," he concluded, looking off toward them.

All right. Wul I could work with. He had a functioning mind. Now if I could just stop absorbing someone else's bad mojo, I might begin to get an upper hand in this realm.

CHAPTER TWENTY-ONE

"Vorc, the masses are becoming restless," Dalfury said respectfully. He was the center seat's right hand, and functioned as an advisor and a secretary. He was a sensitive and thoughtful individual and had served Vorc's mother in that same capacity for eons. Physically, he was cloudy memory composed of cottony, wispy white and gray mists constantly churning in flux. As a demigod he represented— you guessed it—those with cloudy memories. Some godly spheres of influence were pretty straightforward like that.

"And you mention this to me again to what end?"

"To make certain you are well-informed and up to date."

"And you mention this to me again to what end?" Vorc repeated, trying not to smile.

"There *exists* an option in which you intervene, intercede, or otherwise influence the situation. It is potentially, er, destabilizing."

"And what would you have me do?"

Dalfury's vapors churned more than normal. "I wouldn't know, Vorc. I am but a right hand."

"That's it? Nothing more than a nebulous advisor? Really, old friend?"

"And I pray to the Forces I am adequate in that role."

"Ah," he responded, resting back into his pile of pillows. Vorc rubbed absently at his chin. "Let me pose it to you this way. You state you wouldn't know what action to take in this matter. Assume for the sake of argument that you *did* have a thought on the situation. What would it likely be?"

The cloud spun and billowed a few moments. "Well, if I *had* an opinion, it might be that you should encourage our population to proceed as if our escape from this dimension were presently a certainty."

"*That* would quash discontent? But what if Fate does not so favor us? What position *might* I be in, then?"

"A rather poor one. But if we fail to succeed at this time, your position will be as unpleasant."

"Beal's-Point-on-a-pedestal unpleasant?"

"Hardly. But think about it this way. If you say we *go* and we *don't*, you have a problem. If you say we *aren't* going, or simply say nothing and imply the same, you have a problem. If you say we *go* and we *do*, you have no problem."

"So close my eyes, step off the cliff, and hope for the best."

"That is one version of an opinion I might have if I ever had one." The cloud folded to indicate a bow.

"Very well. Call a conclave for the day after tomorrow. I'll announce then that we're going on a rampage."

"I shall be glad to, Vorc. You'll see. I have a good feeling about our chances."

"I care nothing for feelings. I would prefer the poll numbers." He pointed to his assistant intently. "I definitely want the exit poll numbers on my desk by the time I get back here."

"So it will be, even if it takes voodoo magic."

Vorc shook his head slowly. "Dalfury, please don't go there again. I'm still finding beads and chicken feathers in the oddest places."

CHAPTER TWENTY-TWO

The four of us sat around a big fire, resting. We were about halfway through the gauntlet that was a Beal's Point pilgrimage. It turned out my companions had packed Hemnoplop with all manner of food and beverage before they set off. Yeah, small islands have a lot of nooks and crannies to haul stuff. And the added weight was nothing to him. We were feasting on fresh fruits, preserved meats, and lots of intoxicants. *Lots*. Dudes knew how to do it *right*. My kind of picnic.

Hemnoplop ate mass quantities but drank almost nothing. He kept going on about not wanting to destabilize his sedimentary layers with too much fluid accumulation. And if he got tipsy, he'd tip, and it was oh-so-hard to get up unless there were elephants and dinosaurs present to help him. Argh. Dude was turning out to be quite the pansy. Oh well, more for me, right?

As the evening wore on, Wul made it a point to come over to me when the other two were busy arguing. I should say that Livryatous, who was three sheets to the wind, was arguing with Hemnoplop. The island mostly listened and nodded like he found the whole process enjoyable. La-*who*-zer.

"Ryanmax, mind if I sit with you a spell?"

"No. Pull up a rock."

He did just that. "The night is cold but the fire warm. Life is good," he said, as he raised his glass.

I tapped mine to his and we threw the concoction back. I didn't ask the name, since I didn't want to seem unfamiliar with the commonplace. It was definitely fermented and distilled, but it had a bubbly tang. It was nice. "L'chaim," popped out of my mouth.

He furrowed his brow and thought a minute. "Haven't heard that in a long time." He reflected a bit longer. "Associated with the Hebrews, right?"

"Give the man a kewpie doll."

"Did they worship you?"

Never been asked that before. Sure sounded odd entering my head. "Me, no. Someone named Yahweh, last I heard."

He glared at me long and hard. "You speak of matters others do not. I'm still deciding if that's a good thing or not."

"But it's a *fun* one," I said, offering him my glass to toast again.

After a pause he clinked mine, albeit kind of begrudgingly. "Yahweh is not a Force spoken of often. Most are too nervous to say the word."

"Gods nervous about saying a god's name? I never bought into that, friend. Silly superstition."

He angled his head. "If you say so. *I* call it prudent."

"Wul, come on. A god's a god's a god."

"Now I know you're twisting my leg. You can't believe such a falsehood."

Say what? "Help me out here. Are you twisting some part of *my* anatomy?"

"Ryanmax, there are universes of difference between gods. Tell me you know this."

"Let's pretend, because we're friends and bored, that I don't and you explain it like I was four."

He squinted at me, measuring my response. Finally he spoke. "To be a god like we Cleinoids, one must be immortal and have some manifest power, some non-spontaneous ability to act. You know, throwing lightning bolts or prophecy."

"Sure."

"But that we *don't* die doesn't mean we *can't* ."

I gestured broadly to the statues of Beal's Point. "Duh."

"A god like ... like the one you mentioned is very different. They are truly immortal. They possess powers such as omniscience. We do not."

"Yeah, I knew an evil god who we ended. He knew a lot, but he wasn't omnipotent or anything."

That gave him pause. "You knew a god we ended? How is that possible?"

Why did I shake my mouth off? Because I was an idiot, that was why. "Long story."

He pointed to Hemnoplop. "I'm traveling with him. Time I got."

"You finish your explanation, then it'll be my turn."

"Agreed. I'm done. Talk."

"No you're not because I'm still confused. Why stress over saying a name like Yahweh?"

Dude visibly cringed when I said the name. "Because to speak a name has power. It is an offer, an opportunity. Speak a name and that individual might learn of it. They might come to see why you spoke of them. That might be bad."

"There're three *mights* in that sorry excuse for a justification. *Might* cubed makes the odds quite remote."

"You want a Power greater than yours to be standing here angry and bent on vengeance, even if the chances were slim?"

"Well, no, but ..."

"But nothing. You've been warned."

Hmm. Summoning Yahweh actually sounded pretty good to me about then. He'd be able to clear up the entire ancient god threat quicker than an old man slipping on a banana peel.

"The god you knew?" he pressed.

"Ralph."

He contorted his face, considering the name. "Never heard of him. Ralph? Are you certain?"

"Well, no, now that you ask. That's what he said I should call him. He lived in a globular cluster orbiting some stupid galaxy. Are we done here?"

"We haven't even started. A few scouts have slipped temporarily out of our universe into Prime. Yes, we are told they have caused some nuisance damage. But their time is limited and few are able to make the passage."

Destroying an entire planet was *nuisance* damage? Wow, these guys did play hardball. Prime? What the hell was that? My head was spinning. "I wouldn't know about Prime." Not certain what I actually just said, but I spoke with resolve. Resolve was good, when knowledge and options were at a minimum.

"How ... you knew a god in Prime. Are you trying to deceive me?"

"Me? Heavens no." I did my best to seem hurt. Darn near teared up.

"Ryanmax, if you knew a god in the Prime Target, then you were in Prime. You're lying to my face one way or the other." With serious attitude he asked, "Which is it?"

I think I'll title my autobiography, *Spending Eternity Weaseling Out of Problems My Big Mouth Caused*. Yes, most definitely. " I said I didn't know about Prime. Come on, lighten up. I know so little about it I basically *know* nothing. Didn't say I hadn't been there." I set my index fingers next to one another, then expanded them apart. "Two things are big-time different."

He was quiet so long I got nervous. He relented finally. "When you excused yourself earlier to go back and complete some obeisance, I followed you."

"*What?* How dare you, and why?"

"You were obviously trying to do something in private. Ryanmax, no one goes backwards here. The place is a shithole. One moves forward as fast as possible and one never looks back." He looked to the fire. "I wanted to see what you were up to."

"Maybe I wanted to take a dump all by my lonesome."

"Then I'd have seen you take a *dump*, as you so colorfully call what I assume means pass excrement." He looked back to the flames. "But that's not what I saw."

"Yeah?" Oh crap-oh crap-oh crap. I was in for it now. "What'd you *think* you saw, secret squirrel?"

"I saw you repeatedly disappear and reappear."

Dude, I am a god. What's the prob? "Wul, that's it? You saw a god become invisible and you're ready to, what, form a *cult* around me?"

He looked hurt. "You told us before you were the god of warriors."

"Yeah. I am."

"What good would the ability to become invisible be to a warrior?"

Huh? Can I get a *duh*? "I believe a warrior under extreme threat would welcome invisibility. Ya think?" I had to pepper that in. Jerk deserved it.

"Ryanmax, I was beginning to like you. I fancied we might even become friends in time. But you are obviously up to something sinister and you do not want me to know of it." He sniffed loudly. "Such a betrayal precludes friendship, wouldn't you agree?"

On the chessboard of life I just slid from *confused* to *dumfounded*. "Wul, I 'd like to think we are becoming friends. Tell me, please, why invisibility is not an asset for a warrior."

"Our powers help those we expend them on," he said bitterly.

"Yeah, and when your ass is in a sling invisibility is mighty handy."

"*You* becoming invisible in no way helps the poor *soul* with his ... whatever you said."

Oh, *shit*. I had it wrong and I *was* sounding evasive. "Wait," I mostly whined, "are we talking about what's useful in battle, or are we talking about what powers any one of us ..."

"Stop it. This is hurtful." He stood to leave.

Showtime. I stood. "My power is *spearing*. I spear things. If I need to help a warrior in battle, I spear what's causing them grief." I raised a finger and pointed at the nearest large rock. I threw a pulsed full membrane and the rock exploded into dust. "There. Now I'm sorry ..."

"So you *are* a poly and you wish to conceal that fact." His tone was suddenly one of hushed jubilation.

A *poly*? Want a cracker? I was leaping from one fire into the next bigger one with impressive speed. How was I going to figure this one out? "A *poly*? Me? No, you silly goose." Did I just refer to the god of business as a silly goose? Yup. I checked. I had. "I'm as not ... poly as ... as, well, as *you* are."

He smiled conspiratorially. "Sure you are. Sure *we* are." He actually shot a furtive glance around a full three-sixty. What was up with him? He leaned in. "So how many do you have?"

Fingers? Ten. Dicks? One. What the hell ...

"Come on. You just showed me spearing and I saw invisibility. That's two. Wait, you might have been teleporting. Oooh, that's even more powerful than simple invisibility."

"It is?"

He nudged me with an elbow. "No, I do not think teleporting is more powerful than invisibility *either*, Ryanmax." He said my name especially hard. Who the hell was supposed to be taking notes?

"Wul, you been hitting the liquor a bit too hard? I think you're losing it."

His crest fell. "I'm trying to help. I'm also trying to understand. Ryanmax, I've never known a poly. Sure, we all see them from time to time at conclave. But I've never shared a *drink* with one."

"Only Monos?" I ventured a guess.

"Monos? What's that?"

"You know, folks with just *one*." I held up a single digit, because I was *such* a moron.

"You mean a *singlet*?"

Of course, I did. "Of course, I did. I was just messing with you."

"Ah." He smiled nervously. "I get it. Ha."

Not even a ha ha. I think his mirth was forced. "It's no big deal."

Wul literally sat involuntarily back where he'd been. "Not a big deal?" He stared at me like I was, I don't know, maybe a *poly*. "Oh," he offered weakly, "I get it. It's not a big deal. It's a huge deal, right?"

I pointed at his nose. "You got it, big guy. There's no pulling the *wool* over *Wul's* eyes."

He paled quickly. "Are you going to place a sheepskin over my head? Why? Do you mean to end me so your secret is safe? Ryanmax, please ..."

I held up both hands. "Woah, Nelly. It's a saying, an expression." I patted all my pockets. "Do you see a sheepskin?"

"N ... no. But who's to say you don't have that power, too?"

"What, the power to pull wool out of thin air? Are you mental?"

He looked huffy. "It is *possible,* even if it'd be a somewhat useless gift."

"I'm the god of sheep now?"

"You *are?*" He beamed sudden excitement. "But why just temporarily?"

This conversation was officially batty. "I'm not the interim god of sheep. Goats either. Wul, you gotta calm down before you have a stroke, or I give you one."

"You're a health god ..."

I rested my finger over his lips. Thank the maker he stopped spewing nonsense. "I'm *Ryanmax*. I'm the god of *warriors*. That is *it*. Stop now or I'll summon medical aid for you."

It took ten minutes, but I could sense he'd calmed down. "If I'm a poly," I held up a hang-on-a-second palm before he shot off like a rocket again, "and I'm only saying *if*, what's the big deal? It would have to seem completely *normal* to me, right?"

His lips moved silently as he mulled that over. "I guess it would. Look, being a poly is very rare. Even you must know that. If you were, you know, a *poly*-poly, Ryanmax, that would be ... it'd cause ..."

"Any chance you'll just up and say it while I'm still young?"

"You'd be *our* god."

Oh, my. Sorry I asked.

CHAPTER TWENTY-THREE

"I'm not just as stupid as my husband," Sapale snapped at Toño.

"Ah, really? In what manner is your *lunacy* different from his?"

"He didn't have the decency to say goodbye to you. I do. I am."

Toño gritted his teeth and shook his head. "I'll grant that you're more *considerate*," he raised an angry finger, "not that that's saying much, given whom I compare you to. But your act is equally stupid. To march willingly into a trap set by vicious killers is—and you can ask anyone about this—*cited* in the dictionary as an example of stupidity."

"Toño, I've lived two billion years. If I *were* to die due to this foolishness, I'd be two billion years overdue anyway. I've filled my dance card on both sides. My brood-mate is missing and I might," she wagged a finger, "just *might* be able to help him. If I die, who actually cares? I miss Jon, and we'd both die for him, so what's the big deal?"

"There is so much that is wrong with that statement, I don't know where to begin. First, there is no such thing as being overdue to die. You are gifted a very long life and must respect that gift. Use it *wisely*. You have much to offer and our needs are great. Second, if Jon died at their hands, what chance would you stand? And don't bother to say you're just as skillful and lucky as he, because *no one* is. Third, I care. You asked who did, and I'm telling you. Fourth, you're not going after him. He's been gone a year. As I stated clearly before, that either means he *is* dead, or he's well-placed and some cockamamie scheme of his is working. Your arrival will only destabilize his efforts and cannot help them."

"You can't know that," she defended weakly.

"Oh, I can't? So he's dug in like a tick, you show up and are about to be terminated and he's bound to try to rescue you. He has to expose himself abruptly and fly into a hopeless attempt to rescue you from what would have to be their strongest prison. What *helpful* aspect have I overlooked?"

"If you want to see things darkly, darkly you will see them. I've learned in my expansive life that the unpredictable often happens."

"You frustrate me so."

"Not what I anticipated hearing. I'll bite. Why have I frustrated you?"

"Because I will not be able to say *I told you so* when you don't return, after having been killed quickly while providing Jon no assistance."

She pointed a hand at her head. "Make a backup and tell it."

"That's not funny."

"No, but it might be therapeutic for you."

"I will deal with my own therapies, thank you just the same. Now if you are hell-bent on acting out a grievous error, please do so now and leave me in my soon to be shattered peace."

"Wow. That's the best Catholic guilt I've heard since, well, since the last time you played that card."

"And I hope you carry the burden of the guilt long after you pass Davdiad's sacred veils." He turned his back on Sapale.

"Ouch. He really *is* mad."

"No," whispered Toño, "he really is *frightened*."

CHAPTER TWENTY-FOUR

Jonathan Ryan, god of the gods. Hmm. Had a nice ring to it. I mean, I wasn't going to let my new gig affect me, get into my head. Nah. I was going to be a humble, welcoming, and loving god of gods. Magnanimax. Can't forget Magnanimax. Might even have to make that my official middle name. Jon *Magnanimax* Ryan, GOG. No, wait, that'd blow my cover. Ryanmax Magnanimax, GOG. There's the ticket. Man alive, I just couldn't wait to spring that one on Al. He'd positively lay an egg; hell, several species of eggs.

Damn, I hated to admit it, but I missed the bucket of used bolts. I sure could use his analytical input in this Bizarro World. His annoying, grating commentary, too. Sure, I missed Sapale. I missed Doc. But Al and I, we were partners from the get-go. Anyway, I missed him.

Seriously though, these Cleinoid gods were weak in the head. They had a bargain-basement prophecy about how they'd end—*the gods will fall only when three miracles that are one work as two*—and to top that off, they're sitting with their thumbs up their butts, waiting for their god to materialize. Pathetic. Moronically pathetic. But weakness in an enemy was a good thing. Hell, if I did swing the

GOG thing, I could just order them all to off themselves and save everyone a lot of grief.

Oh, great master god, Ryanmax Magnanimax, how best may we serve? they would ask while groveling.

Devotion to me involves but two steps. Find a black hole. Jump into that black hole, I would say with a mother's love.

Not a likely scenario, but a sweet fantasy.

Once we were fed and rested, our odd troop set off again to absorb bad vibrations. Now that I was in tune with the transmissions, I confirmed they did indeed get stronger nearer to a statue. Also there was a variation in the sense I got. Different "sins" must have produced different symptoms. With little else to do I focused most of my time on identifying the nature of the negative transmissions. I knew I was up against the possibility that they were somehow magical, and hence unidentifiable, but it was something to keep my mind occupied. Otherwise, I'd be forced to focus on Hemnoplop's nonstop childish babbling.

A factoid from the past came to mind. The Deft did their shape-shifting using exotic matter. That same exotic matter was the lifeblood of the Adamant Empire. That's why the dogs wanted to make the Deft completely extinct. But, thinking a bit more, that didn't help. I didn't care what the power source was. I wanted to know what the agent causing the feelings was. But I'd done darn near every test I knew of on the atmosphere other than tasting it. If I could ... *Yeah.* That would be worth a try. If I concentrated the signal maybe I could analyze it. I set up a full membrane in the shape of a pointy-at-one-end ice cream cone. The wide opening faced the source, a statue base, and the tiny hole was away from the sender. By toying with the angle of the walls of the cone I could concentrate the signal. That was much the same principle for how a gamma ray detector worked. The particles slid along the edges and were slowly concentrated.

It took maybe half an hour to convince my stubborn self that approach wasn't going to work. Even though it had to work, it didn't. No matter how I varied the size parameters of the system, I detected nothing. That was impossible. I then guinea-pig confirmed that my cone *did* concentrate the awful feeling. I stood at the tiny-hole end and let the signal hit me. Wow, instant buzzkill. I was so depressed I jumped to one side. As I've said many times before, I hated dealing with an impossibility when confronted by one.

What if I slowed the beam down? Hmm. Might help. In a physics lab there was media that could slow speedy light to a walking pace. Seriously. They were clear. I did the experiment once where I fired a laser into one end of the block and walked right alongside the moving light beam without any effort. It was surreal.

But, naturally, no matter how high an index of refraction I subjected the concentrated beam to, it didn't slow down. I was ready to kick something small and helpless. What doesn't slow down? Nothing known. Well, aside from my ex-wife Gloria while enumerating my shortcomings. As I mentioned, even light itself can be slowed to a crawl. For the second time that morning I wished the AIs were present to help me see what I was missing.

Some force emanated from these ugly monoliths that I couldn't detect and that couldn't be decelerated to a speed where I could detect it. With enough energy any particle can be ...

Energy?

Particle?

Can't slow to everyday speed?

Wow. Here's a question. What can't be slowed to a stop? Answer. A thing that cannot go slower than the speed of light. Bingo. The signal had to be in tachyons or some equivalent mystery particle that could *only* move faster than light. As counterintuitive as it might have sounded, one can slow a bullet from fast to zero. But one could only slow a tachyon down to *almost* as slow as the speed of light. It was in the tachyons' nature. They were the Speedy Gonzaleses of creation. They could only go fast. I hadn't detected tachyons, because I wasn't looking for them. In point of fact, I doubted I could prove they were there. It wasn't like I could mosey over to Walmart and buy a tachyon meter. As far as I knew, there was no way to detect them. For a long time they were theoretical particles that no proper scientist actually believed existed. But even in my lifetime on Earth, they were shown to exist. And that documentation had been due only to indirect effects *caused* by the tachyons. Oh well, at least I had some understanding of what was occurring to me. And I had one more tiny insight into the ancient gods' technology.

Based on Hemnoplop's inability to move fast enough to disturb still air, it took us three weeks more to leave Beal's Point. I tell you I could not have been more ecstatic if Gina Lollobrigida and Marilyn Monroe said they wanted a threesome with me. Well, almost. Anyway, we made it back to the main road and there we split up. Hemnoplop said he needed to get back to sea. Fools were lining up to climb his shores as we spoke. With his announcement, Livryatous felt unbounded. He clomped over to my side and dumped a huge pile of horse poop on me, my boots, and the ground around me. He must have been saving it up for days. Then he dropped his tail and charged off into the distance without a word.

That left Wul and me there, staring down at all that manure.

"I'm climbing out on a limb here," I said, "but I'm guessing he never warmed sufficiently to me."

"I believe you could successfully argue that point," replied Wul with a smirk. Then he burst into hardy laughter. I joined in quickly. It *was* kind of funny. Hell, if I was a centaur, I'd have pulled the same stunt.

When we calmed back down, a very serious Wul asked, "So where are you heading now?"

I took a deep breath and exhaled loudly. "To try and soak all the bad karma out of the temple that is my body."

He grunted. "And just how do you propose to do that?"

"I'll use a powerful and concentrated solvent."

His eyebrows peaked.

"With fiery drinking whiskey," I revealed.

He rapped me on the shoulder. "Count me in. I need all the solvent I can get myself."

Because that darn Hemnoplop was so slow, there was no doubt

Gorpedder would have recovered and likely returned to his digs. So it would be profoundly ill-advised of me to go there. "Where's your favorite establishment of intoxicating refreshment, my friend?" I asked jovially.

"My favorite? That's tough. There are a number of such havens."

"Then I suggest we do this scientifically. We'll take 'em down in alphabetical order."

He pointed to my nose. "You are a wise and thoughtful god, Ryanmax. Altruism's Failure just happens to be a short, pleasant walk from here," he signaled to his right, "that way."

"Then why are we just standing here with our teeth in our mouth? *March*," I said, gently shoving Wul in the proper direction.

You know me and dive bars. They're my happy places. Altruism's Failure was hence not my kind of saloon. No, it was posh, over the top to the point of garish, in fact. Clouds lazed their way across the expansive room, gold was the metal of choice for everything solid, and the waitstaff was impeccable. The males were all hunks and the women were all stunning. They were also all buck naked. Gulp. It occurred to me that this *was* a bar for gods. Maybe they all looked like this?

We were seated at a great table, not surprisingly, because all the tables were great. They were all centrally located, but subtly inconspicuous, favoring those inclined to dodgy rendezvous. And all the tables had commanding views of the decor and the stunning vistas outside. Mountains with exploding waterfalls, deep forest canopies, and peaceful seascapes with calming waves. God bars *were* impressive; even I had to admit it.

A woman blessed with spectacular attributes glided up to our table and bowed slightly. "I live to serve only you. How may I begin to make your days the best they could ever be?"

Now, I have to say that in all my days, in all the restaurants, bars, cafés, and hot-dog stands I'd ever visited, I'd never been offered such a friendly, welcoming greeting. I liked the girl immediately. Her commitment to the hospitality industry was palpable. She was a credit to her trade.

"We'll start with a bottle of Zeus Juice and, of course, a bottle of nectar of the gods."

"I will get those immediately. Upon my return please tell me how else I might serve to honor you."

I know what you were thinking. The answer was no, a firm *no*. She was a Stepford waitress, not a real hotty with a fancy for yours truly. I mean, what sane knockout wouldn't want to jump these bones? But this was just too forced, too *convenient*. I should mention Wul appeared to have no similar reservations or pride. No, even through his loose-fitting clothes I could see he was prepared to test the full meaning of our server's open-ended invitation.

She returned with a large bottle. When close enough I could confirm the label indeed read Zeus Juice. Had a caricature of the old bearded guy and everything. Cupids firing arrows and nymphs abounding. Our waitress was followed by a second different-looking but equally over-endowed woman carrying a second bottle, no doubt the nectar. Now I have to say it would have been fully possible for our initial waitress to carry both bottles and several more easily. I think the second babe accompanied the first in case her commitment to the service industry was ... also tested. Catching fish in a barrel with a shotgun was far more difficult than getting laid 'round these parts.

"I'll pour," said Wul, taking the bottle from her hands. "You may leave." He did pat her rump after she'd turned to leave. The #MeToo Moment had a long ways to go in the land of the gods, it would seem.

"When you're ready, let me know and I'll flag one of them down for you," said Wul as he filled our glasses.

"When I'm ready for what?" I asked naively.

"Ready to ... you know, *divest* yourself in the company of one of the staff."

Divest myself. Never heard hiding-the-salami called that before. Live and learn.

"Thanks. I'll ... I'll keep you posted."

He shrugged.

"To a lousy adventure completed," Wul called out as he raised a glass of Zeus Juice.

We toasted and threw back the whole tumbler. Three—two—one. *Zawowzers.* That rotgut burned like I'd swallowed a rocket engine at liftoff. If I wasn't an android, it'd have stripped off my esophagus and begun spewing out the sides of my neck. It had to be *seven-hundred* proof, I'm talking concentrated pure alcohol. I wanted more immediately and lunged for the bottle.

Wul snatched it up first and held it behind his chair. "Huh-uh." He smiled wickedly. "Best to let the first salvo hit your brain before taking another hit."

I rested back. "Whatever. You know this isn't my first rodeo? I'm a big boy. Big boys can hold their liquor. Plus, I'm not driving home."

"Such bold words from the poly. I beg you not to roast me with your wrath." He mock-withdrew in fright, covering his face with his arm.

"Ah, aren't you worried someone'll hear you mentioning that word?"

He gestured about generally. "What, here? No, my friend. No one can hear us unless they're sitting at our table. That's the way it works. You know that, right?"

"Of course, I do. But that cute waitress may pop up under the table without warning, if you get my drift."

"I do and you're gross."

"So I've been misinformed before."

"If she overheard that word, she'd ignore it, just as she will any other gossipy tidbit she'll hear today."

"A real pro?" I teased.

"No, a real *golem.* You know *that,* right?"

"What is this, a quiz? How many questions can I miss before I flunk your class, *teach?*"

"I never can tell when you're joking or not."

I raised both palms. "Duh! Kind of my plan, don't you think?"

He raised one eyebrow. Looked like that old actor-turned-politician Dwayne Johnson. Dude was said to have been a damn good president back when there was still a planet Earth.

"Since you brought it up, let's talk about this poly ability of yours."

"Do we have to?" I whined. "If you let it go I'll pick up today's tab." No freakin' clue where I'd come up with the scratch, but I really didn't want to talk poly.

"Such a *Magnanimax* offer, especially seeing as everything's free. Always has been. I'd say *you know that, right,* too, but I don't need any more of your grief." He poured from the other bottle.

The nectar was extremely viscous. It flowed like a sky-blue maple syrup. Drinking whiskey it was not. The only way to shoot it would be to down the full shot glass.

He picked up his glass and first stared at then sniffed the liquor. It was as if he were recalling long-dead lovers. He was as serious as a husband looking at his wife in bed with his brother. Finally his spell broke. "To new friends, new friend." He offered me his rim.

"To friendship," I returned and clicked his.

Nectar of the gods. What can I say? It was good. I had to laugh on the inside, however, because it didn't hold a candle to Deavoriath nufe. But this thick, sweet, almost pungent concoction was compellingly appealing. Layer after layer peeled open, the longer I held it in my mouth, like a synchronized swimming team. It had the mustiness of muscat grapes, the savory quality of smoked brisket, the tang of a green apple, and hints of cinnamon, clove, and rose water. Wild. It also packed a slow-motion kick of high alcohol. I was an instant fan.

You know how sometimes you see a situation developing before your eyes, but you can do nothing to stop it, and you know it's going to go badly? A train heading for a bridge that's washed away, or a tiny baby seal swimming above a huge dark figure moving toward it? Yeah, picture me raising my hand. Remember the shiny annoying cloud that joined me inside my full membrane when I first arrived in Godville? It just walked through the arched doorway. Well, I guess I shouldn't say walked, because nebulous manifestations don't *have* legs, but you get my point. The thing was back, and it was heading straight for guess whose table. Oh boy.

"Hey," I said quickly, "I need some fresh air. I'll be right back." I started to rise.

"I knew you were a lightweight, Ryanmax," Wul chortled knowingly.

I sat back down. The vague, annoying cloud might blow my cover and result immediately in my brutal death, but no one was calling *me* a lightweight. Yes, I would rather die than live with those words unchallenged in the ether. I slid my empty glass over to Wul. "Fill 'er up, cowboy. I'm suddenly quite thirsty."

He gently rested his palms on his chest. "You don't need to further injure yourself in a vain attempt to impress *me*. We are not children, you and I."

Boy did I want to wipe that smug smile off his face with a blowtorch. "And if I drink, you drink."

That got him to tent an eyebrow. Yeah, bigmouth, what were you getting yourself into? Better think before you spout off next time. Be more mature like me.

He filled the glasses to about one third. I rattled the bottom of my glass as he was setting the bottle down. "You know, my friend, during my brief stay in Prime I ran across a most curious creature. It had feathers, two skinny legs, big wings, and a tiny beak. You know what it was called?"

He shook his head slightly.

"A chicken. You know why?"

He shrugged.

"Because it was afraid of everything, including its own shadow. Do you know what it says?"

He sat deadpan.

"Bwak bwak bwakaaah." I flapped my arms like chicken wings to help the lesson along.

"Are you suggesting that *I*, a god of business and enterprise, am a *chicken*?"

"You said it, not me. But if the shoe fits, cut off your foot before the rumors start spreading." I smiled like only I could. Sassy, mocking, and challenging. It grated on him instantly. *Outstanding*.

"My, my, I seem to have left some vital room at the tops of our glasses, didn't I?" He poured them full to the absolute rims.

"To our good health," I said a microsecond before I threw the whole volume down my throat. "*Ah*, good stuff," I exhaled robustly. Then, because, you know, I was me, I crushed the glass in my hand.

Wul raised his glass to his lips slowly and even more slowly drained his glass dry. Then he stared at it a second. He set it down gently. "Shame to ruin a perfectly good tool." His finger shot up and our waitress basically ran over. "Another glass for my friend and another bottle for us." He smiled like a cat eating shit and angled his head to one side.

"Make that two bottles and two glasses, sweet cheeks." I returned the identical expression to Wul. Maybe it was wishful thinking, but I swear I saw his eyes widen as I finished. Perfectomundo.

"You are getting along ... better, better than you just ... so recently were," said the wavering ball of glitter floating at my side.

"I bet you wonder who my friend here is, don't you?"

Wul scanned to either side of me, then actually rested an elbow on the table and did a three-sixty sweep of the room. "What friend?"

He didn't see or hear floaty-boy? I hated situations where my next move was as unclear as mud. "You don't see my cloudy acquaintance here?" I said, passing my hand through the whatever.

"Is this a setup for a joke?"

"Wul, I *never* make jokes. I'm a somber and sober fellow."

"Now I know you are kidding, because it is impossible for you to be sober." He nodded to what was left of my glass.

I made a show of turning to the apparition. "He claims he neither sees nor hears you. What am I to make of that?"

"You become even more odd when drunk, Ryanmax," Wul said incredulously.

"He could but doesn't."

"My, how typically vague and uninformative a response, yet again."

"I get it," shouted Wul. "You're doing one of those shows, you know, a ventriloquist and his dummy. I *hate* those acts." He fingered his lower lip. "Now I just need to figure out which one's the dummy."

"Which one is ... zzz, the dummy," mimicked the twinkling ball. "Wul is fun."

"You know Wul?" I said, without considering how I might extricate myself from the conversational quicksand I flailed in.

"Yes. All know Wul. He is a good god."

"What'd he say?" begged Wul with significant anticipation.

"Good god," I responded more as a question.

Wul twisted his neck thinking, then burst out laughing. "You *are* good, Ryanmax. I'm a *good god* or *Wul? Good god!* That's rich."

I'm glad he thought I was funny. Of course he'd just slammed down toxic quantities of firewater.

"Wul believes we are ... are fun."

"You mean *funny?*" I said to the vapor.

"Of course I do," wheezed Wul between belly laughs. Guy was making a spectacle of himself.

The mist rose and settled. "Yes. You are more right than ... me. Wul believes you are funny."

"The way you say it, you suggest there's some distance between *belief* and *actuality.*" I had no idea what I was saying.

"No, I said nothing of the kind," defended a suddenly serious Wul.

I looked back and forth from the apparition to Wul like an idiot. Then I pointed to Wul. "Got ya," I taunted.

Thank goodness he was drunk. He burst out laughing again. "Yes, you did, you *son of* a thousand fathers."

"That was not funny," said my annoying shadow.

"Wasn't fun either," I mumbled. I opened my arms to the cloud, again making a show of it. "Why are you here?"

"Why not here? Where should I ... be?"

"Are you here to discuss something or just embarrass the hell out of me?"

"It would take more ... more than embarrassment to remove the hell in y ... you, Jon Ryan."

I didn't recall telling him my name.

"Ryanmax, I'm dying here. What'd he say?" demanded Wul.

"He can't *embarrass* the hell out of me. He says it'd take nuclear weapons, not words."

Wul snickered and gasped. "I have no doubt in that re ... regard."

"Could you please leave?" I snapped at the bobbing butthead.

"Yes."

I waited long enough to realize he wasn't budging. "*Would* you please leave?" I clarified through gritted teeth.

"Yes."

Like the Rock of Gibraltar he remained. "Why don't I see you leaving?"

"Because he's *not*," howled Wul. Such an ugly drunk.

"The god is correct."

"What'll it take?"

"You asked if I would leave. You failed to state the motivation on *my* part."

"What the hell's that even mean?"

"His response, Ryanmax?"

"He said you're as drunk as you are ugly."

Wul flared in anger.

"Hey, his words not mine."

"But you're the puppeteer," snarled Wul.

"No. *I'm* the dummy." I pointed at him again. "Got ya."

He literally collapsed to the floor in hysterics. Man was he a sucker for my *gotchas*. What a moron.

I took the opportunity of Wul's incapacity to speak more freely. "Where were you? You disappeared on me back in the Lower Chambers."

He was silent a bit longer than I expected. "No ... I ... I did not."

"Huh? Are you daft?"

"Likely. But I never left your side. You opened up your force field and we left the chambers together. We came directly here."

A vapor cloud with a cloud-screw loose. Just exactly what I needed least. "No. That was several weeks ago. You and I never left the building together. Trust me."

"Why?"

"Because I'm right, dipstick."

"Does that make him *left* dipstick?" asked Wul, struggling back into his chair.

"Yah, and he told me where he wants to dip it, but he can't on account of your *sitting* on it."

"I'm too old for this level of stimulation and abuse," he protested while giggling.

"Funny, stimulation and abuse were what he was hoping for."

Wul, the *actual* lightweight, hit the deck again in a humor seizure.

"Now look what you've done," said my personal vision.

Was it the Zeus Juice affecting my circuits, or was the blob less ... less blobby than last time? He seemed more *orderly* or something. "You were gone for weeks. Don't you remember that?"

Wul started snoring loudly.

I stood halfway and studied him on the floor, drooling and snoring like there was a wrecking ball in the back of his throat. I wished I had a camera. I could blackmail him forever with that shot.

I turned back to my buddy. Of course, he was gone without a trace. Why wouldn't he be? Hell, if you're trying real hard to complicate my life and torture my soul, what else *would* you do? So there I sat, Wul passed out, cloud-boy vanished, and a naked-golem waitress walking slowly toward my table like this was a typical day's work. Man she was cute. Then again golems, being magically animated mud-beings, weren't exactly my thing. I did, however, consider calling out to her to stop walking and start jogging.

CHAPTER TWENTY-FIVE

"I feel we're fortunate to have documented no attacks or incursions for the last eighteen months," Prime Minister Genter-ban-tol said to the assembled parliament. "I don't know if it's loss of interest on their part or dumb luck on ours, but all has been quiet."

"How would you rate our readiness to defend ourselves?" asked No One Else of the Daxi Federation. The Daxi were a race of simian-looking clones. One genetic female and one genetic male had been copied over and over to achieve a Federation population of over ten billion. Their records no longer documented why this Darwinian oddity of a culture was established or who the Adam and Eve were. Those omissions bothered none of the Daxi. If asked, a Daxi would answer one-hundred percent of the time, "*I* am the original progenitor." No amount of argument or cajoling could budge them from that stance.

"We cannot be certain, No One Else. We know so little about the capabilities of these ancient gods. Estimating what level or amount of defensive forces is needed to defend against them is unknowable."

"That's a guess, you pathetic coward," shouted Densest 87 X105, the new Suriliab minister. She replaced Denser 88 X105a few months earlier, after self-promoting herself by assassinating her predecessor. For the record, she wanted to be minister less than she wanted to kill Denser 88 X105. Suriliab culture was violently inclined.

"Our subcommittee for mutual defense has maintained all along that we are woefully unprepared. They reported to me last week that we are no less *unprepared* currently."

"Unacceptable. I demand you be burned alive and that I be assigned the job you are incapable of performing," spat the Suriliab representative.

First Coequal Di, the one who'd assumed the unrewarding task of trying to hold the Suriliab contingent in check, stood. "There are no protocols for either the incineration of the prime minister or the appointing of his successor. I must ask that you make more effort to abide by our cultural norms. Densest 87 X105."

"No protocol? Look, it's easy. I've torched many idiots in my day. You pour gasoline over them and you strike a match. *I'll* do it."

"Will the prime minister please answer the question posed. I see no need to dignify that last statement with a response," said a very frustrated Di as she sat back down.

"I will paraphrase Densest 87 X105's earlier question as *why are we not more prepared?* I can assure everyone we have exceeded all estimates of how much progress we could achieve. To produce more weaponry or ships would not have been possible. The subcommittee blames no one. They state we simply have not accomplished the impossible."

"Burn them, too," said Densest 87 X105 as if speaking to herself.

"Dr. DeJesus has a rather troubling update to share. I am honestly uncertain if distributing this news widely is the best approach, but the leadership council decided to release the information. The council felt the fullest disclosure might lead to some insights from unanticipated individuals. Dr. DeJesus," Genter-ban-tol invited, as he swept an antenna-like extension across the audience.

"Thank you, Prime Minister. Since we first became aware of the antimatter traps set by the ancient gods, I have spent a lot of time studying them. I was hopeful a better knowledge of the devices might help me understand their technology."

"You *were* hopeful? That doesn't *sound* too hopeful," Santamantasur said loudly. He was a Cholak from Lyra 3. If the Yeti existed anywhere in creation, it was on Lyra 3. Massive, furry, gigantic paws ending in formidable claws, and a disposition that matched their appearance.

"Yes, Master Santamantasur, your observation is correct. My quest came up remarkably short. If I might proceed ..." Toño asked open-endedly.

"Don't stop now. Crash everyone's hopes against hostile rocks," the Cholak replied dismissively.

"As you will recall, the traps were baited with exotic antimatter particles. Gold, platinum, and uranium to name a few. These elements in that form would be extremely unstable and short-lived in our universe. They were made to *appear* stable by basically setting them in micro-bulges from presumably the universe our enemy occupies. I wanted to understand what physical processes and energy expenditures would be required to assemble such a system.

"Naturally, the ancient gods might exist in an antimatter universe. But were that the case, they would never bother coming to our exclusively positive universe. They'd self-annihilate upon entry. So I modeled what conditions would need to be established to project these exotic elements into our universe." Toño breathed heavily. "I could not postulate even *one* mechanism by which what we observed could possibly be reality."

"For us non-fat brains," growled Densest 87 X105 angrily, "what are you saying so ineptly?"

"They perform the impossible."

"What? Are you proposing that they use *magic*?" asked an incredulous Lenty Mo, a Novartoid-equivalent drone. "Are you insane?" Fairly strong words for a three-centimeter-long winged bug.

"If you would like to call it magic, I would not bother to stop you. I will refrain from naming the force, myself."

"Prime Minister Genter," Lenty Mo protested, "defeat is surely our fate with advisors who are idiots."

"That accusation is neither helpful nor called for," responded Genter-ban-tol. "Dr. DeJesus is doing his best to keep us all informed. The fact that the ancient gods' technology is impenetrable at this juncture is no one's fault."

"It is good. I will tell this to my spawn as they die in agony. 'Don't feel badly, loved ones of my lineage. Yes, you die, but it is no one's fault.'" Lenty Mo buzzed from the room.

CHAPTER TWENTY-SIX

I was having no kind of fun. Okay, maybe that shouldn't have been my number-one priority. My universe was threatened. I was trapped in ground zero of kill-the-little-insects central. My current plans only extended far enough to cover the next five to ten minutes. But, Jon here, I was bored. Wul was o-u-t out for the count. I don't know how much nectar and juice it took to lay him low, but it was clearly much less than I cajoled him into downing.

But, God Social Services to the rescue, such a thing was apparently well anticipated. The club had extensive rest facilities. Basically they were posh suites just off the main entertainment space. They were suitable for sleeping one off or sleeping with any number of consenting adults and mud-beings. The expansive pools and spas might have posed an existential threat to the golems. Maybe they were water sealed. I didn't bother asking, as it might suggest I had gross intentions under consideration. I might count among my many conquests some women who were arguably too drunk to tell whether I was *me* or the person they *really* wanted to be with. I freely own that. But doing the nasty with an animated mud pie? Way beneath my heretofore embarrassingly low standards of conduct. As it was, I was never going to look at a dirt road the same again. And when I scraped mud off my boots, I'd likely apologize while doing so for a good long while.

When we were alone I attached my fibers to Wul. I could use all the 4-1-1 I could get. The first thing I estimated was how long he'd be out. Given his body weight, toxin levels, and liver function I figured at least a couple hours. It turned out his full name was—you ready for this?—Wul. That was it. Nothing flowery or pretentious. How refreshing. He was twenty billion years old. Man, here I was thinking *I* was a senior citizen. Wul was ancient before my universe *began* sixteen billion years ago. His species was Nordictalon, his home planet called Exellonum in the Sector of Equivocation. Wul was a god from birth, sired by three—count 'em—three parents. Jaj, Kil, and Das. His people's pattern of naming was declaring itself. Old Wul had been married six thousand five hundred and fifty-eight times. Dude could have avoided all the grief if he'd have started with my ex, Gloria. She'd have cured him of his disease eternally. I couldn't imagine the alimony payments this guy had to be making.

He functioned as the god of business and enterprise, as he mentioned. That involved mostly attending board meetings, networking on developmental plans, and the penning of mission statements. No wonder he drank himself into oblivion the first chance he had. Made me want to do the same, and fast. Interestingly, and to my great relief, it turned out he was really a fairly kind and non-aggressive fellow. The crushing of *as many Leginites as possible into metal canisters* concerned a sour fruit he intended to preserve, not squealing sentients.

Then I almost peed myself laughing. You will never guess what his superpower was. Go on, take a wild shot. Whatever you said, that's not it. No, his power was *negotiation*. Lord, I wished he was awake so I could torture him to death with sarcasm, needling, and potty sounds. I could just picture him on the schoolyard as a little kid. Some big godlet walks up to him and bullies him mercilessly. Wul puffs out his chest and says with composed anger, "If you don't stop this instant, I'll force you to negotiate your disengagement with me." The other kid'd probably disengage by way of collapsing in a fit of giggling. *Negotiation Man, that's me. Instead of a cape, I wear a pad of legal-ruled canary yellow 8 1/2" x 11 3/4" paper.* Out of my way or I'll force you to *compromise.* Ah, everybody *run.* Godzillpromise is stomping in our direction.

I lost it for the better part of a half hour.

There were several sobering factoids I found out, however. Wul had referred to the *Third Transheaval.* Turned out he was in the two before and the one that followed. Another was about to transheave itself on Prime, my universe. Transheaval was their term for massive, all-out, take-no-prisoners, and have-the-time-of-your-life invasion of another realm. The four apocalypses delivered so far were beyond my ability to describe. They were too brutal, too unimaginably cruel, too indefensibly sadistic, and too incredibly easy for the Cleinoid gods. They'd suffered few losses while absolutely devastating, disassembling, and dismembering any and all resistance. If I wasn't so numb learning what was about to befall us, I'd have cried like a baby. We were so toast, so beaten before the first shot. The facts argued in favor of the wisdom of quick suicide by every living thing in my home universe. That, it seemed inescapably clear, was the *best* outcome. Many, *many* worse ones were on the table. Some acts of amorality I reviewed were so dark, I could never repeat them to another soul.

Wul didn't know when the attack would begin. He seemed to assign a great deal of weight to the intercession of Fate, though. Odd. It was almost like Fate had self-determination, options and choices. Sure, that was nuts, but it seemed to be a major tenet of belief for these guys and gals. But he believed the invasion would commence soon. Fate seemed to be moving in a favorable direction. Okay, that meant that an equally powerful force, anti-Fate, was just gonna have to act first. Anti-Fate's name? You got it. Jon Freaking Ryan. *Oorah.*

While I waited for Mr. Lightweight to wake from his beauty sleep, I wove elements and events I'd learned from Wul's memory into my cockamamy excuse for a life story. Knowing a lot of details about the Cleinoid's history would go a long way into making my story very difficult to doubt. I did have one major problem gnawing at me constantly. Tefnuf. No matter how outstanding my slinging of BS was, she'd never buy my story. She was the sole Cleinoid who knew I was actually just a troublemaker from Prime. Or did she? I sprang a trap intentionally, but then I pulled off a godlike disappearing act. But I'd told her my real name and didn't declare my godhood right off the bat. Maybe I could say I was visiting Prime and I used a trap to return home. Why would I do that? I *got* there on my own. Wul was of the opinion I'd been back and forth more than once. Maybe it saved energy? Maybe ... how could I intertwine Fate? Maybe using a trap relied less on the proximity of Fate? And I hadn't let on I was a god 'cause I was messing with her. Wul'd back me up on the fact that I was a kidder. Well, at least I had a series of words to say if confronted. Not too sure I'd like to bet my life I'd be believed, but it was something.

Finally, Wul was rousing. He was entertaining to watch. He rolled over a couple times, groaning. He raised his head a few inches, then let it thump back to the floor. When he sat up, he puked volumes. It was bitchin'. I had ammo to tease him with for weeks to come. Dude made a serious spectacle of himself.

"I don't feel so well," he said. He was as green around the gills as his tone suggested.

"Gosh, Wul, I'm sorry to have dared you into overindulging. Dude, *your* pain is *my* pain." I pounded a fist on my heart to suggest deep empathy.

"Fuck you," was his terse response. Perchance he didn't believe my sincerity. This was so cool.

"In spite of your unjustified insult, may I help you up?" I extended an arm.

"No, but you can begin to make amends by cleaning this mess up." He peered up with one eye. What a player.

"It would be my honor." I nodded.

He was surprised. "Really?"

"Absolutely," I pledged with a hand over my chest. "Here," I stood, "I'll get right on it." I opened the door and yelled extremely loudly, "Cleanup on aisle ten. Wul lost his cookies 'cause he's such a lightweight." I closed the door and slowly returned to my chair.

"I hate you."

"And I hate you, too."

A pair of waitresses slipped in while we bantered and deftly cleaned up what seemed to them to be a pretty routine part of the duties at Altruism's Failure. Then again, they *were* animated clay, like characters in those dopey old videos like *The Seventh Voyage of Sinbad* and *Adventures of Gumby*.

Ten minutes later, we were back at our table. I was having a large meal, not because I was hungry, but because I knew how queasy it made my buddy. For his part Wul stared into a glass of what looked like beer and moaned occasionally.

"I feel weird," he announced.

"It's called a hangover."

"No, I've had those aplenty before. No, I feel different weird. Like ... like I was violated while I was out."

Oh, boy. Trouble.

"Ah, I wasn't going to mention it, but seeing's how you brought it up," I pointed my knife at the next table, "you see that guy there?"

"Yes," he replied in a huff. "I'm nauseous, not *blind*."

"Well, when you were out he asked if he could, you know, *borrow* you for half an hour."

Wul glared at me, then at the guy in question, then back to me. "You *lent* me to *Lorpamoor*?"

I shrugged while chewing prodigiously.

"The *vampire* god, the one with twelve tentacles and four mouths?" Wul held up his fingers in a clawlike depiction. "Teeth like needles and poisonous saliva that can dissolve flowing lava?"

I shrugged again. Then I pointed my fork at Wul. "But I was *firm* about the thirty-minute time window." I ruffed my feathers like I was oh-so-proud of myself. "I had your back the *entire* time, you're very welcome. He was so impressed with my conviction on that matter he had your clothes halfway back on when I burst into the room, *without* knocking, I might add."

He shook his head in disgust. "You're sick. You're also *not* funny." Then he snickered uncontrollably so badly snot dripped from his nose. He gestured toward me as best he could, given his gyrations. "You had me for a second, there. Kudos for that."

"Another of my poly powers and my personal favorite. Bullshitting." I positively glowed as I spoke.

"Will wonders never cease?"

"*Nope.*" I really hit the "P" for effect.

He giggled again. "You *lent* me to a vampire while I was passed out. That's rich. I hope I get a chance to steal that one and inflict it on someone else very soon."

"Good luck with your dreams, sport."

Wul got a very serious look on his face. "Ryanmax, are you The Chosen One?"

Without batting an eye I replied. "Yup."

He recoiled like I'd hit him with a cricket bat flat on the forehead.

"Just ask any woman I've ever been with."

He scowled. "I'm serious. *This* is serious, extremely serious. Can you be, *also?*"

I shrugged again, hoping to both answer and annoy.

"You're not likely to find another soul on this plane as tolerant or openminded as I am. The rest of us take the Words of the Prophet as sacrosanct."

Are written on the subway walls kept looping in my damn head. Curse the SOB. It'd take some serious time to get that one out of my brain. *... and tenement halls ...*

"Sorry. Don't get your knickers in a knot. I'm teasing, because your premise is so absurd." I pointed to my face. "*Me*, a god's god? *No* individual or lost soul would be *that* desperate."

He looked like I'd poured a bucket of hot maple syrup over his head. "Where do you get those idiotic idioms? Knickers? What the hell are *knickers?*"

I directed my knife downward and at his groin. "Pull your pants open. *Knickers* are what you're seeing all knotted up."

"Having a conversation with you is like being waterboarded, only less pleasant."

"From *personal* experience? Hmm?"

"Don't tell me, it's another poly power. Annoying as hell, right?"

I nodded smugly.

"I give up. You want to keep your polyness under wraps, fine. I'm only curious *and* trying to offer my support."

Why would I need his support if I was the Chosen One? Wouldn't I be, like, pre-*chosen* without any outside input? "Sorry, sorry," I said quickly. "You're right—I'm being a bit of an ass, aren't I?"

He wrinkled his face up. "*Bit* of?"

"Dude. I'm a *god*. Humility is not my long sui ... best quality."

"Point."

"So, I know I can pull off a few tricks. That's cool, but I know for positive I'm no messiah. A person'd know if they were," I tapped my chest, "right here."

"I never said anything about a *messiah*," he said as he contemplated the need for clarification. "I said the *Chosen One*. Everyone knows the difference, and it's huge."

In a couple billion years one would think I'd learn to talk without placing my foot in my mouth so frequently and so forcefully. "I used a word wrong. *Sue* me. Come on, I know the difference. I *thought* we were two friends talking, not embroiled in an inquisition. Messiahs are saviors as well as leaders. The Chosen One may be a *leader*, but he, she, or it sure won't be anyone's *savior* but his own." Lord in Heaven, I prayed that was correct and made sense. I needed to take a risk. I couldn't afford for him to start seeing me as too odd.

Slowly he began nodding. "Yes, indeed. TCO is almost certain to rule with an iron fist and enforce whatever vision they have on us all, like it or not."

I raised my glass. "I'll drink to that."

"You'll drink to *anything*," he scoffed, trying to sound annoyed. He toasted me, however, with a big old smile.

While we traded insults I began thinking through just how I wanted to play Wul. We were getting along fine, but I didn't want to cling on to him and scare him off. Then again, I had no idea how we gods communicated, so if we parted ways I might never find him again. He afforded me instant credibility since he was more than an acquaintance, he was a fan. He could introduce me all around until everyone who was anyone knew good old Ryanmax. I decided to stay with him as long as I could. He was too rich an asset for me to try and strike out on my lonesome again.

"When your fragile constitution allows it, my friend, what say we find another establishment for you to hurl in? The golems here are looking kind of dusty, if you take my drift."

"I do not. You wanted to combine the words *golem* and *dust* in one context because you think you're so clever."

"True that," I conceded. "But I know a place where there're real flesh and blood babes." I bounced my eyebrows luridly.

"What a *ridiculous* notion," he snapped. "These tools are for gratification and much-needed distraction," He gestured widely across the room. "Why risk rejection or, worse yet, emotional involvement if rejected by an *actual* woman? You must have a screw loose." He twisted the tip of his finger on the side of his head.

"Because I'm a risk taker, ya big chicken. The greater the danger, the greater the reward."

"I'm not in the mood for either risk or reward. Come, we'll go to a place of my choosing."

"Yeah, and where would that be?"

"Anywhere *but* the Three Last Goodbyes."

Wow. There really was a place famous for fleshie companionship. Android or not, I filed that tidbit away. Ah, in a place for important *cultural* details, mind you. Sapale *did* occasionally review my downloaded memories. I might have been stupid, but I wasn't suicidal.

Out in the fresh air Wul stopped and looked around. "No flying cars in sight. The walk to Blind Faith No More is kind of long."

"How about a magic carpet ride?" I said with a smirk.

He recoiled. "I *hate* those things. I'd rather crawl there dragging my tongue on the ground."

"Carpet-related PTSD?"

He rolled his shoulders. "If you must know, yes. I fell from one as a child and swore to never get near one again."

"Did you really get hurt?"

"Yes. I landed in a pile of minotaur crap right in front of Graselda Mannór."

"Who's Graselda Mannór?"

"The girl I was with. The one with a body made for love and a mind inclined to please. She was also the one who did *not* fall off the damn rug."

"Bet she giggled."

"Oh, she *giggled*," he huffed. "And she told everyone she knew, showed them simages and everything."

What the hell was a simage? "No way," I taunted against what little better judgment I possessed. "They didn't *have* simages that long ago. When you were a kid they carved things into clay tablets."

"Ha, ha. I have a simage for you." He nodded his head at me and concentrated.

Crap, he was sending me a signal. If I didn't get it—and why the heck would I?—I'd be outed. I scanned all frequencies of the electromagnetic spectrum, radiation emissions, and sound pulses. You name it and I scanned it. Nada, zip, nothing. Crapola on a cracker, I was screwed.

For his part, Wul gave me a well-what-ya-gonna-do look, with a hint of impatience.

I swallowed hard. I said a quick goodbye in my head to Sapale and I responded. "You know I saw that picture of your mom way long ago. Yeah, she handed it to me just after she made me take it."

He actually took a step toward me. His face flashed with rage.

Then he relented. "Maybe I deserved that one. Sorry. You're rubbing off on me, I guess."

I pointed at him. "Hey, that's what she said, too. Were you spying on us?" I smiled and elbowed his arm.

"Let's start walking and pray for a ride," he responded.

"There's a couple of magic ponies over there," I kind of squeaked, pointing behind him.

"Do *not* get me started on them," he blurted out, as he stepped away briskly.

CHAPTER TWENTY-SEVEN

"Even now at the eleventh hour, I cannot talk you out of this madness?" The fear was palpable in Toño's voice.

"No, but thanks for caring," Sapale replied warmly. "Toño, we're two billion years old. Maybe now's as good a time as any to die."

"No. I refuse to accept such flippancy." He stopped a second and glanced to one side. "Well, only from Jon. No one else, especially not from you."

"Why? Am I some icon of virtue and worth? The personification of all that's peachy keen?" She shook her head angrily. "I'm not."

"No, because I know your heart. It is good. And you are a friend, a very old and valued one whom I do not want to lose." His head dropped.

She reached back to him, stroking his thin hair. "I'm sorry, old friend. I'll respect your concern with concern of my own. There. Is that better?"

"Now if you'll ..."

"Some favors are too big to ask, too big to agree to. I will find my brood-mate and help him, or I will join him beyond Davdiad's veils. There is no other choice that draws me to it." She withdrew her hand. "Now, unless you wish to risk being my accidental traveling companion, I suggest you step back." She turned and focused on the patch of sand containing the invisible anti-iridium atoms.

"How far back will be safe?" Toño asked acerbically.

Without turning back to him, she shrugged. "I don't know."

"Hmm. So you're vaulting into the unknown with uninformed urgency. That's going to end well."

Her head swung on him. "*Enough*. I am no child and I do not need a heckling crowd. Either shut up or leave." Sapale's eyes all but flared red like an enraged demon's.

"So be it," Toño replied with finality. "As I do not wish the last vision I have of you to be that of you vanishing into the same death as Jon's, I shall leave. Know that I love you. Know that I will continue to do so forever. And know that I acted as I have only because of that eternal love. Farewell, Sapale."

With that, he turned and quietly exited the chamber.

As a tear streaked down her cheek, Sapale said in a voice so faint only she could hear it, "I love you, too, great friend. That's forever."

She extended her probes to locate the antimatter particles. She placed one atom next to another. She repeated the act, setting another fleck of anti-iridium next to those two. Before she could complete the cycle for the fifth time, she was gone.

CHAPTER TWENTY-EIGHT

We hadn't gone far when Wul saw a shuttle and flagged it down. The vehicle didn't—knock me over with a feather—even *vaguely* resemble a taxicab. No, in the land of the ancient gods, *everything* had to be out of proportion, inescapably odd, and without any apparent relationship to the utility asked of it. So, naturally, our ride was personal reflection. You know, when you wax philosophical and recall the good old days, maybe high school and some pretty cheerleader who basically worshiped you? That kind of personal reflection. That's what we opened the door of, sat in back of the driver in, and to whom Wul said, void of emotion, "Blind Faith No More."

What, you rightfully ask, does a personal reflection look like? Damn thing looked like any other thought, only more real in this case, more substantial. And who *drives* a personal reflection? Thank you for asking, because I was dying to say it. A long-lost *desire*. Sure. What else would, I ask you as I contemplate clawing my eyes out so I no longer had to look at it?

"Are you all right, Ryanmax?" Wul asked, with some concern in his tone. "Now *you* appear to be the one ready to hurel."

"No, it's *hurl*, as in throw, not *hurel*, as in mumbo jumbo. And I'm fine. I was just struck by the unsettling image of that Lorpamoor fellow as he dragged your limp body into that empty room." I stuck my finger down my throat after saying, "Kind of gets me right here."

"Why I put up with you is beyond me."

"It's because I'm fresh."

He raised a doubting eyebrow.

"Come on, admit it. I'm fun in a different, novel, and surprisingly *refreshing* manner."

"I will go so far as to say you *are* unique."

"'Ere you go. You now know why I'm so undeniable."

He shook his head and looked forward, in the direction the personal reflection was leading us.

Could I *ever* be annoying in a welcome manner, or what?

We glided up to Blind Faith No More's entrance and the long-lost desire left the personal reflection to open our doors. But Wul was out like a flash and halfway to the club before the desire arrived. I guessed a long-lost desire wasn't a god or anything, by the way Wul ignored it. Maybe it was best if they weren't. I kind of gave the driving emotion a nodding bow, looking like a moron in the process, but I didn't want to seem rude. I caught up with Wul as he stepped inside.

Talk about a different kind of ambience. Blind Faith No More was no clone of Altruism's Failure. Where the latter was garish and ornate, the former was threadbare and impoverished. I was immediately hit with a Wild West saloon vibe. Splintering floors covered with sawdust, smoke so thick the working girls appeared pretty, and employees who exuded an I-don't-give-a-shit-what-you-want commitment to hospitality. Why had Wul dragged me to such a ... such a dive? Wul *was* my brother from another type of mother. He *lived* for dive bars just like I did. Oh, I almost bear-hugged the son of a gun.

"Didn't I tell you to *never* come back here?" a remarkably burly, toothless, and hairy bartender howled at Wul before he was three steps in the door.

Wul smiled as if he was watching his missing puppy trot home. "No, you did *not*," he challenged.

The barkeep swung a massive arm in the air and shouted, "Then come on over and have a stiff one with me."

Wul leaned over to me. "He's really nicer on the inside than he is on the outside."

"Then I can't *wait* to make his acquaintance," I replied. "Or break his jaw."

We bellied up and were served two formidable portions of a thick blue liquid. I could smell that it had lots of alcohol along with an astringent quality. It promised to be horrific. It was. Burned like the section of hell reserved for politicians.

"Queeheg," Wul said, slapping me on the shoulder, "this is my excellent friend Ryanmax. Ryanmax, this is the least appreciative, surliest, and worst-smelling purveyor of rotgut the world has yet had to suffer, *Queeheg*."

"Proud to say I know you," I said, toasting Queeheg's raised glass. I threw back the blue toxin.

Queeheg emptied his glass and slammed it to the bar. As I watched the damn glass filled itself with the blue swill. He nodded to the glass after noting my amazement. "I put a small *spell* on me glass, you know, to saves time and all. Otherwise I'm likes to get so busy I forgets to provide for me own refreshment."

"Very understandable," I said with a nod. "Can I get one like that, too?" I gestured to his glass with mine.

"Ah, sadly that'd be a *no*. You has to pay as you go, so that wouldn't be accommodating to my overall businesslike intentions."

I turned to Wul. "Hey, I thought you said it was all for free?"

Wul, the SOB, smiled like he won the lottery the day he retired.

"Ah, I sees you're *new* to these particular parts and location. The pale offerings at those stuff-up-your-butt bars are *free*. That's on account of it being worthy of exactly that. On the other contention," he passed a proud arm over his dismal establishment, "a place like this being *priceless,* a price must be paid to avail your holinesses of its pleasuralities."

"Don't worry, Ryanmax," Wul said near my ear. "It's not *money* he wants. His price here is easy to pay."

"That's an oxymoron if ever I've heard one," I rebuffed.

"Your friend is, for once in as long as I've been cursed to know him, correct, Ryanmax. I ask little of what you have in abundance and'll ne'er miss the levy."

"I tried that line on a gorgeous hunk of woman once," I chided, as I pointed my pinky at Queeheg.

"And how'd it go?" he responded.

"I'd show you the scar, but we're in a public place," I replied with a wink.

"*Bahha*," he spat-laughed back. "I likes you already. But know that alls I e'er asks in return for my exemplary 'ospitality is a lending of yer magic, if'n when I come to a juncture's looking like it'd be comprehensive to have such aid."

"We barter magic for booze?" I said, gasping. "If that's all you ask, leave the bottle and leave me alone with it." I flipped the back of my hand at him.

"My kind of scum," marveled Queeheg, as he looked to Wul and pointed at me.

"I can still see your ugly face," I said as I filled my glass. "If I'm paying, we do it my way."

Queeheg grunted a laugh as he wandered off to attend to another patron.

"So, that idiot lets you drink for free, because someday he may need you to, what, *negotiate* for him?" I addressed Wul.

"You don't have to be smart to own a bar, my friend. He never even queried what my powers were."

"A trusting man of faith in a business connected to cheap booze and cheaper patrons? What could go wrong in that fantasyland?"

"So many good people suffer in business. You may quote me on that, by the way. I'm sort of an expert."

"I'm sorry, did you just say something I'd care to hear? I was focusing on this fine beverage." I extended my glass toward him.

"You're impossible."

"I know. It's one of my ..."

Jon, are you there, Jon, can you hear me? flashed in my head. *It's Sapale, Jon, are you still alive?*

Color me surprised. *Sapale, please tell me you're not here in Godland?* I flashed back.

You're alive. Oh thank all the gods and powers, Jon, you're alive.

I knew that. Where are you?

Suspended in a space filled with multicolored clouds. Where are you?

Not in the detention area waiting to meet Tefnuf on my way to Triple D.

What the hell's Triple D and who's Tefnuf?

You don't want to know, and you're about to meet the bitch.

Can you get here, like, immediately?

I ... I don't ... yes. Absolutely. I'll ...

"First you blow off the bartender and now you ignore me? Some friend," protested Wul.

"Huh? What?"

"I asked if you fancied either of those representatives of the female persuasion over there. The knockouts waving to us, there." He pointed at two, well, knockouts sitting at the end of the bar waving to us like we were taxicabs in commute traffic in NYC.

"Huh? I'm kind of busy. No time for babes."

What about you and time for babes while I'm about to meet a bad god? Sapale asked, rather harshly.

No, not you, I wasn't speaking to you, I babbled.

Obviously not.

The damn mental links Toño installed had a tendency to bleed the verbal into the electronic signal. I guess it had to do with needing to think a thought before one could speak it. Very *not* helpful on some occasions.

"Ryanmax, I've lost you again. Do you require medical attention?"

"No ... no, I'm fine."

"You are not. If you were *fine*, we'd be walking quickly over to the women."

"I'm not walking over to the hookers," I snapped.

Hookers? I'm about to die, and you want the hookers to come to you? If I survive this, I'll kill you.

No, the guy I'm with is horny. The bar is swarming with accommodating ladies. Maybe they're ladies. Maybe they're clay. I ... "I don't know."

"You don't know what?" asked a confused Wul.

You're gone a year, and now you're with guys? she wheezed.

"I can explain," I whined.

"What? About the girls or that you don't know what, whatever *that* is?" stammered Wul.

I haven't been gone a year. "I've been here two months—tops."

"Two *months*? Try not even two hours," snarled Wul.

You've been gone so long, everyone assumed you were dead. Four hundred fifty-seven days, to be specific.

"I'm not dead."

"You *will* be if you don't welcome the two goddesses who are debasing themselves to come to us."

"I'm not screwing with the babes. I'm a married man."

You're not married, you're dead. Death dissolves a marriage, and I'm killing you on sight.

"We never discussed the subject, but you do sleep with women, don't you, Ryanmax?" He patted his chest. "To each his own, mind you. But it would've been, er, helpful if you'd told me sooner."

"No, I do sleep with women. I've slept with zillions of them. But just not these."

"Why?"

I won't kill you all at once. No, it will be slow, so slow you'll never actually know ... hey, the colored clouds just vanished. Would you believe I'm in a metal cell?

"Tefnuf's coming. Stay calm."

"You won't vanquish those lovely visions because *Tefnuf's* coming to this bar? Ryanmax, you can't be serious? You prefer that abomination to those ... those *not* abominations?"

"I do not want to sleep with Tefnuf. Gross."

That's very reassuring, because some abomination just walked in. If you wanted to sleep with her, I wouldn't be killing you, it would be euthanasia.

Tefnuf's there?

Something that got beat with the ugly stick is. Looks like three pieces of toast with ...

"That's Tefnuf."

Wul spun. "Where? If she's here I'm gone."

"Hi, boys," one of the beauties said, "you two are kind of cute."

The other girl giggled.

I developed such a knot in my gut.

"Kind of cute?" challenged Wul. "Ryanmax, could you set them straight?"

"We're not cute. We're married."

"No, we're not. *I'm* not," he bellowed.

You're not. Remember 'til death do us part?

"I'm not dying. You are not going to kill me."

"Is he speaking to you or to me?" the second girl asked the first.

"Are you speaking to me?" asked a stunned Wul.

"*I* will if you upsets me business regulars," hissed Queeheg. He was slapping a palm with a lumpy bludgeon.

I threw my arms up. "No, I wasn't talking to," and I pointed in succession to everyone present, "talking to *you* or *you* or *you* or *you*."

A fellow at a nearby table looked up at the source of all the commotion; *me*.

"Or *you*," I howled.

He looked away quickly, lucky for him.

She says she's going to kill me, then ask me three questions. She said she used to do it the other way around until some scrawny-assed maniac escaped and she got in big trouble for just trying to kill him. Jon, she has to mean you. You're the only being in creation who can make such a negative first impression.

"Say you're a god," I apparently both spoke *and* thought to Sapale.

All four of my companions pointed to their own chests. As a

practiced chorus they said simultaneously, "Me?" They then looked among themselves for possible clarification. None was forthcoming, of course.

I told those present, "No, I wasn't talking to you. I was talking to my wife."

That not only brought further confusion to my companions, it brought a thorough visual scan of the room by each one independently.

One of the girls was able to say, "I'm a nymph, not a god. Is that okay?"

To which the other girl snapped, "There you go putting yourself down again. Of course, it's okay. It's what you are, and *I* love you."

"I love you, *too*," the first woman replied with unbounded glee.

They joined hands, both gave Wul a particularly nasty look, and left literally skipping out the door.

"I'm *very* confused," said a defeated-sounding Queeheg. Poor guy was stooped over and crestfallen.

"Did you say you were a god?" I asked Sapale.

"I thought you didn't want *me* to," protested Wul. Queeheg was too gobsmacked to parry back.

Yes. The bitch says if I were a god, I'd not have set off a trap. She says nice try, but since dealing with that bony-assed loser she's not buying anything from anybody. Thanks again, love of my life.

I turned to Wul with the least credible grin in the history of smiles. "Hey, I want to go visit Tefnuf. Why don't you come along. It'll be ... swell."

He looked at me not like I farted, but like I was a fart. "Why would I visit that *horrible* woman?"

"So ... we ... so we can visit her *together*."

He scowled. "I fail to see any additional motivation on my part based on that prospect."

"It'll be ..."

"Swell. I know. You said that already."

Because nothing in the life history of Jonathan Alan Ryan could *possibly* go the easy way, Queeheg's eyes brightened and he spoke proudly. "Hey, Tefnuf's my sister. Did you know that?"

Wul and I stared dumbfounded at one another.

She's pointing some device at me. I think she's about to vaporize me or something. If you got anything, no pressure, but now'd be a good time.

Tell her Queeheg says "Hi."

Wul squinted. "Tell who?"

"Yeah. Who'd I just *greet?*" said an angering barkeep.

"Tefnuf," I said quickly.

She says what's that supposed to mean? She's still fiddling with the...whatever.

Tell her your husband is with Queeheg as we speak, and that I simaged you the greeting.

What the hell's ...

Say it!

"Please have mercy, Ryanmax," pleaded Wul. "What is it you want? You're frightening me. I don't want a poly to be angry with me."

"He's a *poly?*" Queeheg said with wonder.

"Yes, but it's a *secret,*" responded Wul.

Queeheg's massive palms covered his chest. "A secret couldn't be safer than with me."

Both Wul and I gave him the once-over for such a preposterous statement.

She seems to have stopped. But she said if that's true, she simaged me a message for her brother, and I better have the right answer or she'll kill me twice. Jon, what the hell ...

I silenced the rest of her message. In a panic I asked Queeheg, "Your sister just simaged my wife a message for you. If she doesn't have the right answer Tefnuf'll kill her twice. What's the answer?"

"Er, uh ... No one's a simaged me, so how'm I suspozed to know?"

"My wife's ... my wife's ..."

"Yes, what about your wife, Ryanmax?" asked Wul.

"She's ... her simager's broken. Yes. That's it. She broke her simager. Until it's fixed she's ... simageless." Man, they were looking at me strangely.

"*Simageless?* In my nearly eternal lifetime, I've never heard that word spoken," said a stunned Wul.

Queeheg rubbed his knuckles on the side of his head. "How'd a thin' like that even bes possible? I mean ... it ain't like it was a moving part."

"Trauma," I blurted out. "Yes, head trauma."

Head trauma? asked a strained-sounding Sapale. *Is that the answer? Head trauma?*

"No *not* head trauma," I shouted, for all I was worth.

"But you just said it was," replied Wul as he sat on the floor. Poor guy really was shaken.

"No, yes, it was. I was talking to her ... er, my wife."

"She doesn't *know* she had head trauma?" asked Queeheg, as he took his seat on the floor behind the bar. I really wasn't clearing the air well at all.

"N ... no," I said feebly. "It was so bad it ... well, it was bad."

"But she said she was a Cleinoid god," whispered Queeheg. "Us gods, we'z don't suffer lastin' damage."

Wait, wait. How'd he know that? I told Sapale, but I was pretty sure I didn't tell him I told her. I said god, not specifically Cleinoid.

I leaned way over the bar. "Did your sister simage you that the prisoner she's holding claimed to be a Cleinoid god?"

He stared blankly at me.

I slapped him across the face as best I could, given the awkward angles involved.

"Yeah, she did. Why?"

Sapale. The answer is that you claim to be a Cleinoid god. Tell her the simage was about that.

But I'm not a ...

Say it and say it now, I yelled in my head. I think it was in my head. I wasn't sure, but I really didn't care at that point.

Wul was weeping softly, sitting there on the floor. "I'm so sorry. I don't know what you want me to say. Please spare my worthless life, oh Chosen One."

I guess I did sort of yell it out loud, too, didn't I?

"He ... he ... he's ..." Queeheg face-planted on the filthy floor before finishing that thought. Right into a puddle of something sticky and brown. Lord only knew what it was, but my assumption was that it was unpleasantly bad.

Jon! She says she'll be damned. That was the simage. She wants to know why a god would be stupid enough to trip a trap they all know about. She asks if I've suffered severe head trauma. Jon, why is she asking that?

My life sucked so badly.

Tell her Jon Ryan says she will indeed be damned. Tell her that I was messing with her, that your husband is Ryanmax, the poly Ryanmax. We both used the trap to save energy. We teleported to Prime on covert missions but used the traps to return because we were ... we ...

We were stupid and wanted to risk death?

Su ... sure. Go with that. I got nothing.

I told her the words you told me to.

And.

And I'm still not dead.

That has to count for something.

Jon, she just turned and left. She said something about how much she hates her job and she left.

Hallelujah and kiss the kids on the forehead, I exclaimed. *Honey, stay put and I'll be there as fast as I can.*

I leaned back over the bar. Queeheg was pushing himself out of the ooze to a sitting position. "Hey, you have a ride I can borrow?" I called down to him.

Rubbing the back of his head, he replied, "Sure. Magic carpet in the storeroom's how I gets 'bout."

I looked back to Wul. "I guess that means you're not coming, right?"

He shook his head weakly. Poor guy bit off more than he could chew, being my friend and all. Lousy luck.

Leaning back over, I asked Queeheg, "Does it know the way to the Lower Chambers?"

That brought me the familiar are you crazy *look I so deserved.* "It's a magic carpet."

CHAPTER TWENTY-NINE

"No, my dearest sister, who happens also to be an idiot, that is not what the sign indicates," Deca scolded Fest.

The two ancient witch gods skilled in prophecy sat hunched over the rotten entrails of a disemboweled carcass. It might once have been that of a pig, but it bore uncomfortable similarities to a person. The corpse was so mangled and decayed that positive visual identification was impossible. The sisters were oblivious to the rank stench. Vorc, who stood in the most distant doorway, was not so immune. He was having difficulty not retching or bolting. But, times being as they were, he needed to know what fate held in store.

"The signs are so clear, Vorc there could read them," continued Deca.

Fest turned to eye him. "If only he'd come a little closer, we would find out."

They had a good cackle over that.

"But, sister dearest, don't you see? The colon has swollen and shoved that segment into the other. That means Fate is forcing its way toward our favor." Deca was resolute.

Fest spat in her sister's face. "Who taught you to read the signs?

You are utterly incompetent. The entrails tell us nothing, nothing one way or another. Fate ignores us."

"*You* taught me, older sister," Deca replied as she wiped spittle from her cheek.

"Then I am a *great* interpreter and a *bad* teacher."

"No, you can't juxtapose great *and* bad in a sentence like that. The qualities of the adjectives must match. Great and good, horrible and bad." Deca poked at the slimy mess with a long stick. "I suppose you could say great *but* bad." She shrugged. "Awkward pacing, then, if you ask me."

"Well, thank the Eternal Darkness no one did, least of all ..."

"Ladies, ladies," chimed in an impatient Vorc, "I need *answers,* not a grammar lesson, threadbare as it is. Please focus on the question at hand."

"Ladies?" Fest quipped. "Are some women standing behind us we cannot *see?*"

Again, they cackled like oversized lunatic chickens.

"How can one of you see a strong positive while the other sees nothing at all?" he pressed with considerable frustration.

"*Hah.* Because one of us is correct and one of us is an idiot," responded Deca.

Fest used her probe stick to whack her sister across the back that Deca had turned to her when she saw the foul weapon coming.

"Vorc, as a layman, you can't see the subtleties. I," Fest rested a proud hand on her withered chest, "a master's master, see whatever is offered up." She touched a green mass that was bubbling slowly with spine-numbing burps. "This is the Organ of Manzy. It was used in life to help digest a fatty meal. It's now more fetid than the rest of this noisome mess." She recklessly slapped at some globs, angry at them for apparently unknowable reasons.

One wad of ooze narrowly missed Vorc's shoes. He hopped like a six-foot rabbit to avoid it.

"If one cannot *digest* a coming meal, one will not *receive* it from all-knowing Fate. Nothing could be *more* blatantly obvious." Fest folded her arms with finality.

"Sisters, please," demanded Vorc. "My position grows more perilous by the day. The general unrest and discontent is peaking to isolated violence. If I do not say definitively that Prime is within reach, I fear anarchy will ensue."

Deca shot up an eyebrow. "Isolated violence? We know of no such acts."

Vorc toyed with the idea of quipping that of course, *they* didn't. They lived in a dark tower with rotting flesh. He wisely let that impulse pass. "Commendra was assaulted and nearly ended last week. The medical gods had a devil of a time reattaching her head before it would have been too late."

Fest set a bony hand over her mouth and chuckled softly. Deca punched at her sister, but her decrepitude dictated she missed widely.

"What? You find it amusing a fellow god was dismembered and nearly *ended*?" Vorc, who actually cared little either way about anyone else's fate, tried to sound haughty and offended.

"It was not civil *unrest* that nearly cost the fool her worthless life," began Deca.

"No, the brood-cow disrespected Bethniak in public," finished Fest.

"Such a foolish thing to do," added Deca.

"I ... why did I not hear of this?" Vorc demanded weakly.

"Why indeed?" parroted Deca.

"Let those with ears *hear* and those with eyes *see*," riddled Fest.

"Those are not answers. Do you mock me?" His indignation was not so much measured as it was halfhearted.

Both sisters glared at him a few seconds, then turned in unison to reinspect the remains. Both poked and prodded at sections but neither spoke.

Vorc finally realized he'd been dismissed. Not wanting to concede that fact and therein lose face, he puffed up his chest and announced, "I will return in *one* day. You had *better* have news by then, or you'll have *me* to answer to."

One of the sisters snickered softly.

CHAPTER THIRTY

My magic carpet ride glided to a soft landing in front of the now-renovated arched entrance to the Lower Chambers. I totally empathized with Wul about the stupid rugs. They were unsteady, the footing was treacherous, and the damn thing seemed to love to dive and pitch at random angles, if for no other reason than to scare the rider. I stepped off and turned back to the wretched rag. "You can go or you can stay, but leave me the hell alone. You got that?"

Magic carpets did not talk.

Sapale, I'm out front. Can you find your way here?

I guess so. Since your girlfriend left, I've managed to get myself fairly lost in this pit.

I don't want to risk running into Tefnuf. She might believe we're gods, but she still may try to extract her pound of flesh from me on general principles.

Yes, Mr. Bony Ass. I bet she would pay good money for the chance.

What is around you? Maybe I can help direct you.

Stone walls, flaming torches, and the occasional demon. At least I assume they're demons. If they're not, there are great career opportunities for them in demoning.

The carpet. It could find her. Duh, it was magical. I walked back to where I'd left it. Rug hadn't budged. "I need you to go into the Lower Chambers and fetch my wife. She's new here and kind of lost."

Nothing.

"Come on, I said go get her."

The carpet slid a couple inches away from me.

A rug with attitude. Nice. Just what I needed. I sure as hell wasn't going to apologize or try and take back my harsh words. The stupid doormat was a deathtrap.

"I have little patience with disrespectful tools," I tried to thunder. It came out rather meekly.

Carpet slid back a few more inches.

Jon, I'm kind of freaking out. A troop of tiny elephants with wings just flew past me. The one who led the column said, "Good morning," the one in the middle said, "Good luck," and the last one said, "Good night." Jon, I need to get out of here now.

That freaking rug seemed to wiggle with mirth. Maybe there was a breeze. "Look, okay, I'm sorry I said mean words. Will you go get her now?"

It slid back one inch then forward one inch. What the hell?

"Please, would you go get her?"

In a flash the carpet shot through the entrance and out of sight. Stupid carpet wanted me to grovel. Man, I wished I had a couple of moths in my pocket for when it returned.

I sent a magic carpet to pick you up. It'll be there in a jiffy.

Jon, seriously, I'm creeped out by this place. No Jon humor, okay?

I'm completely serious. It's ... this realm is kind of different. Trust me.

Jon, did you send a five-by-six red carpet with a paisley pattern?

Did I? Ah, maybe. I hadn't really noticed.

You are such a guy.

Thank you.

It was not meant as a compliment, trust me. How the hell do yooooo ...

Fly one? You don't. There're damn scary, aren't they?

The rug zipped to my side.

"Yes they are," she said as she leaped off the carpet. "Shoo," she said to it with a sweep of the backs of her hands.

"No, don't piss it off. Never know when you might need one, you know?"

"What, you an expert on all things ancient godish now?"

I swaggered in place. "You could say that."

She rolled all four eyes and pushed past me. "Where's home. I need to take a load off."

I bobbed my head side to side. "Well, to be specific about it, we do not have a place, you know, like a home or anything."

She rotated her head back at me. Such a look she gave me I probably never deserved. "You've been here over a year and have no place to call your own? That's pathetic, or you're shacking up. Which of those is it, brood-mate?"

"Wait." I held my hands up. "I've only been here a couple months, tops. Time's different here and back there."

She turned fully to face me. "You've been here *two months* and have no place to call your own? That's pathetic or you're shacking up. Which of those is it, brood-mate?"

Didn't sound any better, did it?

"This place's like Vegas, a twenty-four-seven three-sixty-five kind of roller coaster."

"Never made it to Vegas, never rode a coaster, and I'm never going to buy what you're selling."

"I had a place; well, I borrowed it for a while. Then the owner came out of the coma I'd put him in. Otherwise, I was busy on a pilgrimage and partying," I threw up a finger quickly, "not for fun's sake, but to ingratiate me to our sworn enemy."

"Normally a man'd need a shovel to dig such a deep grave so quickly. You *are* good, Ryan."

"Come on. I'll introduce you to my new bestie, Wul. He'll vouch for every word I said."

She tilted and extended a you-first arm. "This'll be good."

A little way down the road, I felt it was safe to begin speaking again. "Now you're going to love this Wul guy. For a god, he's a good egg."

"He's an egg? An egg god?"

"No, that's an expression. Wul's a good guy. One thing though, go kind of easy on him."

"Because he's an egg?"

"No. Wul is *not* an egg. Probably never was. No, I mean he's kind of skittish around me, lately."

"You mean he's mentally normal."

"No. Well, yes. Look, he is sort of under the impression that I'm The Chosen One." I shrugged. "Naturally, that kind of freaks him out."

"Naturally. By the way, what's a *chosen one*?"

"The Chosen One. Basically their god and savior. Now ..."

"Gods and powers, *no*. Tell me these morons haven't been feeding your ego with aggrandizements. The universes aren't ready for such an overload."

"Someone arrived at my realm rather grumpy."

"Oh, now since you're its god, this is *your* realm?"

"That goal is within sight."

"Now I regret not listening to Toño. Coming here *was* a big mistake."

"What happened to *love honor and obey, good times and bad*? Aren't you supposed to be supportive of your husband?"

"Those are *human* wedding vows. My people do it differently. We *help* our mates. Sometimes that requires a two-by-four to the head, but love is love is love."

"Hey, there's a cab. Let's grab it," I said, picking up the pace.

"That's not a cab. That's a contradiction confronting ignorance."

"It's .. er ... here it can be both. And you're wrong. I'm looking right at it, and I say it's a *beautiful thing*."

"Jon." She pulled me to a stop, tugging at my sleeve. "In *my* opinion, those are one and the same thing."

"You're going to fit in real well here, babe."

"Let's hope not. My plan is to rescue you. We need to get home before you out us."

Hand to chest, I exclaimed, "Before *I* out us? Why would you assume A) we will be outted and B) it'd be *my* fault?"

"Sorry, Jon, I didn't plan this rescue as well as I could."

"How so?"

"I didn't bring a mirror. This is the point where I hold it in front of your face to remind you why I said what I said."

At least I knew this Sapale wasn't a golem sent to fool me. That was *my* Sapale in the flesh. Well, you know what I mean. We availed ourselves of the ride and arrived at Blind Faith No More only a couple of hours after I'd left it. I was hoping Wul hadn't wandered off. Or, actually, hadn't run away screaming, for that matter. Him I needed. I stepped through the doors first, with Sapale just behind me. The place was empty, save for Queeheg. He, the poor SOB, was sitting in a chair that looked like it was about to fail due to the load he asked it to bear. He was hunched over and stared at some indistinct spot on the filthy floor.

"I can tell he's already met *you*," quipped Sapale as she pushed past me. "Hey, big fella, what's a girl got to do to get a drink around here?"

He slowly lifted his head. "A drink it is ..."

Then he sort of noticed me.

"By my mother's love'a me, spare me, Ryanmax. I didn'a e'er cross you. Ya knows that, right?"

"I'll remove the words *has met you* and substitute *knows you*. You are the singular man in forever who could get a troll like that to grovel like a beaten dog." That wife of mine was on quite the roll. A real comedian.

"Queeheg, seriously, no problema. You and me, we're friends," I tried to reassure him.

"I let that worm Wul leave. I told's him a'not to, but he said there was a conclave just called and he a'had'a. I swear I tried a'stop 'im."

"A conclave? I didn't hear about that," I responded. "Why aren't you going? They're mandatory."

"Course'n I know, but weighed again' the very real prospect'a insulting da Chosen One, I elects to hang back in case'a you returns like you's have. My reservations turned out to be *validated*, don't ya sees?"

"You really know how to pick 'em, don't you, Ryan?" snarked my eternal mate.

"Where's the conclave?" I asked Queeheg, who, by the way, was now on both knees wringing his hands like an old woman in church.

"Whe ... ah, it's a test ya be givin' me to measure by weight my fidelity?" He did his best to nod approvingly.

Seriously? I was about ready to change professions, become a dirty-water hot-dog peddler and not a hero of whatever the hell I was heretofore a hero of. My head swam in the strangeness that reality became when I messed with it. I needed a vacation, maybe a sabbatical. Those are typically longer. I needed time, lots of time, to vacuum out my head.

"Yeah, it's a test." I slapped the butt of my palm against my forehead. "Think *I* forgot or something?"

"I don'ts think anything, great one."

That I truly believed. "Let's all three go to the conclave, shall we?"

"By your whim or wish, Chosen One." Queeheg staggered to his feet and went to lock up.

"Did I mention you really know how to pick 'em, Oh Great Chosen Butthead?" That Sapale. Once she was onto a thing, she never let up.

"I'm going with the flow. You might dive in, too; might help," I replied.

"Not flowing there."

"Come on, yaz two, I'm ready as I'll evers be," announced Queeheg as he reentered the room. "I called for a cab, seeing's how we're late to get on."

Out front you will never believe what was waiting to take us to the conclave. I was actually ready to fall to the ground in hysterics. It was a vintage red and white 1958 A8 Checker cab with single headlights, 1953 Chevrolet taillights, and the original thick, single-bar grille. The whole nine yards. Our cab was a *cab*. I felt like railing to the heavens to rain down more of the bizarre, more lunacy, and I'd swear by all I held dear that I could take it. Yeah, I was Lieutenant Dan, and the *whatever* could keep trying with its best shots, because I wasn't going to break.

Instead, I got in the cab last.

The trip to the conclave was short. I had no real preconception of what an all-hands-on-deck assembly of these bozos would look like. Still, I was surprised. Maybe I envisioned a round amphitheater with the principals seated at the low point of the ice cream cone. Or a plush meadow with babbling brooks. Hey, we were talking gods here, right? Nope. It looked just like any tacky convention at the Hilton, down to the cheesy red-patterned carpet and folding chairs no being in creation could be comfortable in. What? Were the Cleinoid gods hard up for cash and needed to do these gatherings on the cheap? Did I mention the undersized chandeliers that sported crystals that shined like plastic and the white tableclothed water stands?

We found seats and settled in. Some fluttering freakazoid was reciting flowery words, so we couldn't have missed anything important. When she rested back in her seat a man I knew to be Vorc stood. He was at the center of a long, gently curved table.

"My friends and fellow gods, I have called this conclave to make a major announcement."

"Couldn't you have just simaged us and cut out the need for everyone having you lord it over us?" shouted some immensely ugly blob of a woman seated near us.

"That Caprahammer never kin hold 'er tongue and let Vorc get to it and be done." Queeheg shook his head in disapproval.

"I personally feel belittled," Sapale remarked blandly.

I looked to her.

She just shrugged.

"An announcement of this magnitude, this import, could not be made via simage. The news ..."

"What, a couple sentences couldn't be sent via the airwaves?" Caprahammer spat on the floor. "Hard to imagine why not."

"Will the guards please assume their customary positions by Caprahammer's sides? She is now just two disrespects from ejection. I believe this is some kind of record for swiftness at being intolerable," Vorc said in a tone suggesting he was less in control than he wished to be.

"No, ass-candy. You already hold that record," she just had to snipe. What a piece of work Caprahammer was.

"Thank the powers she's down to one," Vorc responded gleefully.

The guards inched closer to their prey.

"Yesterday," began Vorc, sounding like every other two-bit politician I had ever heard in the last two billion years, "I told the Prophecy Sisters Fest and Deca to give me *definitive* news on our access to Prime, or else." Dude really came down hard on the *or else* crap.

Caprahammer stood silently and walked to the nearest exit. Once there she turned and shouted, "Or else you'd do what you always do. You'd stick your thumb up your butt and then invite all those present to please add their thumbs or whatever to the party." With that, she turned and left before the guards could even approach her.

I snickered. That one was pretty good. I'd have to remember it, and use it when the need arose.

"When I returned to the sisters earlier today, I reminded them of my demand. They duly informed me that Fate *favors* the Cleinoid gods." He spread his arms in the air, waiting to welcome the riotous response his words would invoke. Someone near the front clapped.

Vorc tapped the microphone with a finger. "Is this thing on?" he asked no one in particular.

The loud thumps confirmed it was fully functional.

"Did you hear me, brothers and sisters? Fate *favors* us."

Queue the crickets.

A free-floating liquid mass rose a bit and said—how, I have no clue, by the by—"Bring back Caprahammer."

"What?" squeaked Vorc.

A pencil-thin man in an ill-fitting three-piece suit stood and bowed slightly. Man did he look to be the god of drab morticians. "As one of the many gods of bureaucracy, it *may* fall upon me to clarify the lack of unbridled enthusiasm you witness, center seat. *Some* present *might* be recalling that you have in the past made similar statements *that*, if taken at face value, proved to be inaccurate in that they predicted events that never *actually* came to be."

Yup, he was a bureaucrat. No doubt about that.

"People," Vorc raged, "we're going to *Prime*."

I could swear I heard a pin drop on the other side of the room. Maybe it was a button, but whatever it was it was small, light, and produced almost no sound.

Vorc spun to face Lusterless, the god who'd just made the clarification.

Lusterless pulled a small book or ledger from a pocket and scanned it quickly. Then he cleared his throat. "It is *generally* accepted by those present that we as a whole will at *some* time in the foreseeable or unforeseeable future make our way to Prime. Such a passage is considered by *most* authorities to be a *certainty*. It is more the *time frame* of the embarkation that restrains current jubilation based on a gross underperformance of *accuracy* on the center seat's part over the recent and remote pasts in demonstrating credibility in any stated or implied commitment to the aforementioned travel."

Just before I nodded off, Lusterless sat back down. I was ready to cheer that.

"Fest, *Deca*, where are you?" howled Vorc.

They stood.

"Tell these *morons* what you told me earlier today."

"Everything we told you?" asked Deca.

"We told you *many* things," added Fest.

Vorc's head recoiled slightly. "No you didn't. You just told me the thing about Fate."

They shook their apple-core doll heads in synch.

"What?" he asked feebly.

"She told you that my bladder control issues were getting worse," Deca snapped, looking angrily at the side of her sister's head.

"And *she* told you her hip hurt too much for *you* to be able to mount her anymore." Fest smiled contentedly.

"I did *not*, you horrible person," screamed Deca. She did her best to tackle her wicked sister. She more or less bounced off.

There was a loud, bone-crunching peal of thunder in the auditorium. When everyone looked back up, all eyes went to Vorc.

"Do not make me repeat that disciplinary action. Clearly the Prophecy Sisters are in a playful and inappropriate mood today. That said, I will ask Deca," he pointed in the direction of the women, "and Deca alone, to tell you what they discovered as a result of *my* mandate to them."

Deca's ancient face turned to regard the crowd. Then she spoke clearly. "Fate favors us. Within a week we will all be able to cross the void and enter upon Prime. *Prime*, you witless toads, is yours."

A deafening roar rose from the audience. The lustful and insatiable ancient gods were about to try and fill the bottomless pits of their desires and their depravity, their cruelty and their callous disregard for all life that wasn't Cleinoid. The ancient gods were about to be unleashed. Hell was coming to a theater near you.

CHAPTER THIRTY-ONE

Sapale and I were lost in a daze as we exited the assembly. One or the other of us would occasionally bump into a reveler, but they never seemed to notice. They were so euphoric it was frightening. I mean, those hateful gods were so enraptured with the prospect of pulverizing a living, vibrant universe. Who's that callous, that psychotically evil? How can anyone live billions of years and come out so completely and jingoistically screwed up in the head? Wait, I could be. I was, in fact. Well, not me but the alternate time line version of me, the one I nicknamed EJ, for Evil Jon. When I hooked back up with him after that period of time, he'd gone completely bad.

Or had he? He was bad, but after leaving him in the custody of a Deft master he eventually came around to being ... er, *not* psycho. That's what Miraya, my sort of adopted daughter, told me, at least. I hadn't seen EJ since the day I dumped him on Cala, the Deft brindas. My mind reeled. Everything I'd come to know and love over my impossibly long life was about to end violently. EJ rehabbed; why didn't these pigs?

You'll never guess what I fixated on the most, what really had me trippin'. Once the ancient gods destroyed my universe, there'd be no more Sunday mornings. Yeah, how odd. Of all the things to miss, I would not have supposed *that* would be my greatest regret. But Sunday mornings were magical. Nestled safely between Saturday's off time and twenty-four hours more of relaxation, I always felt so safe, so buffered against the stresses of life. Sunday mornings I slept in. Sundays I ate a ridiculously big breakfast and it was all good. Bacon, hash browns, five eggs over-easy, maybe a steak tossed in for good measure. And the Sunday funnies. They were quicksilver. Precious but short, gone almost before I started them. But they radiated a gentle magic I soaked up, like dry desert sand does the rain. Once the damn Cleinoid gods were done, there'd never be another Sunday morning.

I had to stop them. I knew then I would open up an industrial drum of whoop-ass on them or die trying. No one was entitled to end mystical memories, mine or anyone else's. I took Sapale's hand and pulled her to one side.

"I am more angry with these pieces of shit than anyone else I've hated, *ever*."

She looked back at me and spoke with strength. "You've hated a lot of people, places, and things."

"But none like these sorry excuses for living beings. These ... these *parasites* will die, and I will kill every last one of them."

Still a vision of power, she rested my hand on her chest. "No you won't."

My hand, the one she held so gently, balled up into a fist. "Why not?"

"Because I'm killing at least half." She smiled and rested my hand on her cheek.

What a gal, that brood's-mate of mine.

"Youz coming back to me place or what, Cho ..."

I shot a stop-sign palm in Queeheg's massive face. "Ryanmax. Call me by my name or die."

It was almost comical to see a creature so big and ugly and

powerful pale as he began to tremble. I say *almost* because for me there would be nothing comical until these wastes of space were extinct.

"Yesz, sir. Sorry, Ryanm ... max. Do you an' the missus plan on comings back or heading out on your own recognizance?"

"We're going to walk," Sapale said to him reassuringly. "You go on. Maybe we'll see you soon."

"I prays we do, ma'am. You're powerful good company."

He took a few steps backward, then turned and hurried away. I started to say to Sapale that Queeheg was okay and that maybe I'd not kill him. But I belayed that thought. I was going to see them all dead. No exceptions. I would show them the mercy they were prepared to show. None. That was fine by me. The simpler the rules, the simpler the warfare.

We stepped out into a fading day. The shadows of the departing gods were long and the air was beginning to cool. It would have been, in another time and place, the start of a very fine evening. "Let's head that way," I said, gesturing off to the west.

"Where are we going?" Sapale asked as she matched my brisk pace.

"No idea. Just away from this horrible place."

"Are you looking for Wul?"

Was I? "No. We're on our own now. If we had time, maybe I'd try and wriggle myself into a position of acceptance and maybe even power. But we're too close to go time."

"So, what? Guerrilla warfare? Sabotage on a large scale? What's the plan?"

I shook my head. "Really, nothing. For now we keep moving and I search for inspiration."

"Sounds like we're hunting for a Jon Plan."

I smiled to her. "We're looking for a Jon Plan. How hard can that be? They're mostly so dumb and so simple there must be a dozen of them out there at any one time."

We walked for hours. We'd left one city, passed through a small town or two, and then marched the wide-open expanse of the barren landscape. Toward dawn I saw the outline of Beal's Point off in the far distance. The twisted nature of the monument and the sad devotion the locals had to pay to it came back to me. What twisted bastards. Forced to adsorb toxic essence from past undesirables.

Wait. *Toxic* might be mighty useful to us. If in small amounts it sickened, there just had to be a dose that would be lethal. It was incumbent upon me to find that dose. The only way to do that would be to collect the bad mojo, duplicate it, and experiment on the locals. That would border on fun in my book.

I pointed to Beal's Point's silhouette. "We're heading toward that outcropping."

"What's there?"

"Something that makes Cleinoids ill."

"Can I get a franchise for myself?" She smiled up at me.

"No, sweet love. We're in business together." I kissed the top of her head, turned, and picked up our pace.

It took us several hours to make Beal's Point. Along the way I filled Sapale in on my road trip there with the others. It took a while to convince her I was *not* kidding about my new buddy Hemnoplop, the walking talking island. I sent her holos and everything, but she still thought I was making it up to get her goat. She finally conceded that it would be stupid even for me to invent such a character, since his being an island and all didn't enhance the story I spun. She could also glean that my annoyance with Hemnoplop's slow pace and loquacious tendencies was genuine.

"So the ancient gods are required to make pilgrimages there with some regularity so they get sick by absorbing the bad mojo from those deemed by management to be bad team players?" The incredulity oozed in her tone.

"Yeah, that's kind of it."

"How is it we're worried about defending ourselves? These wet rat droppings are too pathetic to beat up *anybody*."

"Would that it were so," I lamented. "They have strange rules and strange everything else. But they *are* incredibly powerful, and there are one whole *hell* of a lot of them."

"I trust your take, but so far I haven't seen all that many." She swept an arm across the barren landscape. "Pickings are pretty slim here. And the conclave thing was crowded, but there couldn't have been more than a thousand asswipes there. I mean, the meeting *was* mandatory. That had to be the sum total of their number, right?"

I clicked my tongue. "That's the hardest part to keep in mind. They're gods, magical beings. Everyone was *there*, but everyone wasn't at *that* meeting location."

"You're sounding like an unemployed philosopher who likes to whiff airplane glue."

I gestured my hands forward. "There's only *one* Vorc, *one* large table, and *one* Caprahammer being a turd in the punch bowl. But the Cleinoids can come to the conclave without being there."

"Oh, now I get it."

"Really?"

"Sure. You're deranged." She elbowed me.

"We've flown from one side of our galaxy to the other. We've seen a lot of strange stuff. You know that. This is another example of the inexplicable happening to be the case. I think they pull it off by being there but in parallel dimensions. I got Wul to tell me that much but couldn't press him because he'd get suspicious."

"Yes, he might *suspect* you were deranged."

I tried to look stern, but we both caught a bad case of the giggles.

"So how many are there?" she asked once we'd settled down.

"I don't know for a fact, but I suspect millions. One way I sold my story about not being familiar with the local customs was to say I came from far away. Everyone accepted that straight away. I think this place is *big*."

"Why does it always get worse? We fight the Listhelons, and at the time they seemed formidable. Then we knock out the Uhoor and next the Berrillians. But each new opponent was tougher and harder to defeat than the last. Why can't we face off with, I don't know, Munchkins? Huh? *Them* we could pound and be home for an early lunch."

"Munchkins? Never underestimate those players, honey. They have sharp teeth and are right at groin level. Yeah, try fighting one of those and remaining reproductively intact. No walk in the park, I'll tell you that for free."

"You speak from personal experience?" She hip-bumped me.

I made a show of stopping and looking sideways toward my crotch. "This is my *third* one. Nasty little creatures, those Munchkins. Never cross 'em."

It was midday when we were actually up on the plateau of Beal's Point. That's when the nausea and irrepressible sense of anxiety began to set in.

"You feel that?" I said as we slowed.

"What?"

"Being ill at ease, jumpy."

She looked ahead and angled her head. "I do. Feels like I'm pregnant."

"I wouldn't know," I deferred.

"I could download all my experience to you if you'd like." Man, she seemed awfully gleeful at that prospect.

"Ah, maybe later. It's probably not safe to up here, you know, with the bad air."

"Wimp."

I let that pass. "Come on. Let's see what we're going to see." I pointed to the nearest monument and headed toward it.

"Gal-y-saph-o-lis," Sapale said, reading the inscription. "That's a mouthful and a half. What'd he do wrong?"

"No clue. Wul mentioned a few specifics farther on. Ol' Galy's crimes will have to remain a mystery."

I circled the stone monolith the statue rested on. There had to be an opening or panel. If the stupid structure emitted badness, it had to come from inside. Then again, this was the land of quirky gods. Maybe those rules needn't apply. Finding nothing, I extended my probe fibers. *Open*, I said to the pedestal. The massive structure trembled briefly, then damn if a door didn't open on the far side.

"Hey," squealed Sapale, "you *did* it. Come over here."

"On my way. Stay back. No telling what I've done."

"That's life with Jon's normal condition."

"Very droll."

I stepped in front of her and peered into the darkness within. One thing was certain. The ill effects were much worse with the door open. I really felt like shit. I took that to be a good sign.

"Oh my," said a queasy-sounding Sapale, "I do think I'll move to the other side of this infernal thing."

"Go ahead. I'll call you if I need you. Oh, and try to analyze what the sickening transmission actually is. I couldn't identify it at all last time."

"Where're the Als when you need them?"

"True that. Advanced computers do serve a useful function, even if they're pissy."

I barely heard that from where I am. Switch to comm link, Sapale said into my head.

This monolith is dense. It stopped most of he Nausea Radio and deadens sound intensely. Wonder what it's made of?

The same material that makes up your skull? Such a sweet wife.

Hey, I found something. It's a box or crate. I felt its surface then attached my probe fibers. *What are you?*

You talking to me or the coffin?

It's not a coffin.

And you know this because?

She had a point. Well, what if it was? I'd seen way too much worm chow in my day. I mean, how rotten could it be? And grave robbing might be a useful addition to my résumé. Hey, a job skill's a job skill.

My probes say it's a steel-like metal, hollow, and that there's something alive inside.

They do not, you jerk.

Being together so very long did make it hard to fool her, didn't it? *Well, the first two are correct. I'm trying to get a fingernail in the seam. There. It's ... ahhhhhh.*

Not buying what you're selling, dear mate. What's inside?

No idea. I haven't found the seam yet if there is one. Maybe it's welded shut?

Cut it with your laser.

Good idea. See, I knew I kept you around for a good reason. Toño's been wrong about you all along.

Less mental diarrhea and more cutting, flyboy.

Damn. I think it's working. It took a sec but I think I got through the entire sheet. I'm expanding ... ahhhhhh.

You are not seriously ...

Ahhhhhh ... get it off me ... Sapale, tell the kids I ... ahhhhh.

Sapale broke into a sprint. *If you're shitting me you're dead, Ryan.*

She shot past the pedestal opening and right at Jon. He was writhing on the floor and slapping at his torso. She stood over him scanning for the danger. She saw nothing. Sapale would have vomited up her stomach if she still had one, she was so nauseous. But otherwise nothing seemed amiss.

"Jon," she shouted, "what's wrong, honey? What's the matter?"

"The spiders," he screamed, "get them off. They're ripping my flesh off."

"Jon, there are no spiders. Honey, stand up."

"No, they ate my legs. Run, Jeanna. Save yourself."

Sapale seized him by the collar and began dragging him out. Instantly she felt something on her arm. She shot a glance back. *Falzorn.* There were falzorn crawling up her arm. Those murderous snakes from her home solar system were always ravenous, mindless, and relentless. She released Jon's clothing and smashed her arm against the wall. She went to slap at the falzorn with her free hand. They were gone. She scanned the floor. None. Not one falzorn. *What just happened?* she thought through her panic.

From the ground Jon wailed again. "Rats, now there are rats, too. Ahhhh."

An illusion. That's what it had to be. A horrific hallucination coming from the box. Sapale lunged for her brood-mate's arm. As she tugged the falzorn reappeared on her arm. They multiplied and soon there were hundreds writhing up her arm, across her face, and down her throat.

"It's bullshit," she hissed. "Ignore the vision. You're fine. Keep ..."

Two falzorn squirmed into one of her eyes.

Focus, girl, she shouted to herself, *focus. You can do this.*

In seconds she'd dragged Jon out the door and around to the far side of the pedestal. One by one the falzorn faded. And then there were none. She dropped to her knees. "Jon, honey, are you okay? The rats are gone. The spiders are gone. Jon, *speak.*"

The one-foot-wide spider that had spanned my face started to fade. I was slapping myself hard well after it was gone. I looked at my arms. The rats dissolved into thin air. There was nothing assaulting me. I stood unsteadily and examined the ground. Where'd all the pests go?

"Jon, *easy,*" purred Sapale. "It was all an illusion. When you opened the box something came out that made us hallucinate the worst things we could possibly imagine. It was just a *vision,* Jon. It was *not real.*"

"A what? No. There were spiders crawling up my nose. I could *smell* them."

"Ancient god mojo, honey. We're just fine."

"F ... fine? I'll never be fine again as long as I live. That was intense."

"Then delete the memories. No big deal. We're fine."

I studied my arms and legs. They were perfectly normal, no stain, mark, or tear. But the feeling was so real. No, it was *hyper-real,* more intense than reality. I'd been scared out of my mind before, not often, mind you, but it'd happened. But it was never that ... that *actual*, never that vivid. I never ever wanted to experience that again.

"So what do you think it was?" Sapale asked when it was clear I'd calmed down.

"Wrong, that's what it was."

She rolled her eyes. "Besides that?"

"These evil cockgobblers have somehow purified misery. They've bottled it and can modulate the intensity of the suffering with proper shielding." I shivered.

"Did you get a look in the box to see what it was?"

I stiffened.

"Well, did you? Yes or no?"

"No, but this time I will." I spun on a heel and headed for the door.

Sapale grabbed me from behind. "No, Jon. Please don't."

I stopped but didn't turn. "Why not?"

"Because it's too awful, too all-consuming."

"We need a weapon. Maybe what's inside is one. I intend to find out." I started walking again. "You stay right here. Just takes one of us to check it out."

Sapale hadn't released me. She used my forward momentum to swing around to my side. "No way, hero boy. If you go, I go."

I turned to her and smiled sadly. "We don't both have to suffer."

"Yes, we do, and you know it. Shut up and follow me."

I lifted her hand from my arm and kissed the back of it. "Come on. Follow me, love of my life."

Five minutes later we were outside again. Through blasts of white-hot fire melting my skin off and swarms of scorpions entombing my writhing body, I'd looked and felt in the box. There was nothing in it. Sapale cut a section of the wall and we'd placed it over the hole I'd cut in the box from hell. That modulated but did not totally extinguish the hallucinations. But I had me a weapon, even if it was making me wish I were dead. That was fine by me.

Then, because I was a male, it hit me. I was doing it the hard way again. I placed a full membrane force field around the box. Immediately all horror ended.

Sapale stared at me. "Why the hell didn't you think of that half an hour ago?"

"Me, I kind of enjoyed the feeling. It was like all the rides at the amusement park rolled together."

"Pig," was her initial response. "So, now you have your toy. What's next?"

I scratched absently at the side of my nose. "Something."

CHAPTER THIRTY-TWO

In an antiseptically white room with glaring fluorescent lighting to great excess, three sub-demigods sat at their workstations. Dronus, Borender, and Failos had worked in Control and Remediation for longer than they could rightly remember. They rarely spoke, less frequently did any actual work, and never contributed anything to the common good. Some god at some juncture decided a department to monitor the controls of the inner workings of the Cleinoid dominion was needed. Either that god or some other equally intellectually challenged god felt that if *monitoring* was being done, a *remediation* network and plan had to, by necessity, be attached to that function. Neither thinker of dubious merit took into account that the inner workings in the land of the ancient gods were divinely inspired and magically fabricated. Such implacable systems did not actually *fail*. Monitoring only documented the perpetual perfect running order of all parts. And since nothing ever failed, remediation was but a pipe dream for Dronus, Borender, and Failos. It wasn't going to happen. In spite of all their training, in-servicing, drilling, and potential personal talents, they were doomed to live eternal lives as pointless as a dog with two dicks.

Into their listless careers, one crushingly boring day, came a missive so new, so novel they didn't believe it was real for the better part of an hour. Even then each one looked to the other two workers, non-verbally questioning if anything needed to be done. Half the shift passed before action of any kind was taken by any of the M&R employees. Borender went for a bathroom break. By the time he returned two hours later, Failos had amassed sufficient gumption to ask of his coworkers, "Does anybody else see that flashing red light?"

"I do not *think* I do," Dronus replied, peevishly.

"I refuse to see it unless both of you do before I do," responded Borender. "After all, you two have been present for two hours longer than me since the red alarm began to flash."

"That is only because you took such an extensive bathroom break," chided Failos.

"That is because I have extensive bathroom *needs*," defended Borender.

"So you *admit* you saw the red light before you left just like the two of us did?" fired off Dronus.

"I admit nothing. I was speaking in the hypothetical. You know, *if* I'd seen the light flash *you* would have seen it flash longer and therefore understand it's meaning *better* than I."

"That is definitely not what you said. You stated you saw the light before you left. Since we both saw it too, you are as responsible as we are in terms of reacting to it."

"Fine, fine," snapped Borender. "We all saw a flashing red light a few hours ago at the same time. There, are you two happy?"

"I've never been happy in my entire life," replied Failos. "*None* of us has."

"Stop. Stop it the both of you. Let's agree we *all* saw the light when it started to blink. Let us *further* agree one of you two needs to do something about it."

"No, we *all* do," returned Dronus. "We *all* work here."

"Oh, very well. This discord is driving me insane. Let's *all* do something about the red flashing light."

"I believe we already have. We've discussed it," Failos pointed out.

"I meant something *proactive*. Something we have been trained to do."

"What do you suggest we do, Borender, as the lead party in this crisis?" asked Dronus.

"I'm not the leader. We are co-leaders."

"No, I will only agree that we are co-non-leaders, Borender and I," stated Failos.

"Fine. We are all equally not in charge and not responsible."

The other two agreed quickly to that resolution.

"I suggest someone determine what that flashing red light means," Borender said uncertainly.

"It means there's trouble somewhere in some system," responded Dronus.

"I believe he meant which *system* is associated with that *particular* red light," Failos said softly.

"Ah, an excellent first step," replied Dronus. "Let us all."

They stood and approached the flashing red light like it was an agitated deadly serpent.

"It seems to be coming from the memorial to Galysapholis," announced Borender.

"No," Failos said firmly, "it *is* coming from the statue of Galysapholis. There's no *seems to be* about it."

"Why would there be a flashing *alarm* from one of the oldest monuments on Beal's Point?" Dronus wondered out loud.

"Perhaps it's broken?" replied Failos.

"Perhaps what's broken? The entire monument?"

"Maybe the sensors are defective?" returned Failos.

"That would be the light here." Borender tapped an unlit alarm.

"Maybe there's a storm and the signal is an error?" Failos responded.

"We will not find out what is wrong by *guessing*," said an imperious Dronus. "We have to do that thing they taught us to do, the one where you review the protocols, examine the monument, and identify the problem."

"You mean ... oh, what did they call it? Look into the matter?" Failos said uncertainly.

"*Investigate*. That's it. We need to *investigate* what the problem is," said a relieved Borender.

"Yes, I agree."

"Me, too."

"So, what is the first step in an investigation?" Borender queried.

"Take a break?" replied Failos quietly.

"No, the first step is to await direction from one's supervisor," Dronus responded more confidently.

"We do not *have* a supervisor," noted Borender. "It's just the three of us in C&R."

"Do you mean that *if* we discover a problem and either remediate it or do *not* remediate it, we then report that action to no one?" Failos challenged, incredulously.

"Now that you mention it, friend Borender," said a thoughtful-for-the-first-time-ever Dronus, "we do in fact *not* report to anyone or anybody."

Failos was flabbergasted. "So if we identify a problem and do *nothing* about it, no one will ever know?"

Dronus looked to Borender. Both blinked their eyes a couple times.

"Who's up for donuts?" Failos asked cheerily. "I'm buying."

CHAPTER THIRTY-THREE

Sapale and I had no place to go, which felt weird, but wasn't, really. We had no creature needs like sleep and bathing, so why stress about it? Plus, it sounded like the invasion was on for soon, so accommodations in that realm were superfluous. What we needed to do was find out exactly when all hell literally broke loose and what the process would be. I doubted it would be in the style of the USMC with LCMs hitting the beach and dropping bow ramps. *All gods into the water. Keep your powder dry.* Nah.

The problem, as before, was who to ask and not be outed for posing questions simply everyone knew the answers to. I could try and find Wul, but since the boulder god was certainly home by now, I didn't have free access to one of their comm stations. That kind of left Queeheg. He certainly would answer my questions and never rat me out. No, he was terrified of me. I let Sapale know my thoughts.

"That guy again?" was her underwhelming response.

"And exactly why not? I think he's reliable and trustworthy."

"Off the top of my head a few reasons elbow their way to the front. One, he worships you, which is nauseating to watch. Two, he's a bartender. Bartenders blab any and all secrets. They can't help it. It's in their DNA. Three, I don't trust *any* of these turd substitutes, not him, not Wul, *none*. Four, the joker's a missing link, not a source of reliable information."

"So you're not one-hundred percent behind me on this plan?"

"A safe assumption. I'd put my behindness around minus thirty percent."

"So, you have a better idea how to find out what we need to know?"

"Yeah," she said in a manner almost as cocky as me at my best, "we ask the cum puppet Vorc. Bet he knows."

"You want us, two perfect strangers, to march into his office and demonstrate a suspicious lack of common knowledge? And you think we'll survive? That's not a *bad* plan, honey. It doesn't even rate being called a *plan*. *Bad* just called and said it's pissed being used to describe it, because it's horrible."

"Why not? If he gets antsy or hostile, you release the horror maker and we slip out the back."

Good point. I would kind of enjoy dumping that on him. Hey, he was a politician. He'd put the entire incident in its proper perspective and then establish an ad hoc committee to advise the best action plan to avoid a repeat performance.

"Why the hell not?" I said lustfully.

"How far is his official office from here?"

"This I do know. It's a day and a half's walk in that direction." I pointed to the horizon.

She rose gracefully. "Then let's do this."

"Let us indeed." I offered her my elbow.

She slapped it down. "This is war, not a romantic stroll in the park."

"Cannot the two be combined?" I protested.

"You're the only jerk in existence who'd even think that, let alone say it."

We made good time and arrived to the city center where the civil administration resided faster than I'd anticipated. We had to take a break outside town to avoid arriving before dawn. No sane god would go to the Bureaucracy Center that early.

I recognized the building we wanted based on Wul's descriptions from our pilgrimage. I didn't know, however, exactly where Vorc could be found. We were unlikely to find a directory with crooked plastic letters in the lobby. But, we were all in for a what-the-hell experience. I walked through the wide doors like I owned the place. Sapale was at my side, equally brash.

A quick reconnoiter revealed the tall building had multiple elevators. We strode over to the bank of them. We stepped in. That was when I saw the elevator operator. I then wished I'd told Sapale about the naked golems *before,* because she was going to kind of notice the one that worked the elevator. Guy was buff, looked to be twenty, and didn't have a stitch on.

"Vorc's office," I said in as bored a tone I could. When he turned to pull the lever I put an index finger to my lips toward Sapale.

For her part, she was so darn cute. She faced me, but shot her eyes and the side of her head rapidly at the nude dude as if to say, *do you see that?*

The door swung open at some floor and we exited.

"What the *hell* was that?" Sapale gasped once the doors clinked shut.

I tilted my head toward the closed doors. "That? I think it was a naked man-child."

The punch she landed on my arm was hard, but it was worth it.

"He's a golem. Do you know what that means?"

"Animated clay?" she wheezed. "Ah, Jon, I'm kind of expert on this topic. That was flesh, not mud."

"An expert on naked men. When we're done here, I think we need to explore that claim."

"Not now, Ryan," she said, then growled. Kaljaxians had some great growls in their repertoires.

"Golems are the low-level workers here in God Land; waiters, elevator operators, that type of role."

She pointed back at the elevator. "But why do they have to be so buff and naked?"

I perfunctorily cleared my throat. "Ah, in case the individual being served is suddenly moved by the spirit of romance."

"You mean *lust*."

I shrugged by way of response. "Let's try that direction," I said, changing the subject before someone killed the messenger.

It didn't take long to find Vorc's office. It was the one with the crystalline double doors through which we could see gilt furniture and massive sconces with flaming torches. To-each-his-own didn't cover for his poor taste. Squinting, I led Sapale in. We were confronted by two absolutely gorgeous and, of course, unclothed women.

They started to stand to greet us. "*Sit*," snapped Sapale as she lunged in their direction. "Don't encourage him any more than you have to."

"Honey," I scolded gently, "they're only doing their *jobs*."

There was no mirth in the look she gave me. "We're here to see Vorc. Before you ask, no, we do not have an appointment. But this is important, so buzz us in or whatever," she said with manifest disgust in her voice. I knew then we would not be passing our retirement years in this universe. Pooh.

One of the women smiled cheerily. "You would like us to buzz you into what?"

The other's turn. "We are nymphs and cannot buzz anything. But we will certainly make every effort to summon someone who can."

"Not *golems*?" asked Sapale suspiciously.

"Oh, no, ma'am," said Nude One. "That would never do for Master Vorc."

"A man of more *refined* tastes, is he?" Sapale responded. "Movable, porkable mud's not *good* enough for the master?"

Naked Two's chance to take a swing at a pitch. "He is, and maybe. I'm not certain what pork has to do with the topic."

My dogged mate started to press them unhelpfully. I rested a finger back on her lips. "We need to see Vorc now, please, *nymphs*," I said pleasantly.

I felt a sharp kick to my shin nearest Sapale.

"You may *always* see Master Vorc," beamed Naked One.

Naked Two stood and gestured to a massive painting of Vorc. "There, see him all you like."

"*Sit*," snapped Sapale. "Do you remember the part about not standing?"

They frowned. Two sat.

"No. When I said *see,* I meant *meet* with him in person, now."

"Ah, such is not possible," said N One.

"He is not here," added N Two.

"Where is he?" I queried.

As one they replied, "Elsewhere."

Without needing to glance back I held up a palm to Sapale. "We need some information. Perhaps you can help. Exactly when is our passage into Prime?"

"That is easy. Six days from now the Cleinoid gods march," replied Two.

"As Cleinoids, naturally, we're marching along," I marched in place to demonstrate that I was an idiot. "Where ... where do we meet up, you know, as a group?"

"That is not easy," said One with the first serious look I'd seen on her face. "There has only ever been one point of embarkation. It will be the one you used last time."

"Well, I know it'll be the *same* location, silly nymph. It's just that someone told me last week they heard there was a second, er, *assembly* spot ... in ... into Prime," I muttered. "The other location isn't up to code for the ... I think I'll stop explaining myself now."

"No one told you that," said a focused Two.

"No one would even think that," added an equally focused One.

"I *told* you he was as drunk as you were," scolded Sapale. "When he gets to drinking he loses *perspective*," she said conspiratorially to the girls.

"There is to be *no* use of mind-altering substances from now until the egress," said One, sounding for all the world like my mother when I was in trouble.

"Duh," I said, flicking the side of my head. "I'm mostly a teetotaler myself anyway. No prob, boss nymph." I saluted her. What a jerk I was capable of being. "So, when we *egress*, we do so from ..."

"This universe," said one of them. I was kind of muddled.

"Sure. I think we'll just be, you know, on our way," I said as Sapale was pulling me backward toward the doors.

"What were your names?" called out Two as she most definitely stood.

"I'm Outta Here, and this moron is Toast." Ah, you know who said that, so I'll not bother to actually say it.

As the elevator descended I braved an observation. "Well, that went okay. A real plus, if you ask me."

"Not in the mood, Ryan. World's about to end and you're still trying to be funny."

The golem, normally expertly discreet, turned to Sapale. "The world is about to end?"

"Yes," she said darkly with a growl. "Didn't you hear? Torrential rain tomorrow. I'm predicting a lot of *mud's* on the horizon, dirtbag."

He quickly turned and advanced into the corner.

As we left the building I reminded my mate, "Loose lips sink ships."

"I know. It's ... it's just after forever, you still fry my bacon."

"I still got it," I responded happily.

"Yes, damn it all. You do." She took a deep breath. "So what now? We have six days to stop the egress or somehow join it."

"We're down to Queeheg. He's the only one I can ask the unaskable."

"I hate it, but I agree. At least the man's wavy gravy in the head."

"There's a magic carpet over there. Let's ..."

"*Absolutely* not. No rugs of death. We walk, if that's the only option."

"We'll watch for a cab while we walk."

"I'm not too keen on the cabs here either. Pains in my ass is what they are," she groused as we headed out.

We did get a ride and made it to Queeheg's bar soon enough. I can't say for sure if he was glad to see us or not. One might think they'd enjoy hanging out with their deity, but the reality of it can be more unnerving than anticipated.

"Ah, Sir Lord Ryanmax," he blurted out, even before I was through the door.

"Hey, you old son of a gun, how's it going?" I said, hoping to calm him a bit.

"Of a gun? No, that's nots bes me, but I'll ask around fur ya to find him, boss."

"No, it's just a silly expression where I come from. Queeheg, lighten up."

He slapped his exuberant paunch. "I will if it'll pleases ya, but it's agin' my nature."

"Queeheg," I said with a little frustration, "*hello.*"

Darn if he didn't just look confused.

"What kin I get yas?" he asked back in his bartender mode.

"We'll both have the rotgut you poured last time."

"Rotten your innards sauce comin' up."

He brought a bottle and a couple glasses to our table.

"You forgot a glass for you, my friend," I said.

He reached into a pocket and pulled one out with a grin. "Keeps one handy fur just this typa 'mergency." He imposed himself on a chair that was even-money going to crumble under the challenge.

"Seen Wul?" I asked, to open the conversation.

"Not since ye came here with 'im." He tossed back a shot.

"He's a good man, that Wul," Sapale said as she tossed a shot of her own.

"Amung da best," agreed our host. "That's sayin' a lot round *dees* parts, I can say for a fact."

"Gods can be asses," I said with a thin smile.

"To dat," he replied, and he powered down another belt.

"So, I never got around to asking you. Are you going to Prime in six days?" I asked, staring at my half-full glass.

That brought a loud, juicy sniff. "Nah. Maybe. I dun' know. Haven't asided yet, I guess."

"Apparently," responded Sapale.

"Not your thing, the invasion and destruction part?" I pressed.

"Not no more much." He angled his head and threw his bushy eyebrows up. "Usa be, but na so much a'late."

"What, you feeling old or feeling guilty?" I asked.

He spied at me sideways. "Lill'a both, I 'mangins."

"I've never seen a man your size whisper so quietly. Why I do believe a rabbit sitting on your shoulder would have missed it."

He grunted.

"Makes me wonder if it's frowned upon to not endorse by wild participation an incursion."

"Ryanmax, you seems like the type'a man who'd well keep a secret."

"I actually am."

"I'm even better," added Sapale with a wink.

"It's like dis, folks. Da Cleinoids, as you know, don't brook independent tinking."

"Tell me about it," I encouraged.

"If one was thought to disapproves of a ting like 'cursions, dat one'd not be welcomed like a modder does her new babe."

"This I believe." Sapale nodded.

"But I've never known anyone to be punished for non-participation," I asked more than stated.

"Sure ya do. Well, ya might not knows um, but you seen dare monuments. When ya was wit Wul and de others."

"At Beal's Point?"

"Surin ya know dat?"

"I've never paid much attention when I've been there. I hate that sick feeling."

"Yur spos'a read da inscriptions," Queeheg said rather irritatedly.

"Show this man a rule and he'll break it," remarked Sapale.

"Well, ye secrets safe wit me. Anyhow, seven a da statues are to inaviduls who defied the 'cursions. Da latest was Mol Gar Dor on de occasion a da last 'cursion."

I recalled seeing that one. The odd name happened to catch my eye. "Well, what'd you expect from a squid with a thousand arms?"

"He was a strange one, wan't he? He was a healthy drinker though, so I liked 'im."

"Never actually met him."

"He 'minds me a you, a little dat is."

I spit my firewater back into my glass. "A squid with lots of arms reminds you of me? Thanks for nothing."

"Na. Not hows ya looks, but how yas tinks. He were even more a freetinker n'you."

"He looked more like a nightmare, not a thinker."

"To be certain he could rip most things 'part with those impressive arms. But at de end dare he became quiet and had much regret. At the last conclave a'fore we teleported, he stood and said his piece. Not goin'a kill sweet innocents was he. It was wrong to massacre species so inferior to us whart'nt a'done us no misdeed."

Dissent among the ranks. How very curious.

"We're not too keen on the killing part either," said Sapale. "But we're going for the adventure and to maybe, you know, help out if we see too great an evil."

He rolled his glass in his massive palms. "At's what purchased ol' Mol Gar Dor 'is eternal monument." Queeheg spoke lost in sadness.

"Then he earned it with honor," proclaimed Sapale. She lifted her glass. "To Mol Gar Dor, we keep his memory as was his life. Good, pure, and untainted."

Queeheg scanned the room with considerable alarm. His relaxing face indicated he was satisfied she was heard by no others. "It's n'safe nor wise to say those words wit dat conviction, little lady."

She eyed him as seriously as a frog does the fly. "I praise a good man. That should always be said proudly and defiantly. Those who would hear and deny *him* must be *known*. Those who would hear and deny *me* must be *killed*."

Queeheg stared at her a good long while. Then he grinned. "I likes her already, Ryanmax. You Chosen sure know hows to pick 'em."

I wrapped an arm around her shoulders. "Only the best for this chosen dude." I pecked her cheek. "So, six days hence you, barkeep, remain behind to serve those too concerned or too drunk to make the trip. We, we happy two, will teleport to Prime and see just what it takes to get one of those totally bitching monuments built in our honor."

CHAPTER THIRTY-FOUR

"Someone did *what?*" exclaimed an incredulous Vorc.

"You heard me, cupcake—somebody tore the crap out of a monument up at Beal's Point and stole the intermixer unit." Caprahammer was fuming. She hated even speaking to Vorc, let alone repeating simple words.

Vorc held his head between his palms. "Why would anyone do that? How, in a universe with no mercy for me, would it fall to *you* to be the one who learned this and was tasked with the duty of reporting it to *me?*"

"It didn't fall to *me*, moron. It fell to that sniveling waste of space Boulzeron."

"B ... bu ... but how cou ... could it p ... *possibly* fall to him? And even if it did, which it couldn't, why am I plagued with sitting here looking at *you?*"

"Did you switch to decaf like I suggested a while back?" Caprahammer grinned wickedly.

He slammed a fist on the table. "I did *not*, you reject of hell. Why did the news of the desecration of a monument end up in the lap of a god of *revenge* and *spite* like Boulzeron?"

"Long story, chomp ass."

For nearly a minute Vorc was incapable of speech. He pounded his fists on his temples and slammed his feet to the floor. He also emitted a series of howls, curse words, and gasps. Finally he was rational enough again to interact. "I have time. We don't leave for Prime for two more days. Now, tell me *how* he learned and why *you*, not *he*, are here."

"Because he's a chickenshit coward, that's why."

Vorc's period of convulsions was much briefer. He was cogent again in thirty seconds. "Boulzeron found out about the damage because he's n ... not ... br ... brave?"

"No. What, are you mental? You sure are irrational. I'm here to tell you, cum dribble, because he's too afraid to speak to you. I have zero clues as to why anyone would be intimidated by a section of last week's bowel movement like you, but there you have it. He asked me to pass along the information and I'm just dumb enough to do it."

"F ... f ... fine. How did a god of spite come to know ..."

"You really care, cock puppet? You know. Now you act. End of story." She spit on the floor because she was just that gross an individual.

"I *will* know, bitch."

"Did you just call me a *bitch*? My feelings, frail and fragile as they are, have been shattered, dick breath."

Vorc struggled to collect himself. "If you do not tell me and tell me instantly, I shall be forced to summon *Bethniak* to find that information out. Normally I would be reluctant to do so, but this close to the egress I cannot afford to be cautious."

Caprahammer, as tough a piece of work as there was, paled. She wasn't certain if Vorc would, or even *could*, hold sway over Bethniak. It was not, however, within the realm of possibility that Caprahammer wanted to find out the hard way the puke was serious. "There used to be three cretins in charge of Control and Remediation."

Vorc said the words silently, his lips moving in puzzled twists. Then he recalled. "Ah, yes, Control and Remediation. Not a key department, but yes, there is a small staff allocated to them."

"*Was*, insectophile. Ya listening? They discovered the problem but didn't do squat. I guess they followed your approach to management. Finally someone with a functioning brain found out and fired them all. One of them, Squiggy or something, got pissy and appealed to the limp-dicked Boulzeron for vengeance against, I don't know, his coworkers or the one who ran him off. Anyway, that's the fascinating tale of almost nothing. Can I go now, pus pocket?"

"Please do."

And she did.

Vorc sat wondering what the theft of an intermixer unit could portend. What person, sane or insane, would want to get that close to a *functioning* intermixer unit? It would kill any mortal foolish enough to venture that close. And it would be a worse death than Vorc could even imagine. And no god would be masochistic enough to try a stunt like that, because they couldn't possibly want one that badly. Or at all. It made no sense. With Prime so close, Vorc's stomach knotted up and he was at a loss to understand what he was missing.

CHAPTER THIRTY-FIVE

"The only thing I'm going to miss about this clusterfuck of a universe is this." Sapale held up a bottle of nectar of the gods. "It's way too good."

"Amen, I say to you, sister. Stuff's kick-ass."

"I'll stuff a few bottles down my shirt, sure. But once that's gone, we're screwed."

"Hey, we're gods. We'll snap our fingers and puff some up."

"I'll be *so* glad when you have to stop saying that. Your ego's so large it already requires its own universe. The deity thing only swells it."

"Who said anything about no longer claiming to be divine?" I smiled real cheesy. "I *am* divine. Just ask all the ladies."

"All the ladies in the nursing home, maybe."

In both of our heads flashed, *Sapale, are you here? Sapale, it's me, Toño DeJesus. Where are you?*

"Did you just hear something very *inconvenient?*" I asked as I winced.

"Me, no. I heard nothing." Sapale pulled the stopper out of the nectar, secured her lips on the rim, and turned the bottle upside down.

Toño, please tell me you didn't trip a trap and join us in perdition, I responded.

Jon? Jon, is that you? You're alive!

Thanks for the update. I was just asking Sapale whether I was or not.

"Yes, you are, Jon Ryan, he responded.

Doc, your timing couldn't be worse. The invasion starts tomorrow. We were finalizing our plans. We don't have babysitting time, Toño.

Babysitting? How insulting, Jon. Need I remind you that I am the man who created you? I've been through wars, just like you.

You've been through them, Doc, but not like me. Hell, what are we sparring about? Stay where you are and we'll come get you.

You know where I am?

Yeah. We both arrived in the Lower Chamber. Dark, dank, lots of old stonework, replied Sapale.

That description fits it well.

And if an ugly-plus witch shows up to kill you, then question you, tell her you're a god.

I most certainly will claim no such thing. Jon, you know I'm a good Catholic. I could never ...

Not God, Doc. A god. These dick drippings call themselves the Cleinoid gods. Just tell her that.

"Good thing we stole that cab," said Sapale. "It shouldn't take us more than ten minutes to retrieve the little lost sheep."

"Let's go," I replied, pushing to my feet.

We screeched to a halt in front of the entrance and scrambled down quickly. Doc could get into a lot of trouble quickly with his naïveté.

"Toño, you here?" called out Sapale as we entered the area we'd both landed in.

"Over here," he said with an energetic wave.

"No horrible Tefnuf around?" asked Sapale, as we jogged over to him.

"Apparently not. I've seen nothing, horrible or otherwise."

"Hmm," I mused, "must be close enough to the egress that no one cares about visitors."

"Lucky you," Sapale said to Toño.

"I'll accept all the luck I can."

"Come on. Let's leave in case old Tefnuf's just on break," I said, taking Doc's elbow.

"Toño," Sapale asked, once the car was moving, "why'd you come? You told me I was making a terrible mistake."

"You were. You *did*," he responded.

"But you're not?" she challenged.

"My dear, I couldn't very well allow you to place yourself in danger without helping."

"But you waited days. You can't have it both ways, Toño," she responded.

"I did not. When I left the room I waited just outside the door. Once I heard you depart I rushed over and scrambled the antimatter and disappeared."

"Aw, thanks, Toño. That's sweet. But seriously, I've been here for days."

He shrugged. "Time moves at a different pace here. That's all."

"Well, you could have saved yourself the trouble. The invasion starts at dawn tomorrow. Hell would have presented itself with a ribbon on if you'd have waited a bit longer," I said.

He rested a hand on his hip. "And I would know this how?"

"Easy. By trusting me," I replied with a wink.

"The end of times must be at hand. I'm to trust everything to the likes of you now?"

"You kind of complicated things, Doc, that's all."

"How so? You two are returning tomorrow. I shall join you on your ... shuttle or whatever."

"It's not like that. I'm not sure myself how we're going to do this."

He rolled his eyes. "Not another of your infernal Jon Plans?"

"We really don't have one," assured Sapale. "We found out as much as we dared, but some parts of our plan are kind of *soft*."

"I got some locals to accept me. Sapale is tolerated by association with me, but a third new god no one's ever seen may be too much."

"Then ... then introduce me as your butler," he said haughtily.

Sapale nearly jumped out of her skin. "*No.* No, Toño. You do *not* want to be introduced as a servant around these parts."

"And why not, young lady?"

"Well, for one thing, I'm theorizing you look like shit naked."

"I also don't imagine you'd play well with others 'round these parts in a service capacity," I added with a wag of my eyebrows.

"You two are too much."

"Let's just get back to where we're staying and we can fill you in on what you need to know," I concluded.

Within a half hour Toño was up to speed. He was also fascinated with the whatever I had still contained in the membrane, the make-you-sick machine we stole from Beal's Point. I was still lugging it around because there was no way to stash it away. It was too toxic. Someone'd locate it real quick.

"I have a thought. Sapale can place the both of us in a membrane. You can then safely release the device and I'll take custody of it."

"I don't know. It's really *horrible* what it does to your brain. The way I felt, well, I wouldn't want to go there again. Sapale can vouch for that reaction."

"Come, come. You and I have been through much. I promise I'll contain it quickly."

"All right, but only to be rid of it."

"Excellent. Once we are safely back home I can study it in detail."

"Once we're safely back home?" exclaimed my brood's-mate. "Toño, the odds of that are worse than the chances Jon'll behave himself in public."

"Oh ye of little faith," I defended. "It'll work out. It always does."

Both of them stared at me like I was somewhat off base.

"Okay, honey, place us in a ten-meter square membrane. Keep it up for, oh, five minutes. I'm sure the transfer will take less time, but I don't want to stress."

"Got it. Five minutes. You two stand there." She pointed to the other side of the room. "In three-two-one."

"Okay. The whatever is small, maybe a couple square meters. I, uh, didn't get a good look at it. I'll count down from three and turn my membrane off. The box'll be right there." I pointed to a specific spot on the floor. "Remember, you're going to feel crazy scared and/or sick, so stay focused."

"Not a problem."

"Whatever you see, hear, or experience is *not* real. Okay?"

"Jon, stop being so dramatic."

"You asked for it. Three-two-*one.*" I released the hell box.

I was drowning in shark-infested waters. My lungs burned. Two of the biggest white sharks imaginable torpedoed toward my face. A tiger shark tore at my leg. Blood, my blood, fouled the water so badly I could taste it. I was lurched from side to side by my attacker.

"Anytime, Doc," I managed to shout through my panic.

The nightmare continued. I raised a full membrane around the box. My head cleared in a snap. I was so relieved. I hesitated for several seconds before looking for Toño. Where was he? There. He was clawing at the membrane, trying to get out. He howled like a man possessed, which is exactly what I'm certain he'd felt. But why was he still going on? The brain-deader was neutralized. Then it hit me. I knew exactly what terror, what unspeakable torture my dear friend had experienced.

For millions of years he'd been held captive and abused by the Adamant. They tortured him mercilessly so he'd help their war effort excel. And it drove Toño insane. I was barely able to pull him back to reality. Damn. He was reliving his torment.

"Toño, it's okay. You're fine. I'm here. It's Jon. Toño, can you hear me?"

More mindless terror and bloodcurdling screams.

This was ugly and getting worse by the heartbeat. I slapped him across the face. "Doc, can you hear me? Come on, Doc. It's okay."

Why hadn't I seen this coming? My best friend was suffering the tortures of ten hells. I should have foreseen it. I knew how powerful the damn machine was. I checked my chronometer. We were stuck in here for four more minutes.

I deployed my probes. *Toño, can you hear me?* I said mind to mind. Nothing. His head was filled with the same primal rage and panic it had been the day I saved him from captivity. This was so not good.

Doc, if you can hear me, grab my arm.

For a split second there was nothing. Then he seized hold of my forearm. Man, did he ever bear down. I was a metal man and *still* I thought he was going to snap my arm in half.

Okay, great. Now calm down, Doc. Can you do that for me?

He continued to writhe. Poor bastard, he was in a horrific place.

If you don't calm down, the second Sapale drops her membrane they're going to hear you and we're all dead.

Again, for a few missed heartbeats nothing changed. Then he stiffened. His arms and legs went straight as lead pipes and his neck arched back as if in spasm. His mouth struggled to close over the shrieks trying to exit his lips. Slowly, painfully slowly, he quieted. Occasional ejections of fear and mourning would slip out, then even those passed.

"You okay, Toño?" I asked softly.

"N ... n ... no. Bu ... but I c ... can quiet my ... quiet myself."

"Great, Doc. I'm sorry as hell this happened. I should have known better."

"It was my ... m ... my dem ... mmm ... mand. I will .... will be fine."
He dropped to his knees and was motionless.

That's when the membrane came down. Sapale rushed to Toño's side. "What in the name of Brathos happened?" She wrapped him in an embrace to steady him.

"The damn box brought back his time in hell with the Adamant."

She shut her eyes and threw her head back. "Of course. How stupid can I be? Of course, that's what the worst thing he could experience would be." She held him at arm's length to inspect him. "If he's out as long as last time, we're in deep shit."

"Tell ..."

"I - am - going - to - be - fine," he said with staccato pacing. "There - is - no - need ..."

"No need for what, Doc?"

"Worry."

With his eyes still closed, he stood as unsteadily as a baby crane rising from the egg.

"Easy, my friend," soothed Sapale. "I have you."

His eyes slowly opened. He took a deep breath. After scanning the room, no doubt to confirm the absence of Adamant tormentors, he half smiled. "My, but you two were correct. *That* was intense."

"You think it'll pass?" I asked cautiously.

"I certainly pray to God it does." He shook himself like a wet dog. "I don't wish to revisit that period in my life."

"We're here for you," Sapale cooed as she hugged him tightly.

The rest of the day we just chilled. I wanted Toño to be as well as he could be, come dawn of D-Day for life as we knew it.

CHAPTER THIRTY-SIX

Vorc stood facing a deep verdant valley that cut a swath through a vast expanse of the forested landscape. To his back stood, flew, or slithered the most bizarre and sickening assembly. Figures that could only be dredged up from the depths of a forsaken hell held formation. Anticipation was so thick that the air was electrified. Sparks literally snapped and popped randomly. The wedge of ancient gods that flanked Vorc spread outward to infinity, but never did it thin. As far as any eye could see, denizens of the universe of hate, rapacious consumption, and endless antipathy abounded. All champed at the bit to be freed, lost in a bloodlust for destruction, death, and debauchery.

The time for the egress had come.

Prime was now in their merciless reach.

Vorc raised his arms high overhead. "Brothers and sisters, the time of our sanctification has arrived. Can you feel it?"

The press of the concussive sound that came in response could have flattened an entire city.

"Are you ready to be *gods* to the worthless and the undeserving? Are you set to wreak Armageddon on those whose only role in life is to suffer and to die so that we may find joy?"

An even louder wave of sound struck Vorc's back so hard he nearly tumbled.

"Then let it *begin.*" Spit rained from his lips as he howled. "The advanced reavers may depart. The five ranks of Cleinoids will follow, one at a time. Rage will depart first. Torment second, Wrath third, and Fury fourth. Then ... then *all-consuming* Horror will descend upon Prime, and their fate will be sealed. As is our tradition, I shall personally lead Horror. *This* incursion, Bethniak will stand at my side. She will be the Right Hand of the Gods."

The chorus of howls, cheers, and wails was bone-shattering.

Over the valley a slowly turning vortex of light came into existence. Reds and blues, purples and indigos churned together and sprang apart before disappearing into the center, into the singularity. A sound, as quiet as hope at its onset, began to rise from the disturbance. Soon, the sound declared itself. It was the very opposite of hope. All who could hear felt the wails and moans and sobs and lamentations of lost souls bound to suffer torment for all of time. The sound was to the Cleinoid's ears sensual, erotic, and well past orgasmic.

The whirlpool grew in size and in ferocity. The mass of the calls of anguish increased to match the volume of the storm itself. Soon the vortex darkened the sky and the only light came from the lightning bolts that grew in number. And then chaos broke loose. The formation split like a rack of cosmic billiard balls. Each god acted independently, flying hither and yon. And then the first ancient god, Marropex, a god of atrocities, charged forward. He shot past Vorc and directly at the center of the storm. Well before he reached it, he disappeared. He was gone. He had teleported into Prime.

The first of three reavers was in Prime.

The remaining masses thrummed a chant.

A pair of Cleinoid gods shot into the air and sported around each other like ice dancers. Hartoris and Caliopherous, despair and death, picked up speed and arced high into the darkness. Then they rocketed toward Vorc's back. Just short of that point, a flash of light exploded. Something small but moving at high speed slammed into Vorc with a force sufficient to toss him forward like a bowling pin. He tumbled and slid, then skidded to rest on his back.

He stood, enraged, bent on discovering what had desecrated his great ceremony. But the crowd, the totality of the ancient gods, were gone. Vorc saw only emptiness. He reached out with his mind but it touched nothing. He called out at the top of his lungs but no one heard him, no one called back to him. Vorc was absolutely, positively, and eternally alone. He fell to his knees trembling. His hand covered his face and he began to weep tears of blood. His loneliness was inconsolable. He had been alone forever and always would be.

After the flash, Hartoris and Caliopherous slammed to a halt. Before them were children of all ages and species. The children played, and sang, and each and every one of them had a confident casual belief that their lives would be filled with only joy, nothing but tender love, and they knew above all else, each and every one of them, that the future held limitless possibilities and endless hope. Hartoris shrank before the vision of unbridled positive emotion and charity. He covered his ears so he might not hear the happiness. He clawed at his eyes so that he might not see the wonder. He struck his noses so that he might not smell the sweet treats and plentiful candies. Hartoris lay down on the dirt and ended, such was his misery, his loathing, *his* despair.

Caliopherous, an icon of death, stood aghast in disbelief. She saw before her nothing but life, verdant, boundless, and energetic life. As far as her eyes could see there was no other emotion but love, hope, and happiness. And she was left breathless by the level of endless, immutable peace. It went on forever and it could not be ended. Hers was a universe of growth, fertility, and most painful of all, no boundaries. She clutched her stomach and vomited with such might it hurled her backward, where she struck Vorc.

For his part, Vorc felt the blow but could not see the source since his universe was empty. He felt the burning vomit spill across his face, but he could not see the liquid because there was nothing, not even vomit, in his solitude. He crumpled to the ground and wished that he had never been born.

All the ancient gods near enough to the small box that rested on the ground near Vorc experienced their own personal hells. Antorphij, the prideful bearer of the flag of deceit, saw a million fleas lift him up and carry him back to the army he'd just betrayed. The dead souls only then rising from the corpses saw Antorphij coming. They wiped away the bloodstains and the excrement that tainted them and they swelled toward the traitor. They would rip his great body to shreds and he would join them, lost forever in death.

Fenorl was an amphibious cyclops. His role was to collect the bodies of those who died at sea. He would then bind their souls to their dead corpses so they could never know an afterlife. His greatest joy was to stack the lost souls like cordwood in a cavern at the bottom of the deepest ocean. There they would remain for all time. The only escape came when he consumed one. Fenorl was a despicable god. But at that moment in time, he was no longer a happy god. He lay on his back facing up to the burning desert suns, three of them, each hotter than the next. The noonday suns were frozen in place over him. He would never again know darkness or moistness, or taste the abominations he had amassed in his larder. His scales burned and his lips cracked, but his scales and lips grew back just fast enough to never vanish yet never heal. His only companions were the footlong red ants that stung him and ripped bites of his flesh off. He knew with utter confidence he would lie desiccating there in the parched desert until the end of time.

Into the chaos, into the unbearable fear, walked a child. Her pace was even, her face showing no emotion, and her eyes looked blandly at the small box sputtering on the ground near Vorc. She reached down almost daintily and picked the intermixer unit up. In defiance of belief, she showed no ill effects from her proximity to the hell-raiser. As casually as you please, the child smashed the intermixer unit to dust between her palms. Its noxious effect ended promptly, but its victims' minds only very slowly returned to reality. The little girl's gaze swept over the writhing gods strewn about like trailers after a tornado.

After I slammed the hate-box against Vorc, I began to smile like a kid in a candy shop with a charge card. The asswipe gods crumbled and bawled, and made perfect fools of themselves. It was the most beautiful sight I'd ever seen in my entire life. I was about to turn to Toño, to make sure he was far enough away to be spared the horrible reaction he'd had the last time he was exposed to the device's effects. He shot me two thumbs up. Sapale added her thumbs-up, too. She sported the hugest grin. We couldn't know the long-term outcome of our act of terrorism, but we sure as hell felt good right then.

Out of nowhere appeared a little girl. I hadn't noticed her before, but she was tiny, especially compared to the many gargantuan gods. She was walking right toward the box. She should have been running from it, not approaching it. The power of the evil illusions might easily kill a child, especially a sweet young girl with a pink pinafore dress and the cutest matching bonnet I'd ever seen.

I rushed toward her. She was maybe thirty yards away. As I cut the distance, I noticed a shimmering appear directly between the child and me. Soon I could see it was the ever-so-annoying shiny blob I'd all but forgotten about. It was materializing along my path. Like the last time it had darkened my doorstep, it was in general taking on some shape. Well, let's just say it was no longer a globular blob. No, it was a pickle-shaped blob.

"*Move,*" I shouted ahead. "Get out of my way."

In the most non-ethereal voice I'd yet heard from my tormentor, it yelled, "Run."

"Out of my way."

"Run, Jon Ryan, run."

The blob appeared to fly sideways and dim significantly. Never did that before. I picked up my pace. I was just about ready to snatch up the girl and save her.

The shimmer returned to block me. "Run, Jon. All of you, run."

Then the blob was gone; it just vanished. Good riddance, I reflected as I reached for the child. Funny what sticks in your mind. Right before I tried to grab her, she had the cutest demure little smile, just a little crooked. So sweet.

As my arms closed around her, she seized them. With the power of a Saturn 5 at liftoff, she rotated and slammed me face-first onto the ground. Any living being would have been pancaked to death. Me, I was only confused and trying to reboot about five hundred systems.

She grabbed my hair and lifted me like a rag doll.

Okay, child or not, playtime was officially over. I extended my fibers. *Sleep*, I said into her head.

Fuck you, came back loud and clear, like she was designed with the same unit.

What are you?

Instead of the usual stream of information, I heard, *Your worst nightmare.*

Worrisome, reflected I. My fibers retracted. I turned my finger laser to maximum and fired at her right eye. The beam arrested mid-flight. I shoved my hand closer to her face, but the beam still stopped at the same spot.

She whipped me around her head like I was an athletic hammer, and she threw me to the feet of Sapale and Toño. They were impressed.

"Run," I stammered as I stood.

I got no argument on that count. We started out at top speed. I noticed the gods were slowly recovering. Many were on their feet or whatever and beginning to mark the action.

"Scatter," I shouted widely. "They have another device." I hoped we could lose ourselves in the ensuing panic.

No such luck. Most gods held their ground.

Then we ran right into the cute little girl who wasn't looking so cute to me any longer. "Stop now and I will not destroy you immediately," she said with convincing authority.

I pushed my companions to one side, and we ran for all we were worth. "I'm putting up a membrane," I yelled to them. "Three-two-one."

We were instantly isolated. We stopped before we could impact the far wall.

"That should hold the baby bitch out for now," I said.

"Who was that?" shouted Sapale.

"No idea. Badly in need of a spa ..."

Before I could finish the sentence, the membrane we were in began to rise and fall. Clearly someone outside was shaking it. I deployed my usual tricks. Ribbons of membrane dug into the bedrock below us. We held steady.

"Good. They know where we are, unfortunately, but at least we're s ..."

That time before I could finish, one spot on the membrane began to change. What we normally saw looking outward from a full membrane was perfectly nothing. As I watched in horror and disbelief, perfectly nothing began to change color. It began as a dull red, then bright yellow, then it was blindingly blue white. I set a probe fiber on the spot. Two *thousand* degrees Celsius. Nothing was amazingly hot. Then the edge of the membrane cracked like an eggshell.

"That is not even remotely possible," wheezed Toño.

"I'd agree if I thought it'd help," Sapale responded.

"Here, I'll throw up one just inside the original." I produced a nothingness that eclipsed the failing membrane I'd deployed. Of course with a full membrane in the way, my force field would have vanished instantly.

We three stared at the spot right in front of where the first membrane broke. Sure enough, within a few minutes the whole red, yellow, blue color repeated. Wash, rinse, repeat.

"Doc, we can't keep this up forever, but maybe, just maybe, neither can they. Run a calculation as to energy expended and time intervals to each temp. See who'll win this game of chicken," I said with uncertainty.

An hour later Toño sighed deeply and cleared his throat. "I see neither a decay nor an increase in the speed of their assault. I think we must face the fact that they can do this forever if need be."

"So do we wait and see or surrender?" asked Sapale. "Kaljaxians are not big on surrender, you know."

"I know," I replied as I ran a nervous hand through my hair. "If we hold out, we'll eventually lose."

"In approximately three days," added Toño.

"If we go down in a blaze of glory, we can't help our universe. We've learned a hell of a lot so far that could be critical."

"So you're saying we should pray they take prisoners?" Sapale was not pleased.

"I say it's the best way to help our people. I'm willing to accept a vote," I said. "I say surrender."

"I say *fight*," snapped Sapale.

"I say I hate you both. Putting an old friend in such a position," protested Toño.

"Hey, look on the bright side. Only fifty percent of your crewmates will hate you. The other half'll consider you almost as smart as they are," I quipped.

Without allowing time to develop regret, Toño said, "Surrender. It's the only choice that might allow us to help our kind. I'm sorry, my dear," he said to Sapale.

"No prob," she said stiffly. "Works for me. Every time it gets worse, I can tell two people *I told you so*." She smiled. "At least I'll die happy."

We all lay facedown on the floor, spread-eagle. Then I extinguished the membrane. Immediately we were rushed by nothing short of a horde. Everything that fell on us was large, smelly, and pissed. Two or three creatures grabbed each one of us separately. We were raised overhead and paraded around in triumph. Our captors howled and roared and the crowd cheered and hissed. I could say that for my part, I was having no kind of fun.

CRAIG ROBERTSON

The mob stopped at the feet of the little girl who'd been so bad. They clearly feared her. Based on my experience, they were wise to do so. We were gingerly set on our feet in front of her.

Her fists rested on her hips. Vorc stood a good three feet behind her and looked to me to be shaking like he was made of rubber. He was clearly abdicating any current leadership role to the girl.

"I am Bethniak. Please know this is the worst day of your lives. I will discover your conspiracy and then you will all die miserably."

I started to stand. From nowhere a force slammed me to the deck and held me there like a building had landed on me.

"You will do only what I say you will. *Speak* nothing on your own. Do not *move* of your own volition. Do not even *think* without my permission."

I formed a membrane. It was in the shape of a sphere at the end of a long stick, a hinge halfway along the length so it could move back to front. With all the force I could will, I aimed the ball at the back of her head. It hit with something in the range of the force of an adult rhinoceros on a full charge. Damn kid was tough. She flipped over once but landed on her feet like she planned it that way.

"*Fool*," she bellowed. The back of my head was struck with massive energy, and my face imaged itself in the hard dirt.

My next blow was to the back of her heels. That one worked better. She awkwardly vaulted backward and slammed the back of her head on the ground. A gasp rose from the crowd. I think they were surprised anyone would fight toe-to-toe with this bitchlet.

She rose unsteadily, which was a beautiful sight. But I had to know she was madder than before, especially there in front of her peeps. "Do that again and I will dismember your friends."

I tended to believe her intent and ability. She did waver a bit, however.

"You, the male in the center, may stand."

I did so slowly, like I was waking from a nap. I dusted at my clothes. "I'm Ryanmax. I, like you, am a poly."

A much louder gasp rose from the audience; a few murmurs, too.

"I doubt that very much. To be a poly you must be a Cleinoid god, for one. I do not presently know what you are, but one of my kin you are not."

I set up a full membrane and dropped it instantly so I flashed in and out of visibility. Then I silently pointed at a nearby rock and lifted it a meter off the ground and pulled it into my hands. I smashed it to pebbles with a fist. "A poly's what I am. And know that some have whispered The Chosen One in my presence."

Boy did that draw an energetic reaction from those watching. I sensed a little genuine excitement.

"The Chosen One wouldn't throw an intermixer unit at the feet of those about to egress. They do not hide in a shell. Pranks and parlor tricks are not harbingers of that individual. You will not say the name again. Tell me now, who are you and why do you delay us?"

I touched my chest. "Ryanmax. I didn't hit you that hard, did I?"

Someone in the distance guffawed. She pointed at the person without looking that way and he rose into the air, legs flailing and arms flying. Then he accelerated quickly and shot out of sight.

"Your purpose in delaying us?"

"I wasn't delaying you. I was trying to get everyone's attention." Man I thought on my feet well. Bullshit was my stock and trade.

"I believe you have," called out a very squeaky Vorc.

"To what end?" demanded Bethniak, "oh, great Chosen One?"

"To announce myself."

"I'm getting extremely bored with your vague rants," she said in a manner I fully believed.

"As we embark on our latest mission of conquest, I wanted all to know who the strongest poly was. It is me. I expect to be kept informed as to how the invasion is going and what plans are being made." I wished I had a better line there. That was weak cheese.

"You sad little rodent dropping. And did I see you even enlisted the help of that decrepit old ghost? That's shameful."

"What ghost?" Wait, the shimmery blob.

"The one that tried to stop you. The one I cast out." She laughed like a lunatic as if on cue.

"Oh, that ghost. No, he's a fan, that's all."

She closed her eyes and sucked in a powerful breath through her nose. "This ends now. If we wait much longer, all the ancient gods may not be able to egress. You are no god. Even if you were, you're not Cleinoid."

"Maybe an antigod?" I said robustly.

The crowd really reacted to that one. Screams and shouts erupted. People began to bolt.

"If you are I will kill you with even greater joy."

I wagged a finger. "Ah, ah. Not *kill*. End, yes, but gods don't die."

She hammered me backward like an ocean liner struck. She was most uncool. "One last time. Why did you try and slow the egress?"

"Because I want you all to stay. If y'all leave I'd be so lonely."

Sapale whispered, "Do you think it's wise to bait her so energetically?"

"Hey, if she can kill us she will. Why not make her suffer a little first?"

"You are the man for *that* job," she responded quietly.

"We are through. You are having fun defying me, fool. I will therefore exact an equal amount more in suffering from you, as I remove you from existence."

"Hang on. That last sentence was fairly convoluted, and you used a lot of overly large words IMHO. Could you repeat what you said in the language Normal, not Stick-Up-Your-Ass?" Without waiting, I gave her my best shot. I drove a membrane sphere down on her as hard as I could and fired my laser finger at her—right between the eyes. I also extended my probes not because I thought they would help but because, what the hell, I was all in. They couldn't *hurt*.

I think the impact distracted her just enough that the fibers stuck. Before when I used them on her, I tried to control her and she proved uncontrollable. This time I shoved as much electric charge as I could through them. The only thing I left off was a prayer to Azacter, the wannabe local god of war. I'd met him. He was a total wank.

And what did my beast accomplish? A hell of a lot, but not nearly enough. Her knees buckled under the blow of the membrane and she nearly fell. She held up a hand and stopped the laser beam. The electric charge was the sweetest. Her hair puffed out like in the cartoons and sparks shot from her eyes. Maybe if I could have delivered ten times more juice I'd have done her in. I would never know. My probe fibers slipped off her and she lunged toward me.

The crowd gasped to see anyone so openly defy Bethniak. They were even more impressed because I was semi-holding my own. Apparently that was a first in Godland.

Bethniak grabbed me by the arm. I hit her hard in the face with my free hand, but that barely fazed her. She hammered me on the ground like she was using me to kill a mouse that frightened her. After a few seconds, the world faded to black.

EPILOGUE

I awoke feeling *most* disoriented. My brain was fuzzy, I felt upside down, and my left leg was constricted. Above me I began to see a shifting red circle and my face was hot, very hot. Whatever was happening, it was new to me.

"Toño, I think he's coming around," said a soft voice. Sapale?

"It's about time. He's been out so long I was beginning to fear the worst." Yup, that was Toño's voice.

"Jon, can you hear me?" Yup, that was Sapale. It hit me. Why was it people always ask if you can hear them before anything else? *Are you okay?* was a much better initial question. And if you answered yes or no, they'd know you heard them. Two queries in one sentence. I wonder why a thing like that seemed important just then?

"Yus. I cun her you fun," I managed to reply.

"Why are you speaking so oddly?" shot back Toño.

"Tink my jaws dissvocaed." I grabbed my lower jaw with both hands and pulled out and down, then released it. "There, better. Man, that bitch kid packed a punch."

"Sure looked like it to us," observed my life mate. I think she was laboring to suppress a giggle.

"So, did I win?" I asked halfheartedly.

"No, kind of the opposite, in fact," quipped the love of my life.

"But you made me proud in your efforts," responded a more upbeat Toño.

"You know, if I could have hit her with more electricity, I think I could have offed that douche canoe."

"Maybe next time." Sapale couldn't suppress a giggle.

"What?" I snapped. "What's funny about *next time?*"

"Jon, are your eyes working?" she replied.

I looked around. I was upside down. Yeah, I was hanging over a pit of bubbling lava, suspended by my left ankle. "Yes, I see fine, now."

"Hence my uncertainty regarding the possibility you'll get another shot at Bethniak," she responded.

"Or anyone else," added Toño.

"You guys," I returned, "what quitters. I think I have 'em *right* where I want 'em."

They both snickered.

"In fact, I *almost* feel sorry for them."

Most definitely to be continued ...

GLOSSARY:

Al (1): The ship's AI from Jon's initial *Ark 1* flight. He kept it with him until his dying day and then it elected to hang around. Good AI! Full name is Alvin. Those engineers and their lame naming.

Als (1): The Als is the surname for the "married" AIs Al and *Blessing*, given them by a pissy Jon Ryan.

Ark 1 (1): The subluminal, or slower-than-light-speed, ship Jon took on his very first flight. He was searching for a new home for humankind. The story is revealed in *The Forever Life* by this author.

Battle of the Periphery (1): The decisive battle where the combined forces of the free planets along the periphery of the Milky Way soundly defeated the Adamant armada. Of course they were greatly aided by the magical dragons of Nocturnat. Shortened to TBOP.

Beal's Point (1): An area of monuments to disgraced Cleinoid gods. All living gods must visit to be made ill so they stay loyal.

Bethniak (1): Evil, powerful child-appearing god. A real piece of work. Do not date this girl!

Blessing (1): Vortex Cragforel gifted to Jon. Our hero renamed it *Stingray* because pronounced in Deavoriath *Blessing* sounds like "crash."

Brathos (1): Kaljaxian version of hell.

Brindas (1): High master of Deft tradition and psychic ability.

Brood-mate/brood's-mate (1): Male and female members of a Kaljaxian marriage.

Calfada-Joric (1): The Deft master brindas on Rameeka Blue Green. Went by Cala also.

Calrf (1): A Kaljaxian stew that Jon particularly dislikes.

Central Seat (1): The official leader of the Ancient God's conclave.

Cleinoid gods (1): Ancient and malevolent mix of gods. They have destroyed many universes before and are eyeing ours now.

Command Prerogatives (1): The thin fibers Jon extends from his left four fingers. They are probes that also control a vortex.

Cragforel (1): Friendly Deavoriath Jon met after he first escaped the Adamant in the far future.

Davdiad (1): Kaljaxian divine spirit.

Deavoriath (1): Three arms and legs, the most advanced tech in the galaxy, and helpful to Jon.

Deca (1): One of the witch gods skilled at prophecy. Sister of Fest.

Deft (1): A shape-shifting species from the planet Locinar.

Di (1): Coequal head of the Joint Galactic Parliament. Basically an elephant seal with tentacles, rudimentary legs, and an extendible tongue lined with razor-sharp barbs.

Evil Jon Ryan/ EJ (1): Alternate time line version of the original human to android download. Over time, he turned to the darker side of his nature. He studied "magic" under a Deft master.

Fest (1): One of the witch gods skilled at prophecy. Sister of Deca.

Genter-ban-tol (1): Prime Minister of the Joint Galactic Parliament. A Bezathy, basically the Galaxy's largest snail species.

Golem (1): Creatures animated by the Cleinoid gods. Traditionally composed of mud.

Gorpedder (1): Boulder god defeated by Jon.

Hemnoplop (1): Demigod of Fool's Island. On pilgrimage to Beal's Point with Jon.

Hirn (1): A Kaljaxian dialect.

JCFIDAC (1): See Joint Council for Interplanetary Defense and Cooperation.

Jaccash Bimdulo (1): Scientist in the Joint Galactic Parliament.

Jonnaha (1): Prime minister of a main country on Vorpace. Agreed to try and form a united defense against the Adamant onslaught heading to their region of the Milky Way.

Joint Council for Interplanetary Defense and Cooperation (1): Group of allied free world fighting the Adamant.

Kalvarg (1): Planet Jon took the orphan Kaljaxian population to as the Adamant were destroying their home world. An island solar system long ago ejected from the Milky Way galaxy.

Livryatous (1): Centaur god who accompanied Jon on a pilgrimage to Beal's Point.

Locinar (1): Home planet of the Deft in the Milky Way galaxy.

Membrane (1): Space-time congruity manipulator. A super force field.

Nufe (1): A magical liquor made by the Deavoriath.

Oowaoa (1): Home world of the Deavoriath.

Peg's Bar Nobody (1): First reference in The Forever Quest. A true dive bar Jon loved. A total Dump, and Peg was one tough cookie.

Quantum Decoupler (1): A most excellent weapon that pulls the quarks apart in a proton. The energy released is amazing.

Sapale (1): Jon's Kaljaxian wife from his original flight to find humankind a new home. At first just her brain was copied, then, eventually, she was downloaded to an android host. Traveled with the corrupted Jon Ryan from an alternate time line.

Stingray (1): Name Jon used for the vortex *Blessing*.

TBOP (1): See Battle of the Periphery.

Tefnuf (1): The first ancient god Jon encountered. She was saddled with an uncanny ugliness and a profoundly bad temper.

Toño DeJesus (1): The creator of the android Jon. Became his lifelong friend.

Triumph of Might (1): The massive spaceship Mercutcio ruled. Jon first met the Adamant there. It was, in part, an extermination ship.

Visant (1): The proper name for a pair of Deft joined in hollon.

Vorc (1): Current central seat of the conclave. Generally humanoid.

Vortex Manipulator (1): The intelligence inside the vortex. Not actually an AI, but similar.

Wul (1): God of business and enterprise. Humanoid. Befriended Jon.

AND NOW A WORD
FROM YOUR AUTHOR
WHO DOESN'T LOVE THAT?

Thank you for continuing your journey through the Ryanverse! Along with this series, please check out *The Forever Series*. Beginning with The Forever Life, Book 1, learn Jon's backstory and share his many incredible adventures.

The second series in the Ryanverse begins with Embers. Learn what happened to Jon and his companions long after humankind safely left Earth.

Audiobooks, you ask? Why yes, there is the entire Ryanverse is available on Audible, and it's superb. It starts with The Forever, Part 1

Along with joining by reading, hop aboard the bandwagon. There's plenty of room. Follow me at Craig Robertson's Author's Page on Facebook. Partake of the conversation and fun. Best of all, sign up for my Mailing List by emailing me and asking. contact@ craigarobertson.com That way you can stay abreast of news and new releases. You'll be so glad you did. Finally, I love emails. No, I'm not that needy. I just love emails. contact@craigarobertson.com.

A final favor. Please post a review for this book, especially on Amazon. They are more precious to us authors than gold.

Craig